# DEFENSIBLE MURDER

# DEFENSIBLE MURDER

## NO. 5 IN THE MAVIS DAVIS MYSTERY SERIES

## SUSAN P. BAKER

REFUGIO PRESS

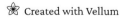 Created with Vellum

## DEDICATION

*For Ezekiel (Zeke) Reyna who is is always cooking up something, whether a game strategy or actual food.*

# PRAISE FOR SUSAN P. BAKER

"Mavis Davis is a great character: smart, funny and stubborn enough to make an efficient P.I." An Amazon Vine ™ Voice Reviewer

"Nothing complicated or flowery – just a good entertaining mystery." Another Amazon Vine ™ Voice Reviewer

About *My First Murder, No. 1 in the Mavis Davis Mystery Series:* "I really loved this Texas-based P.I. murder mystery. Mavis Davis is a hoot. She's gutsy and glamorous and fearless. She's determined to get her P.I. agency up and running, and this is her first murder case. She's been handling employment investigations, insurance claims, and other boring jobs, but this is a bonafide murder investigation. It's a bit more dangerous than she expected, but her intuition and instincts are great, and she stirs up more than one hornet's nest on her way to a solution. I'll definitely read more of the series. Fast and fun. Great read." An Amazon Verified Reviewer

"Mavis is a strong and resourceful protagonist, and Baker is a strong and resourceful writer. They make a good team." David Pitt. ALA

"These well written and realistic stories will keep you reading all night." An Amazon Verified Reviewer about Books 1-3.

# CHAPTER
# ONE

I was at my desk in the back of the building when the bell above our front door chimed. No one had an appointment, so I didn't pay any attention to the bell, figuring one of the staff, Margaret or Candy, would handle whatever was up.

A minute or so later, a woman I'd never seen before stuck her head around my door jamb and said "Mavis Davis?" The woman was middle height, plump like she was some months pregnant, and had huge, bruised circles under her bloodshot eyes.

Yes, that's me. Private Investigator. Former social worker. Employer of two women, one my age—thirty-something—and one not yet twenty. Tenant of a repurposed house in an older neighborhood of Houston, Texas. Single woman with a cop for a boyfriend.

Who else would be in my office? I wanted to ask but didn't. My mother raised me to be more polite than that. "Yes, ma'am, that's me." I coughed. "I've tested negative for Covid so don't worry. This cough is left over from some other crud I caught from my assistant, Margaret. Did she send you in here?"

"I couldn't find anyone in the front, so I came on back." Her chin trembling, she said, "I hope you don't mind."

I was going to kill Margaret and/or Candy, whoever was supposed to be staffing the front desk at that time for letting someone come back without notifying me. They were supposed to work out who occupied that space when one of them had other obligations, though the front of the office was mainly Margaret's terrain.

I had slipped in through the back and hadn't checked to see who was handling the front desk. Hadn't paid attention to any vehicles parked behind our little house-office. Not normal for me. Though I was recovering from whatever had ailed me, my focus hadn't returned one-hundred percent.

I hadn't wanted to be bothered with new cases for a few days, until I was better. I was doing some reading and research until I got my energy back. Without visibly sighing and without offering her a chair, I asked, with hope in my heart the pitiful-looking woman didn't want to hire me, "What can I do for you?"

She glanced at one of the chairs positioned in front of my desk. "May I sit down?"

I almost said, *if you must,* but refrained. "Please." I'd let her sit, but she wasn't getting a smile out of me. I coughed into my tissue, and by the time I looked up, she was ensconced on the edge of a chair, her oversized handbag resting on the side table.

"Have you tried that stuff you squirt up your nose? It's supposed to really help the cold not be so bad."

"Yep. If I hadn't, I'd probably be home in bed. So, anyway..."

"I heard of you and know you do kidnapping investigations. Not too long ago I read of that big case where those kidnapped teenagers' mother had lied about their father and gotten him thrown into prison."

"You needn't go on. I remember it well." In fact, the money I'd been paid—including a nice bonus—had enabled me to pay some bills and be choosier about what clientele I took, but I wasn't going to tell her that.

Her eyes wide with hope, she said, "I want to hire you."

"Uh-huh." She must have mistaken my grunt for one of interest, because she kept talking.

"Someone has stolen my babies. My twins."

Oh shoot. Twin babies. How low could a person go? I didn't mean the baby-stealers, although that was beyond low, I meant the story—how could anyone resist helping a person whose twin babies had been stolen? I really needed to develop a thicker skin. I blew out a long breath—no cough, yea. She had me. "Tell me more," I said in a raspy voice. My laryngitis had improved over the past week. Any earlier and she wouldn't have been able to hear me.

She grimaced, her face scrunching up, her eyes full of tears. I didn't blame her. If I'd had even one baby stolen, I would have cried for days. Not that I had any babies. I did not now and didn't intend to ever have any. I pushed my almost-empty box of tissues to her and waited for the dam to burst. Instead, she took a lot of short breaths like I've heard women must do when they're going through natural childbirth.

"I promised myself and my husband I wouldn't cry. I've cried a river since last night."

I nodded. No tears. Good. "So, if you want to tell me about it, I'm eager to hear." Hate to admit it, but it was true.

"My babies were born six weeks ago today. Fraternal twins, a boy and a girl. Fred and Frederika."

No comment on the awfulness of the names. Who was I to judge, with the name my mother had given me? I pulled out a yellow legal pad. "Fred and Frederika?"

"They're named after my great-uncle, my German great-uncle Friedrich, who left us some money in his will."

Had she read my opinion of the names in my mind? Or on my face?

"Oh, my goodness, I'm so sorry. You're asking for our last name. I forgot to introduce myself. I'm Connie Wite. No H." She held out a lavender-smelling hand for me to shake.

"I don't think you want to shake my hand right now. I don't think I am, but I could be contagious. What does that mean, no H?"

She withdrew her hand. "W-I-T-E. Wite with no H. Fred and Frederika Wite are the babies' names. And my husband is Dave."

"Number one, you want to tell me what happened? And number two, have you gone to the police?" Private investigators were not supposed to involve themselves in active cases. Not that I'd ever let that stop me.

She settled back in the chair, but her shoulders were still up around her ears. "Well, I feel so guilty, but the fact is, after six weeks of crying babies, my husband and I were at our wits' end. Last Sunday, we asked Dave's sister, Louise, if she would babysit for us just for a few hours, so we could go out to dinner and a movie on Wednesday, that would be last night. She usually goes to church on Wednesdays, but she agreed so long as we didn't mind her taking the babies to church with her."

"And you and your husband went out?"

"We loaded her car up with both car seats and two diaper bags full of diapers and several bottles of milk—I nurse the babies, but I express enough for several bottles extra just in case."

My boobs cringed. I did my best to continue keeping a straight face.

"When we returned to our home—Louise was going to go back to our house after church and meet us there when we were through with our date—Louise was pacing up and down the sidewalk outside in the dark. She was near hysteria when we stopped the car and got out. Someone had taken the babies from the church nursery while the little girl who attends them was in the bathroom."

Astounded, I sat back and took a moment to just stare at her. If I were a lawyer, I'd be wondering whether Mrs. Wite could sue the church for negligence for losing her children. But I wasn't. Just a P.I. So now I'm wondering whether my energy is back enough that I can help this lady and, also, what the police were up to. "Y'all did call the police?"

"They did at the church, but no one called us. My husband's own sister. Can you believe that? She thought she should come home first and tell us in person and let us handle it. Sometimes I don't believe her stupidity."

Was she saying she and Louise didn't see eye-to-eye on things? And was that relevant?

"Not long after we arrived home, the police showed up and took a report. I could hardly talk, but my husband told them what they needed to know."

Stating aloud what I'd already reminded myself of, I said, "You know, private investigators aren't supposed to get involved in active police investigations."

"Oh." She collapsed like a deflating balloon, folding in on herself.

"Is there some reason you don't want to let the police handle this? Did they say they wouldn't look for your babies? I can't imagine that."

"The one officer was nice, but his partner looked at us funny and asked a lot of questions that made me feel like I'd done something wrong. We're worried he'll focus on us and not search for them."

"Like how did he behave?"

"Frowned at us. Looked at us with an eyebrow raised, his eyes squinting, just like you see them do sometimes in the police shows on television." Her voice grew higher and louder the more she talked. "Like he didn't believe us. Like maybe we or Louise had done something to our babies."

Nuh-uh, he did not. Not in this day and time. With all the human trafficking that's going on, especially in Houston, Texas? My blood pressure rose. Where was that blood pressure cuff when I needed it? "Since last night, have you heard back from the police?"

"Dave and I went down to the station first thing this morning and confronted them to see what they were doing. We're the kind of people who aren't going to sit around and do nothing even when told to stay by the phone and wait for a ransom call."

"That's what the police said to do?" Not quite a rhetorical question.

"But Miss Davis, we're not stupid. We're educated people. Someone could sell our babies and get more money than we could come up with for ransom even though we're both working and making good money. We read. We know what's going on in the world. We know Houston is practically the capitol of human trafficking."

She could probably read the surprise on my face. "And I suppose you have cell phones, so if there was a ransom call, if anyone could even get your cell phone numbers, you could take the calls on your mobiles."

"Of course. And I think the police are doing exactly nothing."

"They did, at least, put out an Amber Alert?"

"Yes. I must give them credit for that."

"Were other children taken as well?"

She shook her head. "No one else brought kids to church last night."

"Huh, back to Louise. They interviewed her separately?"

"Yes. Apparently first at the church and then again at our house."

"The police went to the church and—"

"Talked to the minister and the little girl who was supposed to be babysitting. They also talked to other parishioners or whatever you call them in that Holy Roller church."

Holy Roller church? "And got nowhere?"

She shook her head. "Got less than nowhere."

"Hmmm. I don't usually mess with investigations where the cops are involved." This time I said it aloud. My legs were crossed under my desk. She would have seen my fingers if I'd crossed them.

"Oh, please, Miss Davis." Her voice squeaked. "If you could just ask questions and look around, maybe they missed someone or something. We would never tell Officer Ryan and Officer Tyler you were helping us."

She couldn't have been more sincere. Her big brown eyes welled up with tears. Then I registered what she'd just said. "Officer *Tyler*? Lon Tyler?" OMG. My arch nemesis.

"I think that was his first name. A kind of piggish cop, if you excuse the pun. You know him? He's the one who acted like he didn't believe us." She covered her mouth in disgust. "Are you friends?" She stood.

"Oh, *please*, sit back down. We are definitely *not* friends." But if it was Lon who was doing the *alleged* investigation, it would not bother me one bit, not one teeny-weeny (again no pun intended) bit to help poor Mrs. Wite.

So, against my better judgment, which some people say can be questionable—but I won't go into that—I decided I'd at least do some inquiring. Okay, to be perfectly honest, I decided to let her hire me. I couldn't let her and Dave be victims of Lon's doltishness, assuming the case wouldn't be handed off to someone more competent. "Tell you what, I'll go over there and look around for you." I wrote a not-small sum on a piece of paper. "Here's my fee, for starters. This amount will cover a couple of days. If my investigation runs longer than that, my fee will be more. You can bring the money back here before five this afternoon and give it to Margaret or Candy, okay?"

"Margaret or Candy?"

"The two women who also work here" (allegedly, I thought, since neither of them was actually in the office), "one of whom was supposed to be sitting at the front desk when you came in."

"Okay, Miss Davis. I'll have to make a trip to the bank to transfer some money around, but I'll bring in cash by the end of the day." She handed me a pink Post-It Note. "Here's the name and address of the church and my sister-in-law's name and address. And let me give you my card." She held out a white business card with a red apple embossed on one corner. "I wrote my husband's cell number on the back." The card listed her name, address, phone number and "Freelance Writer. Former Teacher."

"Where's your husband right now? Why isn't he with you?"

Her eyes shifted to the right. I'd have to look up whether that meant something. Or was it eyes shifting to the left that meant something?

"He had some business to take care of. He dropped me off at home after we left the police station. I drove my own car over here."

"I'll need to meet him pretty soon." I stood. "I'll do what I can. You don't have to tell me that time is of the essence, Mrs. Wite. I know it is, especially with little babies. By the way, when they took the babies, did they take the milk and diaper bags? I hope they have enough stuff to take care of them."

"No. They just took the babies and their blankets. They must have bought some supplies—diapers and formula." She let out a sob. "They'll have to feed them formula. I wasn't going to ever feed them formula."

A twinge of anger coursed through me at the heartlessness of the situation. "I'm so sorry. I'm sure that's not the way you intended to wean them from the—the—breast. One more question, you said Holy Roller church, and I see from the name that's what it sounds like. Are you and your husband not members of the same church as his sister?"

Her lips stretched thin. "Oh no. No way we could buy into all that —we're atheists."

An atheist brother and an evangelical sister. Interesting, but none of my business. My business was finding those babies as quickly as possible. I walked her to the front door. "I'll get back to you this evening. Why don't I come by and meet your husband and report on anything I find today?"

She nodded, wiping away a tear with her sleeve as she went out onto the sidewalk.

After closing the door behind her, I punched Candy's number into my cell phone. I hoped she and Margaret weren't up to any mischief.

# CHAPTER
# TWO

A baby bawled somewhere in the back of the house, sounding angry—or hungry, maybe.

Candy Finklestein stood at the front door, her helmet under her arm. Her blue-streaked, collar-length hair rippled in the breeze as she rang the doorbell of a one-story, flat-roofed, orange brick house. After she'd counted to sixty, Candy rang again. The baby still cried. She'd wait, give the defendant time to tend to the baby, give it a bottle, or change it, or whatever baby wanted.

For a few moments, the baby's cries stopped but almost immediately began again.

Luckily, the season was late fall, approaching the holidays but still on the mild side in Houston, which had been suffering from what used to be called unusually hot weather for the last few years. Now more normal. The neighborhood the legal papers required her to go to was one where she could ride her Moped. She never had to enter any of the freeways. Though a suburb, almost out of Houston, the area was still in Harris County and easy for her to navigate without her phone directing her, compared to some in the city. The streets had numbers instead of names, so she could locate addresses with no problem. Not that she'd ever served papers there before, but she wouldn't mind if she had to go again. Nothing was scary. No creeps on the street.

Mavis had always told her if the people were freaky or if anything made Candy uneasy, to get the heck out of there, and either Margaret or Mavis would serve the papers later in a car. Mavis, most likely. Mavis liked to act like nothing frightened her, but Candy knew some things did. Fire ants, for instance. Fire ants had once left little scars on one of Mavis' ankles.

Candy listened for other sounds. All she heard was the rustle of the magnolia tree leaves coming from the left-hand side of the yard. No music. No voices. No vibrations or closing doors. Just a crying baby who sounded angrier and angrier as the moments fleeted by. Candy could tell the difference between an angry cry, a hungry cry, or an I-need-my-diaper-changed cry. When she'd been in elementary school, she had become a big sister to a baby girl born to her mother and the man who had taken Candy's father's place. The following year, a baby boy showed up by the man who took the place of the man who took the place of Candy's father.

Being a big sister, many times Candy had been charged with the babies' care. Yeah, she knew the difference in a baby's cry, and she wished whoever was charged with the care of the crying baby would hurry up, take care of the baby, and come to the door. At that point, she didn't care whether it was the defendant or a babysitter, but at least answer the door and let her know one way or the other.

After ten minutes of ringing and waiting, she considered giving up. The defendant might have figured out Candy was a process server, even though she wore her school uniform, the ugly maroon polo-style shirt and beige slacks. Any idiot could see she was a schoolgirl. She had parked her scooter at the end of the sidewalk leading up to the house and trotted to the door with her backpack on. She couldn't look any more like a high-schooler unless she wore a letter jacket, which she didn't own. No way anyone would think she was a process server. She'd figured that out the first time she'd served papers right after she'd turned eighteen.

Backing down the front steps, Candy continued to hold out hope someone would come to the door. Someone had to be inside to take care of the baby. She didn't want to think about the possibility the baby was alone. She went back to the sidewalk and pulled her cell phone out of her back pocket so she could call Mavis.

Candy had started out working for Mavis as a junior in high school, running errands, copying papers like depositions. Really, Candy did whatever Mavis asked her to do. And, yeah, some things Mavis told her not to do.

Her cell rang, and Mavis' picture popped up. Keeping an eye on the front door and the small driveway that led to a detached garage in the back, in case someone tried to leave in a vehicle, Candy punched the answer icon.

"Hey, Mavis," she said. "No one's answering the door."

"Oh, so that's where you are? You're serving process?" Her voice sounded nasal, which was to be expected since she was still getting over a cold.

"Didn't Margaret tell you? I couldn't get to it yesterday before I had to go to class, so I came out here first thing this morning."

"How long have you been there?" Mavis' voice sounded low, annoyed.

"At least ten minutes."

"Damn. I've already tried twice to get that woman served. I thought maybe she'd come to the door for you."

"Maybe she knows they're divorce papers. Maybe she doesn't want to get a divorce."

"That's her problem. We've been hired to serve the papers. The nature of the case, or the defendant's feeling about it, is not our problem."

Candy had heard that line before. "What do you want me to do?

"She still had two more papers that were supposed to be delivered. She could do them and try this one back in the evening after her math class at Houston Community College. The lady might not be expecting anyone in the evening. "I could come back after I do the others, when I get out of class."

"Yeah. No. I hate for you to have to go all the way back there. Did you have any trouble finding the house? Any problems getting there?"

"No. Easy peasy. I just love navigation systems. Once I looked at its map, I could get here without having to see it every few minutes."

"Good. I don't like the idea of you driving and looking at your phone at the same time. I'm glad it wasn't difficult."

"Is it really important to do today? I mean, I don't know. I didn't look at anything but the citation, but would it hurt to put it off for one more day? Maybe Margaret would have more luck tomorrow. Or I could come back tomorrow at a different time. Maybe hide out down the street or something and catch her coming or going."

Mavis blew her nose into the phone. "Yeah. Time is of the essence. There's a hearing coming up. I promised the lawyer I'd get her served long enough out that she couldn't get a continuance."

"How much time have we got before the lady will be able to continue the case?"

"Ummm, a day, maybe two. But I'd like to get her served and go about our business."

Candy felt the same way. It was so much better if they only had to make one attempt to serve people, though that was unrealistic in many cases. Playing Tom-and-Jerry with a lot of people was part of the job. She caught herself tapping her foot and stopped. "I can come back tonight after class. In fact, if I can't get her served tonight, if you want to let me use your old car, I can do a stake-out. I'm not sure I want to drive my clunker all the way out here. How about that?" She'd been trying to get Mavis to let her do a stake-out for months, ever since she'd graduated from high school, but Mavis kept saying she was too young. "I know what you're going to say—that it's too dangerous—but I'm thinking this neighborhood is safe. Is there any reason this lady would want to hurt somebody?"

"I guess not. The case is a child custody thing. Okay, tell you what. Come back to the office now, please. I've got to go out, and since Margaret is in absentia, I need you in the office. If Margaret shows up this afternoon, you can get started on the service for the other cases before you go to class." Mavis cleared her throat. "After class, you can try to serve that respondent again—rather, tonight. Maybe she'll be home later in the day. I hope I'm making sense."

"Unless this lady is staying somewhere else so her husband can't get to her."

"They do that sometimes. Anyway, we're going to get her. We'll talk this evening about how."

Candy's pulse speeded up. "Woohoo. See you tonight." She wondered whether the baby who was crying was the subject of the lawsuit. That would make sense since Mavis said it was a child custody case. Hard to believe a man would want custody of a little baby, but you never knew these days. Maybe the mother did something he didn't like, or he wanted to get back at her for something so he was asking for the kid.

"Hey, before you hang up, do you know where Margaret went? A woman came in to see me a while ago, and Margaret wasn't out front. The woman has been gone for a few minutes, and I still see no signs of Margaret."

"If she told me yesterday, I don't remember. I came straight out here and haven't heard from her. No reason why I should since I brought two other papers home with me last night to serve after this one."

"All right. You'd have thought she would have left me a note or texted me or something. See you later."

Candy clicked off. She walked back to the front door and took one last shot at perfecting service, leaning on the doorbell. Still, no one came. She'd already peered into the one window where the blinds weren't all the way closed and not seen anyone. Now, she'd go to the back of the house, and then she was out of there. If there was no one in the back, she'd possibly get to do her first stakeout. Alone, she hoped.

She wanted to do the stake-out, but really, it was inconvenient. Although she'd get the experience, she didn't get paid any more than her regular salary no matter how many times or ways she tried to serve people. Neither did Mavis. It was all part of the business.

She traipsed around the back of the house and heard the baby again, but the crying sounded farther away. Walking up the opposite side, Candy realized the crying came from the neighbor's house, not the defendant's or the respondent or whatever you called people in custody cases. So much for that particular kid being the subject of the case. Time to leave, but she still wished someone would take care of the baby so it would stop crying. Much as she wouldn't admit it to anyone because it would affect their view of her, hearing a baby's cries did something to her insides.

# CHAPTER
# THREE

Margaret didn't answer her cell. Even though Margaret had a reputation with me for doing goofy things sometimes, she didn't have a history of not advising me if she couldn't work. I was beginning to get worried. Had she even shown up that morning? I'd been so wrapped up, literally as well as figuratively—due to the cool weather—that the morning was foggy. Figuratively, not literally.

I plopped down in her desk chair. There were no notes, no bits of paper, no Post-its attached to the computer screen, nothing to give me a hint of where my best friend from girlhood had absented herself to. The computer had not been turned on, so I stared at a blank screen. The situation hadn't been helped that Candy had no clue as to Margaret's whereabouts either. Couldn't she at least have texted me?

I hated to leave the office unattended, but I'd promised Mrs. Wite I'd start working on her missing babies immediately. The babies were more important than my office being closed until Candy returned. I grabbed a piece of printer paper and a fat, black permanent marker from the coffee cup impersonating a pencil holder and wrote in large letters: CLOSED FOR A FUNERAL. PLEASE CALL BACK. That should, hopefully, cause any walk-ins to be sympathetic to finding the door locked. Then I taped up the sign and locked the door. I left the lights on, hoping that would indicate someone would be back in the immediate future.

Back at my desk, I texted Margaret that I needed her in the office immediately, packed up my purse and tissues, grabbed a jacket, and headed out the back door with Mrs. Wite's info in hand.

Throwing my belongings into the passenger seat of my new SUV —new to me, anyway. Who could afford a brand spanking new SUV? Not a poor P.I., though I had come up with enough dinero to put a hefty down payment on the one I did buy as well as buy a Moped for Candy.

In order to use my phone through Bluetooth, I plugged it in before asking Siri for directions to the church. I was getting used to Siri navigating, and she almost always got it right. Now was not the time to point out all the slight errors she'd made that had taken me in roundabout routes to my destination.

Pulling into traffic, I headed to The House of Charity Community Church of the Gulf Coast, quite a mouthful of a name if you ask me, but "ours is not to reason why," Alfred, Lord Tennyson, once said. I often keep that quote in mind.

I headed south, my trusty tissue cube on the seat beside me. Luckily, it was around lunch time and rush hour hadn't begun. Of course, in Houston, when rush hour began and ended was a matter of opinion. Rush hour could be considered 24/7/365, though some people thought traffic didn't qualify unless it came to a dead stop at least half a dozen times.

Anyway, I found the church, which was in one of those tin build-ings often used for start-up businesses when they can't afford a real building, either to build or buy one. The parking lot looked like it would hold about a hundred cars, having been cleared of any shrub-bery or trees and nicely paved and striped. Unfortunately, it was empty. I should have looked on the Internet to see if the church had a web site and whether said website listed hours.

So, I drove back to the freeway and pulled into the first coffee shop I saw. Although I had a recent model cell phone, courtesy of my boyfriend, HPD Lieutenant Ben Sorenson, who had given it to me for my birthday, the 5G didn't work any better at always opening webpages than the 4G had. Not to say I fully understood what modern technology was supposed to do. I didn't. Maybe it's not supposed to do that. Candy had tried to explain it to me with limited success. I did think 5G was advertised as being better than 4G, though I didn't know what the G stood for. Luckily, this coffee shop had free Wi-Fi. Is it free everywhere now? I'm not sure.

Anyway, I purchased a hot tea and was able to open the church website and was pleased to see the church opened at one o'clock on Thursdays. I had plenty of time to get a coffee shop sandwich and a bag of chips and check my email. Fortunately, I could return and catch someone without having to go all the way back to my office and return another time. So, that's what I did.

At approximately one fifteen, when I turned onto the road that led to the church, I spotted a red pick-up truck in the church parking lot. Taking my purse, cell phone, and keys with me after I parked, I approached The House of Charity Community Church. The front door was locked. I walked around to the side and found an unlocked door almost at the back of the building. Entering, I was immediately hit with a musky smell. Did evangelical churches burn incense? I didn't know the answer to that. While standing just inside, I did a visual.

To my left was the sanctuary, which looked like it seated about the same number of people as the number of the cars which would fit in the lot times two, for passengers. The floor was carpeted with gray utility indoor-outdoor carpet, sorely in need of a deep clean. The walls were the same metal as the outside, with no insulation or sheetrock. I didn't know much about construction, but it seemed to me there should be walls inside, at least something to keep the elements out. Right now, the weather was moderate-to-cool since we were approaching the holidays. How had they stood it in the summer?

There were no pews, but brown, plastic stackable chairs were stacked against the walls. Piles of hymnals stood on the floor next to the chairs. Down front was a small stage, a podium, a microphone, an antique upright piano, a piano bench, and another one of the plastic chairs. A spotlight aimed at the podium hung from the ceiling. Two black speakers about the size of a construction worker's lunchbox hung on the walls, one on each side of the room.

The clanging of the door had echoed, so I knew someone must have heard it. Moments later, a spindly, bald man about my height came out of a room and greeted me. He appeared to be about fifty, give-or-take.

"Hello," he said as he walked toward me with his hand outstretched. "How may I help you?"

I hesitated because of my cold but went ahead and shook his hand because I always try to get the measure of a person by their handshake. Doesn't always work, though. There was nothing remarkable about his handshake, unlike some I've had. Not cold and clammy. Not hot and sweaty. I was glad of that. "I'm looking for some information on the missing Wite children. I've been hired by the parents to help find them. By the way, I hope you have some hand sanitizer handy. I don't have Covid, and I don't think the remnants of my cold are contagious, but still..." I shrugged one shoulder. "Sorry. I couldn't possibly put off this case until my cold goes away. I'm sure you understand."

One eyebrow hiked up as soon as I opened my mouth. He looked at his hand and dangled it. "I do. Your name is?"

"Oh, sorry again. Mavis Davis. Let me give you my card." I rummaged around in my purse until I found my card case and retrieved one for him, holding it by two fingers so as not to get many germs on it.

He took it from me with two fingers. "'Private Investigator?' I thought the police were investigating who took those babies."

"That's what Mrs. Wite said, but I'm afraid she doesn't have a lot of confidence in the police officers who have been assigned to the case, or at least the ones who met with her. So, I'm assisting in the search. Your name is?"

"Timothy Markham. I'm the pastor here at The House of Charity Community Church of the Gulf Coast." As if I didn't know the name already.

He motioned for me to accompany him down the hall. He led me through a reception office that held a small, antique-looking wooden desk with a file cabinet behind it, a couple of chairs, and pictures of religious figures on the walls in addition to a cross eleven or twelve inches tall. I followed him into what appeared to be his private office behind the reception area. He circled a black, metal desk that had seen better days and indicated for me to sit in one of the, again, brown plastic chairs facing it. He, at least, had a comfortable-looking executive chair, though it bore some wear and tear. The office, fortunately, didn't have the same musky smell as the sanctuary, but, instead, the aroma of oranges. I wondered whether he'd just peeled and eaten one. The smell was that strong.

"Do you want me to get the door?" I asked as I continued my survey of the room.

"No. No. We're alone here."

I wasn't sure whether that was a good thing or a bad thing, but it was a thing. I'd have to cope with it. He didn't look all that dangerous. However, looks can be deceiving. He took a moment to squeeze out a glob of hand sanitizer from a bottle the size of dishwashing liquid that sat next to a landline, an old-fashioned, black desk phone, buttons and all.

Next, he picked up the receiver and pushed said buttons.

"Wait, what are you doing? You're not calling the police, are you?"

One side of his mouth curled up in a smile. "No. I'm calling Mr.

Wite's sister—she's a member of our church—to verify who you are. I want to be very careful in a case such as this."

I shrugged. "Of course. I don't blame you." I sat back and crossed my legs and coughed into a tissue. When I was through, I stuffed the tissue into the other pocket of the jacket. I didn't think it would be acceptable behavior to put my germy tissue into his trash can.

"Louise. Pastor Tim," he said into the phone. "Have you spoken to your brother or sister-in-law-today? There's a woman here who tells me she's been hired about the babies." He glanced my way and then down at the blotter on his desk.

While he was on the phone, I continued looking around. There were two diplomas framed in black dime-store frames probably from back when we still had dime stores, as they appeared a bit yellowed. A brown, wooden two-shelf bookcase, the kind that came with the set of encyclopedias that door-to-door salesmen sold, stood to the left of his desk. A Bible, worn around the edges, a hymnal like the ones I'd seen out front, several binders filled with papers, and a family photograph filled the bookcase. The picture depicted the minister standing with a blonde woman with a big updo. Two grown young men, who resembled the minister, stood between the couple. Two grown young women, again with sculpted blond hair, sat in front of the standing people, three children clustered around them. Nice family.

Nothing else in the small office warranted my attention except for a stand of bottled water in the back corner with stacks of cups on a little table next to it.

After a short few minutes, in which he conversed with the person on the other end of the line, who I assumed was sister Louise, Pastor Tim clicked off the call, apparently satisfied about me. He'd been leaning back in his chair and sat up.

"Okay, Miss Davis. Louise confirmed what you said, so what can I tell you?" I didn't know him well enough to know whether his now friendly attitude and smile were sincere, but I needed to plow ahead.

"I wonder if you can confirm what Mrs. Wite told me about what happened, what you know about it, what the nursery babysitter said, and, if you'd be so kind, show me the nursery."

"I can do all of that. Of course, we're all very alarmed that someone could waltz into our church and grab some children in a matter of a few moments when someone had looked away."

"Not quite looked away as I understand it. She went to the restroom."

"She told me she was only in there long enough to urinate and wash her hands, and she hurried back to the nursery as fast as she could."

I wondered whether those were her words, but I wasn't going to quibble. "Please relay in your own words what happened."

He rocked forward in his chair as he nodded. "You've seen the sanctuary. It's a bit of a distance from this hallway. There's the door through which you entered and the front doors. People generally enter through the front doors. I always enter through that side door. The nursery is next to my office here, and we have a small kitchen, which I'll also show you. There's a door in the back of the kitchen, leading to an alley-like area where the dumpster is located. The restrooms are across from the kitchen."

"Okay, I understand. No outside access to the nursery?"

"No. People come in the front doors and bring any children down the aisle to the nursery. I was in the middle of giving my sermon at about six-thirty last night when our babysitter screamed like she'd been attacked. Of course, at first, I didn't know it was the babysitter. Sometimes a parent will check on their child in the nursery during the service. Could have been a parent that somehow got hurt."

"Then what happened? Did you run back here?"

"One of the ushers did and returned, quite quickly, and beckoned and hollered at me to come right away. I stopped what I was saying, told everyone to remain calm while I ascertained what was going on, and ran here and found the babysitter hysterical. When we got her calmed down, she told us the babies were missing."

"Is she the same babysitter y'all always have?"

"Yes. We pay her to come to every meeting in case there are children. There aren't always. But we have her just in case. If we don't have any and it gets to be halfway through the service, she's allowed to come into the service or go home. I don't allow her to leave until then in case some stragglers come in. Usually if people are late, they're here by the time I start my sermon, after we've sung and prayed." He pressed the side of his bent forefinger to his lips as though trying to remember everything as it had transpired.

"Were the doors or the door leading into the sanctuary closed? Are they usually closed?"

"Yes. In case a baby is crying. We don't want the congregation to be disturbed by noises coming from the nursery or the kitchen."

"I understand. Was anyone in the kitchen? I'm assuming your church has coffee at the ready for discussion after the service. Or maybe not. What's the custom here?"

"Yes, but one of the ladies in the auxiliary sets up the coffee to be ready at the end of the service, so no one was in the kitchen. When we have more money, we'll run a speaker into the kitchen and the nursery so any adults who can't come into the sanctuary will be able to hear the service."

From what I'd seen, they needed money for a lot more things than speakers. How about an inside wall, for one? I wondered how long the church had been opened that they hadn't raised money to complete the interior of the sanctuary. "Okay, so the only people who should have been back here were the babysitter and any children, correct?"

"Correct. Of course, if a congregant needed to use the restroom during the service, he or she could have come back here for that reason and returned to the sanctuary afterward."

"Anyone do that, or do you know?"

"I didn't see anyone leave the sanctuary. Up front it's just me and the pianist facing the sanctuary, and the pianist isn't really facing that way, but could have seen movement with her peripheral vision."

"You didn't see anyone?"

"As I said, no." His forehead drew together for only a moment and then his face became placid again.

"Did anyone ask the pianist about that?"

"I'm not aware but probably. Wouldn't the police have asked if anyone saw someone leave the sanctuary?"

"That's what I'm wondering. So, to reiterate, only you and the pianist could have seen someone, unless, of course, someone down front left and walked down the aisle past the folks in the back and then everyone would have seen them."

"That's right. Just so you don't think I'm holding back, I do want to tell you that sometimes I'll have a choir member come up and lead a hymn or a congregant come up and lead a prayer."

"But wouldn't you be sitting in that single chair I observed on the dais? But it's directly behind the podium, is it not?"

He nodded. "Just about—a little off to the side, so I have a view all the way to the back of the sanctuary."

"So, you would have seen anyone who left while the hymn or a prayer was being led."

"Yes, but I didn't have anyone do those things last night."

"Well, sir, what about the usher? Would he have seen anyone?" I wondered whether there was some reason he didn't mention where the usher had been.

"Oh, yes. I forgot. He stands inside the sanctuary, in front of the double doors."

I was now wondering whether he was holding back something else. "Anything else you can tell me about the event?"

"Only that when I reached the nursery, the babysitter was in hysterics. The usher, who had first checked on the scream, ran out the side door to the parking lot but didn't see anything. I tried to calm the young lady who was babysitting. The usher said he'd checked the restrooms, but they were empty, and no one was in the kitchen."

"And then what happened?"

"People came running. I yelled for someone to call 911. My wife took the babysitter in hand, pulled her to a corner where she could comfort her. I instructed the congregants to return to the sanctuary, that no one was to leave."

"And waited for the police?"

"Yes. We waited between five and ten minutes. Then two officers showed up. Then they called it in, and more officers showed up. Eventually after speaking to the babysitter, everyone's names and other information was provided to them. They said they'd be in touch this week to get complete statements from everyone."

"So, then everyone went home?"

"Except me and my wife. I stayed and spent more time with the officers and my wife cleaned up the kitchen. Then we went home."

I crossed my arms and stared at the front of his desk for a few moments trying to think of anything else I could ask him. My imagination was running wild as I thought of all the possible scenarios that could have gone, and were still going, on. "Do you have any idea who may have taken the children?"

"Lord, no. I'm just astonished by what happened. Who would even have known we had twin babies in the nursery other than the babysitter and anyone who observed Louise bring them in before the service started?" He did look genuinely distressed. And maybe he was, but I'm so suspicious of everyone. I think I was born that way. Right now, though, he'd get the benefit of the doubt.

"Pastor Markham, I appreciate your taking the time to go over the events with me. This whole thing is so very curious."

"I know. Those poor people. I've been praying for them ever since. I hope you or the police will find their babies soon."

I stood. "If you'll just let me get a look at the nursery and the kitchen, I'll get out of your hair—" My eyes went to his bald head. "I'm so sorry. I was speaking figuratively, of course." He hadn't even winced. I guess he was used to it.

"That's all right." He came around the desk. "Just follow me."

He led me into the nursery, which was not much more than a room with a couple of baby beds and other bits of furniture. The kitchen, however, had some of the latest appliances and two long workspaces. I spotted the door to the dumpster on the far side. Anyone could easily skirt around those counters and out the door unimpeded.

"Is there anything else I can do at this point?" He stood with his hands behind his back.

I hesitated. "Well, yes, actually. Could you give me a list of the names and the contact information on your congregants and the babysitter? I'm assuming you've already provided that information to the police."

"Well, the people themselves did. I'm not sure—"

"I promise I won't harass them. Just simple interviews. If you can indicate on the list who the usher was that was first on the scene, so to speak, that would be helpful. I could talk to him after I see the babysitter."

He held his hands up to his mouth in an attitude of prayer and closed his eyes. His lips moved for a moment or two. I suspected he was praying over my request. I was praying he'd grant it, though I gave no outward indication that I was doing so.

"Okay, Miss Davis. I'm uncomfortable with your request, but I'll give the membership list to you. Just a moment while I print it out." He passed by me and went into the reception area. After a few minutes, he returned with the list and a photocopy of a group picture of the church members. "Just so you'll be able to identify them," he said when he handed it to me.

Eager to review the membership list and get started, I left, thanking him profusely and reassuring him I'd keep him posted.

# FOUR

Mid-afternoon Thursday traffic once again tested my courage, but I finally made it back to the office while the sun still shone. When I pulled around to our parking area in the rear of our office, whose car did I spy? The soon to be deceased Margaret Applebaum's, unless she had a good explanation for her earlier absence.

I did not fling open the back door. I was most ladylike when I pulled it open and crossed over the threshold. No stomping. No yelling. Certainly, no cursing—I had given that up recently—at least when anyone else was around, most of the time. Anyway, I entered my personal space, which is adjacent to the back door and across from the restroom, plopped my purse and phone on my desk, and calmly headed down the hallway.

To get to the front of the office, I had to walk past the kitchen. The kitchen is pretty much Margaret's domain, since she's the only one of the three of us who knows how to cook, or is willing to cook, I should say. She's been known to bake some strange concoctions and once in a while some pretty good eats. Unfortunately, if Candy or I happen to be in the office when Margaret's in the mood to play

Martha Stewart, we're required to perform taste tests. I don't even want to think about the last time I tasted an original recipe of Margaret's.

So, as I strolled past the kitchen and happened to glance in, what should I see in the middle of the table that doubles for an island, but a wedding cake with a tiny bride and groom standing on top. There was no question it was a wedding cake. My insides almost became my outsides in reaction thereto. Who, what, where, when, why, and how? I didn't even want to imagine.

I didn't get a chance to arrive at the front of the office where Margaret's desk faced the entry. She almost knocked me over when she skidded to a stop from running toward me.

Stepping back, I assessed Margaret, who has not only been known to experiment in the kitchen but has experimented with her appearance in the past. I will never forget the time she bleached her hair white. Absolutely the only other time I'd seen anyone or anything with hair, or fur, that white was an albino squirrel our high school class saw when we were visiting a park in Washington D.C.

Margaret stood, wide-eyed and breathless, and stared at me apparently expecting me to lambast her for her behavior, or lack thereof, that morning. I, however, stood in awe of her attire. She wore a pale pink dress with a matching jacket and two-tone (pink and white) t-strap stilettos that were probably five inches high. Her face was fully made up. Her hair, coiffed and in a color as close to her natural color, which I'd last seen in high school, mousy brown, now had really pretty highlights.

I wasn't sure what I was looking at wasn't an illusion. I was speechless, absolutely speechless. Turning toward the kitchen, I pointed at the wedding cake, then pointed at her, and waited, with my mouth hanging open, to hear her explanation.

On closer inspection, I then noticed her blood-shot eyes had dark shadows under them. Still speechless, I took her in my arms for a tight hug. "You want to tell me? Or should I guess what is going on?"

I said into her hair. "By the way, nice outfit. You didn't look this good at our prom."

She burst into tears. I can't say I wasn't expecting tears, because plainly something was amiss. On the way back to the office, I'd been hoping, though, to put my feet up for a few minutes on my still somewhat new couch and get a bit of a rest. Guess that wasn't going to happen.

We stood in the hall for two or three minutes. Finally, I let go of her and retrieved some tissues, so she could smear the makeup all over her face while mopping her tears. When she finally calmed down, I led her into my office. We huddled together on the sofa while I waited for her to start.

"Barry and I were going to get married today."

"What!" I would have swallowed my gum if I'd been chewing any.

Her lower lip trembled. "I would have told you, Mavis, but I knew you'd talk me out of it, so we kept it a secret from everyone. We had planned to go to one of those chapels on the outskirts of town, one of those that look like a little church. He rented a limo and picked me up. He looked so nice in a black tuxedo. He brought me a bouquet of red roses."

"Sounds romantic. I guess."

"We had the limo driver take us to that little chapel. We had made reservations a couple of days ago. When we got there, we were third in line, so we had to wait in a really sort-of grungy reception area. The sofa seat was sprung. The coffee table was made of thin black plastic." She stopped to wipe under her eyes and sniff and blow. "Two collapsible chairs like you see people sitting in at ball games were against the wall with two other people sitting in them. Well, I won't tell you anymore about the decorations, but while we waited, I wondered whether we were doing the right thing. Whether *I* was doing the right thing."

I nodded like I do when a new client takes forever to tell me what the heck they want me to do for them. Little nerves tingled around my body. I scratched the side of my face and the back of my head.

"I remembered we'd always said since we were in high school that if either of us ever got married, we'd stand up for the other one."

Goosebumps sprouted on my arms. "Yeah, we did, but I told you even though I never wanted to get married, I'd still stand up for you no matter what. So, what happened?"

"I felt so guilty I hadn't told you. That you weren't there. That I hadn't even given you a chance to be there or Candy either, much less my parents who I know wouldn't have come, but I didn't even call them and tell them what I planned on doing."

"Go on, finish your story."

"Don't be mad at me."

"I'm not mad. Really, I'm not. I just wish you'd at least called in sick, so I'd have known you wouldn't be in today. I didn't have anyone to cover the front, and I had a real need to go out."

"Yeah, I saw the funeral notice on the front door. Who died?"

I guess that was a natural conclusion, though she knew me well enough to know if someone had really died, I would have told her about it. "No one died. I just put the note up there so people might not get as aggravated when they found the door locked. Assuming anyone wanted to walk in and give us a million dollars. But I want to hear the rest of what happened."

"I could hear the people in the other room saying their vows. I looked at the other couple and wondered whether they were really in love. She looked like she was about six months pregnant, so I guess it didn't matter. They were just doing the right thing. Then I looked at Barry who was so handsome in that tux. I got up and walked around and started thinking about what I was doing. Was I being too impetuous? Should I have told you? Or at least Candy, knowing she couldn't keep a secret and she'd tell you? I guess you could say I was having second thoughts."

That was understandable. I'd never given marriage a first

thought. She stood and began pacing. "I like Barry, I really do. In fact, I think I may even love him."

"You think you might love him?" That wasn't the way it should work, was it?

She flapped her hand at me. "Let me finish, okay?" She stomped her foot. "Mavis—"

"I know. I can be annoying sometimes."

In a louder voice she said, "Let me finish! So, it finally became our turn, and we went into the little office that didn't look a whole lot better than the reception area. He had my ring in his pocket. I had his ring on my thumb. We walked up to the woman who was going to perform the wedding, and she asked for the license."

"'License?' We asked. She said, 'you did go to the clerk's office and get a license, didn't you?'"

"I was so nervous I had forgotten all about the license even though we had gotten one yesterday. I had given it to Barry to put in his pocket, because the envelope was too big for the little formal bag I was carrying."

I was wondering how much longer this never-ending-story was going to take, but I refrained from any overt action that would reveal my feelings.

"So, Barry took the license out and handed it to the lady. I guess maybe she's some kind of justice of the peace or something or maybe she got one of those licenses to perform weddings that you get on the Internet. Anyway, she opened it up and looked at it front and back and looked at the other papers the clerk had given to us when we got the license and she said, 'I can't marry you today. You didn't get a judge to waive the three-day waiting period.'"

I'm afraid I let out just about the biggest sigh ever. Margaret gave me a look.

"So, she sent us to the courthouse to get a judge to sign the waiver and said we could come back late this afternoon, that she had time this afternoon."

"You didn't get married, then?"

Margaret shook her head. "No."

"But you can still get married this afternoon if the judge waives the waiting period? Is that what you're going to do? Did you have second thoughts about not inviting me to your wedding, and you're here now to ask me to go home and put on a fancy dress and come to your wedding?"

"Nope, Mavis. Once we got into the limo, I said to Barry, 'Barry, I don't want to get a judge to waive the waiting period. I don't want to get married today. I think we should wait. We've rushed into this too quickly.' Barry was really nice about it. He said he understood, so he had the limo driver take me home, and I knew you'd be mad that I hadn't come to work, so I got my car and rushed right over here without even changing my clothes. I brought the cake I got at the grocery store yesterday. There's plenty of sugar in it, so you and Candy can go to town." She stopped in front of me, smiling like she'd just found a prize under a scratch off. "Okay?"

I nodded and stood and hugged her again. "Okay. I'll take you up on that cake. There's just one thing I want to know, though. Who is Barry?"

# CHAPTER
# FIVE

Margaret's brows drew together in what I took to mean she had put on her thinking cap and was deciding what to tell me about Barry. I didn't tap my foot while I waited, but I thought about it. I wanted to know where she found this Barry guy, but my mouth watered for some non-wedding cake. We also needed to get to work on the Wite case.

"Okay, well, you know how I've been on some dating sites?"

"Yes, though I've forgotten how many over the past year."

She shrugged. "Well, I've also been on this site that's about looking for missing people. I joined, in fact. It's called WebDetectives."

"A Facebook group or what?"

"There's a Facebook site and a website. I started out just looking around both of them and then I joined. I met Barry on the Facebook site."

"And when was that, pray tell?"

She licked her lips and rolled her eyes. "I know what you're going to say, Mavis."

"You can't know what I'm going to say when I haven't heard the answer to my question. But based on your demeanor, I take it you aren't that well-acquainted with him."

"Not as well-acquainted as I started thinking we ought to be this morning."

"Which is?"

"Okay. I really liked him right off. We met online two months ago. We met in person one month ago."

"And decided to get married when?"

"You mean when did he propose to me? Last week."

I put my hand on her forearm and squeezed. "You made a wise decision, Margaret, to put it off for a while."

She did a double-take. "You're not mad at me for keeping him a secret?"

"I'm not your mother. I'm your best friend. I'm a little hurt, but I can understand. You were afraid I'd give you the third degree and discourage you if I didn't like what you told me, or if you introduced me and I didn't like him. I apologize. I know I'm often too hard on you."

"Often?"

"Yeah, how about frequently? I'm frequently too hard on you. And Candy. I'll try to do better."

"I appreciate that, Mavis. I really do want to tell you all about him."

"And I want to hear it but not right now."

She looked slightly aggrieved.

"Really, I do want to know all about him, but while you were out galli—"

"Mavis..."

"While you were out this morning, we had a walk-in. A new client. A lady who has hired us to help the police find her twin babies who were stolen from a church nursery last night."

"Oh, wow! That's why that woman brought that money. She didn't say what it was for. Oh, my goodness! That's terrible." She spun around.

"She's already brought the money? Good news. Good to know I've been paid since I've already been working for her."

"I made up the deposit slip, too. I'll take it by the bank when I leave here. So, what can I do to help? Tell me what happened."

"Tell you what, let me go to the restroom and then get a piece of your cake and then you come into my office, and I'll clue you in."

"Okay. Do I need to take notes or anything?"

"No, but I do have something I need you to do ASAP. So, maybe go get some paper."

She hurried to the front of the office. I took care of business, and then put a little bit of water in the kettle and put it on to boil. I cut myself a decent slice of cake—if I was going to make it into the evening, I needed some sugar. I was feeling so much better than I had been that morning. I'm not an adrenaline junky, but ever since Mrs. Wite had come into the office, it was like I was operating on an adrenaline rush. I know they don't last that long, but I did feel stimulated. Did that mean my cold was really at an end? Was I even making any sense?

Margaret nestled in one of my client chairs before I was even able to pour hot water over the teabag. One thing I loved about Margaret was that she brought her eagerness to work just about every day. Sometimes so much so, I was overwhelmed.

Anyway, while I waited for the kettle to boil, I informed Margaret about what Mrs. Wite had told me. I gave her my notes and asked her to make a file for Mr. and Mrs. Wite. Then I told her about my trip to the church and my interview with the pastor.

"Did he exude righteousness?"

I laughed. "He didn't come across as someone who was overly religious. I was surprised. He did pray over whether he should give me the list of his parishioners. That was interesting. I watched, but his prayer only took a minute or two." I handed her the list.

She took a gander at it. "Shouldn't there be a lot more people on it than this?"

"It's a new church and rather small. I'm betting he's worried this event will cost him some parishioners, too."

"I guess he is. I think I'd go elsewhere."

"So, first, make two copies of that, one for me, one for you, and put one in the file. Then you can start checking up on everyone on that list. Find out whatever you can."

"All right. I can work on that. I'll make the deposit tomorrow morning on my way in."

"Well, you can't get through it today, but do you mind staying a little late?"

"Not at all, Mavis. Those poor people."

"I know. What a weird thing to happen." The kettle began whistling, so I skirted around my desk to go to the kitchen. "As soon as you can, bring back my copy to work from. I'm going to call some of the people right away. We need to act quickly."

"Sure. I'll get busy. And thanks for not yelling at me."

"You know I love you, Margaret."

"And me, you."

"Before we get too mushy, let me show you the names of the two people I want you to start with." I put a checkmark next to the babysitter's name and the usher's name.

"I'll get right on those." She went back to the front of the office, and I went for my tea. While I was enjoying my tea and cake, I devised a plan. Should I talk to the babysitter and the usher on the phone or make appointments to see them? Make appointments. My calendar showed I had nothing pressing in the next few days. I had said I'd meet with Dave Wite that night, but I could get started on the first two people right away. Tomorrow morning, I'd start on the others. Candy could take care of any errands and serving papers. Margaret would help when I needed her, beginning now with the background checks.

As soon as Margaret brought my copy of the list, I pulled out a legal pad and wrote the name of the first person: Laura Kate Allison. I knew nothing about her. I probably should have asked the pastor how old she was. I was starting from scratch.

I punched in Laura Kate Allison's phone number. After three rings, the call went to voicemail. I left my name and number and what I wanted. There was a second number for her, so I called it. A woman answered right away.

"May I speak with Laura?"

"Laura Kate is still in school. This is her stepmother, Amy Allison. Is there something I can help you with?"

"I don't know, ma'am. My name is Mavis Davis. I'm a private investigator looking into the kidnapping of the Wite babies. I understand—Laura Kate? That's what she goes by?"

"Yes, that's right."

"I've been told by Pastor Markham that she was the babysitter last night when the children went missing."

A sigh on the other end of the call. "Yes, she was, I'm sorry to say. So, you're helping the police find the babies?"

"I've been hired by Mr. and Mrs. Wite to assist the police in this matter. I was hoping to speak with Laura Kate. What is she, a senior? Does she have off campus privileges? I could catch her during sixth or seventh period if they have that at her school. I guess it's too late to catch her for home lunch, if she has that?"

"She's a good girl and has all the privileges, but we, especially her father, would want to be present when you talk to her. I'm not going to apologize for that."

"I understand. Will y'all be home tonight? I could come by then."

"She's told the police and everyone everything she knows. I don't know why you would want to talk to her about it."

"Well, ma'am, sometimes another person can have a different perspective."

"I guess. I'm sure those people have a good reason why they're bringing you into it instead of waiting for the police to find the children."

First of all, her calling the Wite's "those people" didn't sit well with me. I wondered if she meant something by that. Secondly, I wasn't going to give her a summary of my experiences with Officer Lon Tyler and his ineptitude. I didn't know the other cop, but hopefully he had some modicum of intelligence. And the thing is, I didn't even know if they were the cops assigned to the case or just the ones who caught it the night before.

"I don't know the parents, Mr. and Mrs. Wite," she said. "I know Louise, Mr. Wite's sister, and she's a good person, so I guess it would be okay."

Why did I think she'd be calling Louise to check on me before dinner? Speaking of whom, I needed to talk to her in the worst way, too. Maybe I could catch her this evening as well. "Thank you, Mrs. Allison. I appreciate it."

"Laura Kate has been too upset to even think about going out anywhere except school, so she'll definitely be home. I guess it would be okay if you want to come out here after dinner. I'm going to make sure her father doesn't object and call you back if he does. Otherwise, come on when you can. We have dinner at six."

"Thanks. By the way, were you at the church on Wednesday evening?"

"I made the coffee and set out some cookies for after the service and went into the sanctuary after I checked on Laura Kate."

"Well, then, I'd like to speak with you about it also. You'll be home this evening?"

"Of course."

"Was your husband at church on Wednesday night also? I'd like to talk to him if he was."

"Mmmm. No. Jimmy doesn't go. He doesn't belong. But he'll want to be present when you talk to Laura Kate. You know she's only seventeen, right?"

I didn't tell her seventeen qualifies a kid to be handled as an adult in a criminal case in Texas, but knowing her age was good information. I would have asked this evening. "Mrs. Allison, while I have you on the phone, I wonder if you could answer a few questions for me."

"I'll certainly try."

"Laura Kate's the regular babysitter for the church, right?"

"Yes. She has a little friend who will do it if there's a school activity or something that would get in the way, but Laura Kate is most often the babysitter. She took over last year when the other girl graduated from high school and went off to college."

"I see. So, I take it Laura Kate has had a lot of experience babysitting?"

"She babysat here in the neighborhood before she had the church job. Even little babies, but I wouldn't let her if we weren't going to be home. I wanted to be available for her if the baby was really young."

As an experienced babysitter, Laura Kate must be considered responsible if she'd been doing the job for a year. I wondered if there had been any other incidents, anything anyone would have been concerned about, but I decided to wait to ask that until we met in person. "Well, thank you very much Mrs. Allison. I'll see you around seven this evening."

"Okay. You should have no trouble finding us. We're in a subdivision."

"I have a navigation system, too, and your phone number if I get lost. Take care."

The phone call felt perfectly normal. A stepmother being protective of the child in her care. Of course, I couldn't see her, but I didn't detect anything suspicious in her voice except for that one statement. Being as how the Wites are white, Anglo-Saxon, though not Protestant, was there any reason Mrs. Allison would refer to them as "those people?" The only explanation I could think of was that the Wites were not religious. Would the fact they were atheists have anything to do with the children being missing, or was I making a lot out of two little words in a telephone call?

# CHAPTER
# SIX

J ust as I was at the back door, leaving to grab a leisurely bite to eat and head to the Allison's, the babies' mother, Mrs. Wite, phoned me. "Are you still coming over this evening, Miss Davis?"

"Mavis, please. And yes. I was planning to bring you up to date."

"Dave's home, Mavis, if you're ready to come now."

"Good, that way I can tell you both what I've been up to." My early dinner could wait even though my stomach would have an opinion on that. "See you in a few minutes."

The Wites only lived twenty minutes from my office even with late afternoon traffic. Judging by the young adults who were mowing lawns and milling about, the garden neighborhood was one for working professionals. The Wites' house wasn't exactly cookie cutter, but similar in architecture to all the others in the subdivision with two-car garages and short driveways. I'd guesstimate a three-bedroom-two-bath and maybe a den or a study. A small SUV similar to mine sat in front of the first garage bay, on the driveway. The garage door was open, and a BMW sedan occupied the second bay.

Connie Wite answered the door after one ring. "Glad you could make it." She lowered her voice. "Dave is in the kitchen. I'm hoping you can reassure him that you'll get to the bottom of this and find our children."

I was hoping so, too. She led me to a family room, which held a big screen television attached to the brick wall above the fireplace. Two oversized sofas, facing each other, looked so cushiony I suspected if I sat back, I'd need help getting out. A large, oak-framed, glass coffee table and matching end tables were arranged so they'd be an easy reach from the seating. The aroma of what smelled like take-out fried chicken permeated the room. I perched on the edge of the closest sofa.

Connie had disappeared and reappeared with a clean-shaven man with a full head of blond hair, dark eyes behind gold-rimmed glasses, about my height, that being five-foot-ten, slim but not thin, dressed in a brown and beige plaid sport shirt under a dark brown blazer over a pair of khaki chinos and loafers. I wondered what he did for a living. He held a beer can in one hand, switching hands to shake mine. Of course, his grip was icy cold and firm but not bone crushing. He did not smile when we were introduced. Not that I was really surprised at that. In his situation, I wouldn't have been smiling either.

Dave sat across from me with Connie by his side. "I hear you've already been working on finding our children?" The muscles in his jaws flexed.

"Yes, sir, I've been to the church and spoken to the pastor to get his perspective. I managed to get him to give me a list of all his congregants or parishioners or whatever they call them at that church—members, anyway. He has no idea who took your kids."

Dave swallowed from his can of beer twice while I talked. I wondered if he was on the way to getting drunk on purpose or if that would be his only alcoholic drink that day. "You believe him? I mean, come on, how could he not know what was going on in his own church?" His face had grown pink.

"Well, sir, he was way down front—"

He took another drink of beer. "Yeah, but—"

Connie squeezed his elbow. "Let her finish, Dave."

Dave crushed the beer can in his hand. I thought he was probably thinking of doing that to the perpetrator. I couldn't see how developed his muscles were with what he wore, but, still, he was a man. "I'm just so—so—" He jumped up and passed me by. The can made a racket when it went into the trash can, at least that's what I thought he did with it. He returned with another can of beer. "It's just so unbelievable! How can someone waltz into a church and steal children?" His face had gone from pink to red.

"I'll do everything I can to find them. I have an appointment with the babysitter, Laura Kate, and her parents at seven. I don't know how well the police questioned her, but I'll ask in great detail what happened. It is hard to believe she could have been just down the hall in the bathroom and not heard anything."

"When I find out who did this—who took them—"

Connie gripped his arm and pulled him back down on the sofa. "You won't do anything, Dave," she said, her voice a higher pitch than earlier. "The authorities will prosecute the person."

"If you don't mind my asking, I'd like to get a little more information on the two of you. You never know, but it's possible whoever took the babies had some kind of vendetta against one or both of you."

"But how could they have known where Fred and Frederika were Wednesday night?"

"I don't know. That's something we'll eventually find out." I pulled my cell phone out of my purse and tapped the notebook icon. "Mr. Wite, what do you do for a living? Where do you work?"

"I don't see how any of that has anything to do with the kids."

Connie squeezed his arm. "He works at the University of Houston."

"Thanks." I dictated his name into the notebook and tapped out the information. "And what position do you hold, Mr. Wite?"

"Assistant Professor in the mathematics department. I don't see how anyone at the University of Houston could be involved in this."

Ignoring his outburst, I asked, "How long have you been there?"

"Five years. In another two, I could be promoted to Associate Professor. That's what I'm working toward." He glanced at his wife and almost smiled. He patted her hand, which was still clutching his elbow. He set his beer down on the end table and sat back.

"Anyone there have it in for you? Any crazy students who would want to get back at you? You haven't been there long enough to become real competition to any other professors, have you?"

"There's always campus politics," Connie said. "But Dave has many friends there. You haven't made anyone angry, have you, honey?" She leaned forward and peered into his face.

"No one I can think of. I try to mind my own business. I mean, yes, there are some irate students sometimes. Most of those are angry about their grades, but when they come to see me, I explain to them what they need to do to bring them up and tell them how they're in college now and have to be responsible for their own behavior."

I remembered getting a lecture like that my freshman year. What a rude awakening.

"So, you teach what, freshmen and sophomores?"

"Sometimes I sub for advanced classes if there's some kind of emergency and they need someone to cover for one of the Associate Professors. Someday I'll be one of them, I hope, and not have to deal with sniveling kids."

"Be nice, now," Connie said. "Mavis, he comes home sometimes worn out from trying to get the kids who are required to take math for their degree to understand any of it, much less like it."

"But I've never had any kind of a violent run-in with a student, so I'd rule out anyone from the school having a vendetta against me."

I tapped my own form of shorthand into the notebook, enough for me to remember later what was said. I could write it all out when

I had the time. "What about you, Connie? Do you work outside the home?"

She nodded. "I'm on maternity leave and I'm—I was—taking the rest of the year off. I'm a music teacher at an elementary school."

"I didn't know they still had music programs in elementary schools. I guess that's a dumb statement. Of course, they do, otherwise who would play in the bands?"

"And we have choirs, of course. I love my job. The kids, especially the ones from more disadvantaged homes, get so much from music education. A lot of them don't have—well, they do have music in their homes, but not a good foundation in music." She shrugged as if to say she was trying to be politically correct.

"I understand. Same questions for you as your husband."

She shook her head. "I can't think of anyone who would be angry with me. I've been there since I graduated from college. I found the position right as the previous teacher was retiring. Very fortunate for me."

"No angry parents?"

"At open houses, the parents are always excited their kids have the chance to take music class. So, I'd have to say no."

"And no spats with other teachers?"

"No. I know it sounds too good to be true, what we're telling you, but we've talked about it, and we can't think of anyone who doesn't like us," Connie said.

"Probably there are some, but if so, we don't know about it." Dave took another swig from his beer. He'd grown calmer over the course of the conversation.

"What about neighbors? Any property disputes? Any fights at the HOA meetings? I know those can sometimes be contentious."

"Well, we did have a dispute last year over our back fence. The HOA had the shrubs on the other side of it cut down without talking to us. On the other side of the fence is the street opposite the elementary school for this subdivision."

"That the one you work at?" I raised my eyebrows at Connie.

"No. I work across town."

"So, what happened? Were the shrubs on your property?"

"That wasn't it," Dave said. "The fence was old with a lot of boards with rotted places in them. We knew that, but the shrubs were so thick that no one on that side could see the holes. Once they cut down the shrubs, the holes in the fence were glaringly apparent."

"The fence looked awful," Connie said. "We wouldn't have minded so much what they did, but we were just pregnant. Our focus was getting our house ready for a baby. Later we found out we were having two babies."

"Once they cut down the shrubs, they sent us a notice that we needed to install a new fence, or the HOA would fine us." Dave stood up and then sat down again. "I called the president, and he said they voted and decided the shrubs were too thick and unsightly, and that we should have attended the meeting."

"So y'all got into it?"

Dave looked like a sheepish child. "Yeah, well, I had some choice words for him—for them. Paying for a new fence across the back of our property was not in our budget. You know what wood costs these days?"

"They didn't have a fistfight or anything," Connie said. "The President of the HOA is a deputy sheriff. He's usually pretty nice, but he can throw his weight around when he wants."

"Would he want to see any harm come to your family?"

"I don't know why he would," Dave said. "We put the new fence up right away to avoid the fines. We've seen him since at National Night Out, and we've shaken hands."

"That's the only falling out with any neighbors?"

"We didn't discuss that matter with any of the others, so yeah."

I was coming to the end of my questions about possible suspects.

"Oh, I'm so sorry," Connie said. "I'm so rude. I should have asked you if you wanted anything to drink. Can I get you something? A soda or some water?"

I realized I hadn't coughed since I'd entered their home, but my throat was past dry. "Some water would be good, thanks." Connie left me alone with Dave. "Dave, absolutely no one else comes to mind who would have it in for you? You can't think of anyone?"

His lips were stretched thin across his teeth. He covered his mouth with his hand and shook his head. I wondered whether he was going to cry. Wouldn't be the first time a man shed a few tears around me, but I can't say it's my favorite thing to witness.

"Would you tell me about Louise, your sister? As I understand, she's a member of that Holy Roller church, and y'all are atheists, right? How does that sit with her?" I wanted to see if he'd react to my calling it a Holy Roller church.

He sniffed and swallowed and sat up straighter, looking like he was glad for a change in subject. "She's tried to convert us, but we don't believe in that fiction."

"How did it happen, that y'all ended up in two different religions? Not that being an atheist is a religion, but you know what I mean."

Connie returned and handed me a bottle of water wrapped in a paper towel. I nodded my thanks.

Dave's laugh wasn't nearly genuine. "My sister—I love my sister, but she has a way of getting involved in things. I think she's searching for answers, often in all the wrong places."

I remembered a song that went kind of like that. I took a swallow of water, grateful that Connie finally thought of it. I hadn't wanted to be rude and ask. "How long has she been a member of this church?"

"A couple of years. This pastor started it up in an old, closed down office supply store. They rented the space. Louise met him somewhere. I'm not sure where or if one of her friends got her to go. I've forgotten."

"Her friend Carmen asked her to go with her," Connie said. "Remember when Louise came back and told us that people were rolling around on the floor and making strange noises and how it scared her?"

"Oh, yeah, that's right." He snorted. "We all had a good laugh about that. She had never heard of people speaking in tongues."

"Is she younger or older than you?"

"A lot younger, but still, she's an adult. She had a bad time with drugs for a while and had gone into a recovery program," Dave said, with a glance at his wife. "When she came out, Carmen, who she had been friends with in high school, appeared back on the scene. I don't remember where they ran into each other again, but they started hanging out. Then one day Louise went to church with Carmen."

Connie said, "We thought it was just a one-time thing. She went a second time and came back and told us that the pastor said if she didn't believe the teachings of his church she was going to hell. Louise was really confused, but she was still recovering from the recovery program, if you know what I mean."

"They caught her at a low point in her life?"

"Yeah, they did. Pretty soon she was regularly going to church with Carmen or by herself. Then one day she told us she'd been baptized in that church and had joined," Connie said, shaking her head.

"And that was that? She's been going ever since?"

"Regularly. She never misses a service."

"But the church isn't in that old building anymore. It's in a— what I call a tin building in kind of an out of the way place," I said.

"They raised the money to buy the land and then borrowed to build the building. We went with her when they had the ceremony about the building. I forgot what they called it. Do you remember, Dave? What I remember is that people gathered around us and started asking questions and asking us if we were going to join."

"They were nice and welcoming. So nice and welcoming, that we got out of there as soon as possible," Dave said.

"They were like doll people," Connie said.

"Doll people?" That was a term I hadn't heard of before.

"Too nice. Too sweet. Unreal like. No one is truly like that. I don't care who they are," Dave said.

"So, you asked Louise to babysit even though you knew she'd be taking the twins to that church." Not really a question, I suppose, but I was curious about it.

"The twins are too little to be influenced by that sort of people. They're only six weeks old. And besides, Dave did have someone do a background on the pastor, and he came back as being okay. We didn't think anyone would do anything but take the best of care of the twins. Louise loves the babies."

I chewed on a cuticle for a moment. I probably would have more questions later, but I needed to digest what we'd discussed. I also needed to get to the Allisons'. I drank some more water and tried to think of anything else I might need to know in the next day or so. Nothing came to mind. I edged my way toward the front door. "All right. I'm headed for the babysitter's house. I'll keep y'all clued in on anything interesting I find. And will you let me know if you hear from the police? If they learn anything that I might find useful?"

"Be sure to tell us as soon as you find out who did this," Dave said, his tone back to the angry one he'd used when I'd first arrived.

Connie pushed herself in front of him. "Go back inside," she said. "Thank you, Mavis." She whispered, "I'm trying to keep him under control."

# CHAPTER
## SEVEN

I breathed a sigh of relief as I drove away. That Mr. Wite was past being intense. I hoped I'd find the perpetrator before he did.

No sooner had I pulled away from the Wites' when I received a call from Candy.

"Mavis, I've been trying to get you. Didn't you check your voice-mail?" She sounded stressed and breathless.

"Sorry. I was interviewing clients. Where are you? Have you talked to Margaret?"

"Yes, I'm at the office. In my office."

Some months earlier, Candy had asked, and I'd agreed, to let her turn our storage room, where we housed the copier, into an office for herself. She'd said having her own space made her feel like a real part of the staff.

"It's getting late, and I need to know whether you want me to stake out that house and try to serve that woman from this morning, or whether I can make plans with my friends."

"My mind has been elsewhere. I take it Margaret brought you up to date on her own life and told you about the case we were hired on today."

"Yes to both. She's crazy sometimes, but at least we have cake. I'm glad she didn't get married to someone she barely knows, like someone we haven't had a chance to check out."

"Me too. Pretty scary. So, go ahead and see if you can get that woman served if you don't mind."

"You're working on that new case? That's terrible about those twins."

"Yeah. I'm headed to the babysitter's house to see what I can learn from her, and possibly anything her stepmother might have seen or heard, then I'll call it a night. I'm worried that every minute that goes by gives the kidnappers more time to do something with the babies, but I don't know what else I can do this evening."

"I'll check in with you after I get to that neighborhood and see if that lady is home. Will you keep your cell phone on? At least so I can text you?"

"Okay. I'll feel better anyway with you being out in the field. Take care of yourself. And watch the traffic."

Candy laughed and disconnected.

The address for the Allisons' that I'd gotten from the list proved to be in a Houston suburb a few miles from the church. The neighborhood was another subdivision, like the Wites' but with more modest and cookie-cutter older homes with one-car garages. Most of them were well-kept, give or take one or two that had overgrown grass.

I blew my nose, pocketed the tissue, and drew a deep breath. I'm in the business of questioning people, but often I'm a little nervous about it. I knew from my years as a social worker that you never know what's behind the door to a house. In this case, the front door was opened almost before I'd finished ringing the doorbell.

"It's after seven," a petite brunette woman, who looked to be in her early thirties, said.

I took it she was the stepmother, Amy Allison. "I know. I'm sorry. It took longer than I thought to get here. May I come in?"

She backed away from the door. "Of course." She was dressed in a short-sleeved red sweater, winter-white slacks, and black flats. She pointed into the house. "Go on in the dining room. Laura Kate and Jimmy are waiting for you at the table."

"I often forget how bad the traffic is on Thursdays—in every direction." The dining room was just large enough, if you squeezed between the walls and the chairs, to hold a table about six feet long. A teenage girl and a large, muscular man who looked to be in his forties, were talking quietly with each other when I entered. The man sat at the head of the table, the girl adjacent to him. I approached them and held out my hand.

The man stood. He was dressed in jeans and a long-sleeved blue-plaid shirt. "I'm Jimmy Allison." He was considerably taller than me. I'd bet he weighed every bit of three hundred pounds, almost all of it muscle. I could tell by the thickness of his shoulders and neck.

"I know I sound nasal, but I'm not contagious, I swear. This is just the dregs of a cold."

He shook my hand briefly, squeezing but not smashing my fingers, and sat back down. "This is my—our—daughter Laura Kate."

Laura Kate feigned a smile and didn't shake my hand, which was no surprise since most teenagers don't. She had long, straight blonde hair parted in the middle, blue eyes, a perky nose, pert lips, and a few extra pounds. A cell phone sat on the table next to her elbow.

Mrs. Allison said, "Have a seat, Miss Davis. Do you need anything before we begin?"

"No, thanks. I just finished a bottle of water." I was starting to feel the urge to use the facilities but thought that would be an awkward thing to ask right off the bat. I sat down across from Laura Kate. Amy sat to my left. I quickly got the message that the parents weren't going to give me any alone time with her.

"Now, what is it you want to know?" Mr. Allison asked.

"May I make notes on my notebook app on my phone? I won't record y'all, but if I make a few notes, I'll be able to remember better later without having to call you back."

He nodded. I glanced at Mrs. Allison and then Laura Kate, and they both gave tacit agreement.

I opened the app on my phone and asked some preliminary questions like how old Laura Kate was, what school she went to, what grade she was in, and what her experience as a babysitter was. Just trying to establish some rapport. Then I turned to the stepmother, "As I understand it, Mrs. Allison, you drove Laura Kate to the church last night."

"Yes. I always drive her and stay for the service."

"Just in case you're wondering," Mr. Allison said, "I'm not a member of that church. I don't go to church. I'm not a religious person, but I don't interfere with other peoples' beliefs."

"Good to know." I turned back to Mrs. Allison. "Did you see anything unusual when you arrived in the parking lot? Or any people you didn't recognize?"

"No, but we always get there a little early so Laura Kate can make sure everything is as it should be in the nursery, and I can get the coffee things ready."

"Do y'all enter by the side door near the kitchen, the office, the nursery, and, I guess, the restrooms? I'm afraid I don't remember exactly where the restrooms are situated."

She nodded. "There's no sense in us parking near the entrance and then having to walk all the way through the sanctuary to get to the back."

"No one was in the back when y'all arrived? Or was someone there?"

"Pastor Markham was there. He's always in his office until the last minute, working on his sermon. But I didn't see anyone else, did you, Laura Kate?"

The girl shook her head and fiddled with the top button of her blouse. "The doors to the restrooms were cracked open and dark. No,

I take it back, someone, a man I recognized, was coming out of the men's room when we got there. No big deal. He went into the sanctuary." Her eyes flickered at her phone.

"Okay, so nothing unusual in the parking lot, no strangers in the back of the church. Was that back door to the kitchen locked or unlocked?"

"Locked," Mrs. Allison said. "I always check it to make sure if anyone's been in the church between Sunday and Wednesday night that they didn't leave it unlocked. After the service when I put out the trash, I always lock it back."

"Last night, after the—the taking of the twins, did you try the back door to the kitchen?"

Her eyes teared up. "It was unlocked."

I glanced at each of their faces. "So everyone's concluded that whoever it was left by the kitchen door?"

All three nodded.

"Laura Kate, I'll ask you the same questions as your—as Mrs. Allison. Did you see anything or anyone out of the ordinary last evening?"

"No, ma'am. I've thought and thought about it, but everything was like it always is."

I couldn't see under the table, but someone's knee was vibrating. I suspected Laura Kate, because if it had been Mr. Allison, who had a snug fit at the head of the table, the whole table would have been shaking. I could see why Laura Kate would be nervous. If I'd lost someone's babies, I'd be quivering in my boots.

"What was the nursery like when you arrived?"

She shrugged and glanced at her father. "Like how I left it on Sunday. Then Louise—Miss Wite—came in. She held a baby in each arm. She asked me if I'd go out to her car and get the diaper bags. She had parked outside the back door, too. So, I did."

"Still didn't see anyone or anything unusual out there?"

"No, ma'am. I locked her car and went back inside. By that time, she'd put one baby in each baby bed with their blankets. They were a little restless, but they were okay."

"Then what happened?"

"Louise—Miss Wite, gave me a few instructions and left to go into the sanctuary. She wanted me to give each baby about half a bottle and thought they'd go to sleep then."

"Is that what happened?" I took out my tissue and blotted my nose.

She nodded. Her eyes went to her cell phone again. I knew from Candy, and others these days, that eyeballing one's cell had become as natural as blinking for some people.

Mrs. Allison said, "Laura Kate was sitting in the rocking chair and feeding one of the babies when I checked on her before I went into the sanctuary. Everything looked fine."

"So, Laura Kate, you fed one baby and I guess checked its diaper and laid it down to sleep and then you fed the other baby and did the same and laid it down to sleep? They were both fine, not fussing or anything?"

"No, ma'am, once they had their bottles, they were calm. They were good little babies. So cute. The kind of babies anyone would want." Her cheeks grew red. "I mean if someone had a baby. I know that didn't sound right." She clasped her hands on the table and stared at them. One tear rolled down her cheek.

Mr. Allison laid a humongous hand on his daughter's arm. "It wasn't your fault, honey. You had nothing to do with what happened."

"Mr. Allison, just out of curiosity, where do you work?"

"Pipefitter. I work in Texas City."

"Regular hours?"

"Shift work. Does that matter?"

"No, sir, except I'm wondering whether anyone at your work might have any reason to want to get your family in trouble. Just a fleeting thought."

Shaking his head, he said, "I don't think anyone at the plant even knows where I live or where the girls go to church. We only see each other at work and at the union hall or other union activities throughout the year."

"And Mrs. Allison, same question."

"I'm a housewife." She sat stiffly upright, her chair not fully under the table, so she was slightly turned toward me, and her hands rested in her lap.

Old fashioned way of saying it, but I knew what she meant. If she'd said domestic engineer, I'd have thought she was a feminist, maybe, but I had the distinct impression that she was nothing like a feminist. Did they even have any of those in evangelical churches? Didn't know and didn't want to find out unless it pertained to the case. "Mrs. Allison, since you make the coffee on Wednesdays, I take it you're one of the more active members of the church. Like in a ladies' auxiliary or whatever they call it."

"I'm in a circle. We raise money for groceries for poor families at Christmas time. And one of the older ones is teaching knitting to those who don't already know how, so we can knit things for charity. The church isn't that big. I know all the other ladies, but I'm best friends with just two other ladies. Louise and Carmen are my best friends."

"I haven't met Louise yet." Carmen's name had come up earlier. "Is there any reason to believe Louise or Carmen would be involved in this kidnapping?"

Her eyes grew wide, and she clasped her hand to her mouth. "You think that could be possible?"

My gut told me something in her response was not quite authentic. She didn't answer my question. I looked at Laura Kate and Mr. Allison. I got no read from Mr. Allison and Laura Kate still stared at her hands. The roses in her cheeks had turned blood red. "I'm just asking questions. I don't know those ladies, so I have no reason to think they or anyone in your church had anything to do with the kidnapping."

"Oh. Okay." Her hands had gone back into her lap and were holding each other so tightly her knuckles had turned white.

"Who all knew the babies were there or would've known the babies were in the nursery? Louise and any others?"

"Well, I suppose Louise could have mentioned it to someone. When I went into the sanctuary, I told the lady I sat next to that Laura Kate was babysitting Louise's niece and nephew and how cute they were, but she certainly didn't have time to tell anyone."

"Laura Kate, did you know you'd be babysitting the babies before you arrived that evening? I mean, did Louise call you ahead of time?"

Her eyes met mine. "No, ma'am. I never know if there will be any kids. I just show up and I get paid even if no one brings a kid."

"That's what I understood from the pastor. That's probably standard in all churches, isn't it?"

"I don't know about that. I've never babysat in another church."

I sat for a moment contemplating whether or not Mr. Allison would allow me to question Laura Kate alone. He leaned toward her protectively, still with his hand on her arm. I knew police were supposed to have a parent present especially if a kid was a suspect, but Laura Kate wasn't a suspect and I wasn't the police. "Mr. Allison, I don't suppose you'd give me a few minutes with Laura Kate alone?"

"No way. What for?" His expression was much like I'd expect a papa bear's to be. "Anything you want to talk to her about can be said in front of us."

I thought so. I directed my attention to the girl. "I just wanted to ask you, Laura Kate, about when you went to the restroom."

Her eyes darted to her father and then to her stepmother. She touched her phone like she wanted to pick it up and do something with it. "I was only gone a couple of minutes."

"Okay, all right. I'm not accusing you of anything. Were the babies asleep when you left to go to the restroom?"

She nodded. "Sound asleep. The restroom is just down the hall. I was only in there long enough to—to pee and wash my hands."

"And you didn't hear anyone in the hallway while you were in there?"

"No, but the hallway is carpeted. If you've been there, you know that." Her chin jutted out, her lips drawn together.

"You did your business, washed your hands, and rushed back to the nursery and the baby beds were empty? And then what happened?"

"I knew they were too little to have crawled out. That sounds crazy, I know, but I glanced around the room and into the hall and then it hit me and I screamed." Tears began gushing.

Mrs. Allison said, "She screamed bloody murder. I knew it was her. I ran back to the nursery. I was right behind Darrell, the usher. I saw she was okay, but she'd started sobbing and pointing and I looked in the nursery and could see the beds were empty." Mrs. Allison's eyes began streaming.

Mr. Allison's face was drawn up into a scowl. I had the feeling I had overstayed my welcome.

Through her sniffles, Mrs. Allison said, "Darrell ran outside into the parking lot. He came back and said he didn't see anyone. The church became loud with people talking and yelling. You probably know from the pastor what happened after that."

Sighing, I said, "Listen, I know this has been a traumatic experience for Laura Kate and, well, all of you." I stood and slipped my phone into my pocket and picked up my purse. "I'm not trying to make it worse. I'm just trying to help Mr. and Mrs. Wite. If you think of anything else I might need to know, please give me a call." I pulled a card out of my other jacket pocket and laid it on the table. "Thank you for your time and cooperation."

I thought Laura Kate's expression held a plea, but that was probably wishful thinking on my part. I wanted her to tell more than she'd said. As I made my exit, I came up with an idea on how to find out if she was holding anything back. I was eager to get to my car and put that into play.

# CHAPTER

# EIGHT

S ince there were several cars parked across from the house of the woman Candy was supposed to serve, she had parked her clunker around the corner. She knew she was taking a chance on having someone accost her and question her about what she was doing, but she sat on the grass on the far side of one of the cars, where if the woman was home, she couldn't see her. From there, Candy kept watch.

The sky was just about dark. The temperature had been moderate during the day, but a cold front was supposed to blow in that night. She was warm enough in her jeans, long-sleeved shirt, tennis shoes, and socks. If she got cold, she could walk back to her car and get her hoodie. She'd been there for forty-five minutes and exactly nothing had happened at that house.

The house next door, however, the one where the baby had been crying previously, had seen a lot of action. People, mostly men, had been coming in and out every few minutes. No one had a baby with him or took a baby or any other child away. But they definitely were in and out. Candy was convinced it was a drug house. She contemplated contacting the police anonymously, otherwise she wouldn't be able to hide out and serve the neighbor or, heck, anyone. If the drug dealers found out who she was, Candy might not even have a future. She would think about it and maybe call after she was long gone.

She'd shut off the ringer to her cell but left it on vibrate, which it started doing. Mavis' name appeared.

"What's going on? Did you serve that woman?"

"Hey, Mavis. No, I'm still waiting for her to come home. Are you back at the office? Your voice sounds weird."

"I'm in my car. Are you sure you want to keep waiting? It's nearly eight o'clock."

"Yeah, like, I know that, but you said I could stake her out, so that's what I'm doing. I don't want to have to come out here tomorrow if I don't have to. Or Saturday or Sunday, either."

"You're not allowed to serve anyone on Sunday, anyway, except in certain kinds of cases, and this is not one. Maybe she'll be home on Saturday."

"Not if she's staying with someone else." Candy really didn't want to spend her Saturday waiting on the woman, even though she was glad Mavis had given her the opportunity to do something close to a stakeout. Saturday mornings, Candy liked to spend with her friends, if her mother didn't make her take care of her little brother and sister. She wanted to serve the woman that night if she could.

"We're only required to make so many attempts. Why don't you go get something to eat and go back and try one more time and if she's not there, we'll return the service. The lawyer can try to get her served some other way."

"I hate to do that. It makes it look like I can't do my job."

"Happens all the time. Don't worry about it."

"I'll think about it. What are you doing? Are you going back to the office?"

"Just for a few minutes. Margaret said she'd do some background on some of the people at that Holy Roller church. I just want to look over what she's found. I'm thinking I might go over to Mr. Wite's sister's house and talk to her."

"Mr. Wite is the father of those twins?"

"Yes. His sister's the one who took the kids to the church. I have several questions I'd like to ask her. Then I'll probably go home. I'm tired, and I don't want to have a relapse of this cold."

"You sound better except because you're on Bluetooth your voice sounds like it's hollow or something. You haven't sneezed once since we've been talking."

"I'm mostly feeling better. I think I've kicked this thing. I don't want to wear myself out, but I do want to find those twins. Speaking of which, I have something I want you to do on this case. I don't know how you'll accomplish it, but it's important."

Candy straightened her shoulders. She'd been slumped on the curb behind the car and her rear end was starting to go numb. Her shoulders were feeling cramped, but she was up for anything Mavis said was important. "What is it?"

"I just left the babysitter's house. I was able to get the babysitter and the stepmother's stories. The babysitter's name is Laura Kate Allison."

"Yeah and?" She kept one eye on the houses across the street.

"I think the babysitter hasn't been completely forthcoming."

"You think she's lying about something? You want me to find out what it is?"

"Exactly. If you can get her alone someplace, you might be able to find out what she didn't say. The father wouldn't let me talk to her without his being present."

"Maybe he knows what she'd say."

"Either that, or he's just being protective. The latter, I think. Also, I think the stepmother is holding back, too, but I'm hoping Mr. Wite's sister will fill in that blank. That's why I want to talk to her tonight. She may not have given the whole story to her brother and the police."

"Huh. So, how do I meet up with this girl?"

"Yeah, that's the hard part. I don't know. Tomorrow's a school day. You could try to catch her at school."

"You know how hard it is to get past security at some schools without an ID? And I wouldn't know what color uniform they wore at her school. Do you even know what school she goes to? How would I explain what I was doing there if I got caught?"

"Okay, okay. Well, then, I'm pretty sure she'll be babysitting at the church on Sunday."

"Didn't you tell me they're evangelicals? Like, are they far right?"

"Right, but I'm not sure how far right."

"You're not asking me to go to that church, are you? No way."

"No, I wouldn't do that."

Candy laughed. She knew Mavis better than that. Of course, she'd ask her.

"If you don't think you can manage it, I'll figure something out."

Oh, she'd manage it. She'd sleep on it. She wanted to show Mavis that she, Candy, could get things done. "That's all right, Mavis. I'll give it my best shot. Let me think about it overnight. In the meantime, I'm going to do what you said. I'm going to get something to eat and come back, and if this woman is not here then to heck with her."

"That'll work, kid. Let me know how it goes. And be careful."

Mavis clicked off, and Candy stood and stretched. She looked up and down the street and didn't see anyone. She wondered whether the neighborhood, which at first had seemed like an okay neighborhood, wasn't as safe as she'd thought it was. No one was walking their dog or jogging or riding their bikes. It had gotten dark, but not totally dark yet. There were streetlights. She'd do exactly what she told Mavis. Eat. Return. Try to perfect service. Leave if she couldn't accomplish her task.

After downing a hamburger, Candy pulled her hoodie on since the cold front had begun blowing in while she was eating. The temperature would probably be in the low sixties by the next morning. When she turned onto the street where the woman lived, there were lights on in the house. Candy hoped she could simply ring the doorbell, hand the woman the papers, and say, "You've been served."

It pretty much was like that. The woman sighed and shrugged. "I knew he was going to file. I just didn't know it would be this soon." Two toddlers came from behind the woman and peered at Candy.

"I'm sorry to do this to you, but I'm only doing my job."

"I know that hon. I was just hoping my husband would come back. You see he went down to Cancun with his girlfriend last weekend. I thought he'd get her out of his system, but I guess not."

Candy shook her head. "Doesn't look like it. Be sure to read over the papers. Divorce papers have a lot of stuff in them about court hearings and filing answers and stuff like that. You'd best get a lawyer."

"Well, thanks. I guess."

"By the way," Candy said. She glanced at the kids and whispered, "Are they dealing drugs out of that house next door? Something like that went on in my neighborhood last year." Her neighborhood was no better, in fact way worse, than the one she was standing in. She couldn't wait until her little brother and sister grew older so she could move out and not worry about them.

"I believe so. I'm afraid to call the police. I'm afraid they'd know it was me and hurt us."

"I heard a baby crying when I was here the first time to serve you."

"One of the young girls who hangs out with one of those icky men brings her baby with her sometimes. She looks haunted, and I worry about the baby, but what am I supposed to do?"

"Okay, well, just take care of yourself and your kids. Do you rent or own this house?"

"Rent. I guess now I'm going to have to move. We won't be able to afford a house, me and the kids. Anyway, that's not your problem. Sorry to talk your ear off."

Candy shrugged. "It's okay. I understand. Sorry I had to serve you with the petition for divorce." She walked back down the sidewalk, her eyes fixed on the house next door. She'd decide in the morning whether or not she'd do something about it. Right now, she wanted to get out of that neighborhood as soon as she could, go home, and get warm.

# CHAPTER
# NINE

I searched for Louise's apartment in complete darkness. She lived in a complex of what looked like fifty or so red brick apartments. Since the sun had set by the time I'd arrived at the Allisons', a chill I hadn't dressed for had set in. I waved my flashlight at the corners of each building in my search for her apartment until I found the correct one. Turning off my cell flashlight and ringer, I pushed her doorbell.

Louise had huge bags under her eyes. Her dark hair was like a rat's nest. She wore a wrinkled gray tee shirt, stained red sweatpants, and dirty beige wool-looking clogs. She held a coffee mug in one hand. "Who are you and what do you want?" Her breath smelled decidedly like bourbon, which, I realized, also held an aroma of coffee. What a combination for an evening cocktail.

I put my foot in the door and said, "Mavis Davis." I held out my hand, but Louise didn't take it. She probably heard the nasal quality of my voice that was a dead giveaway that something was going on in my sinuses.

Louise turned her back on me and said, "My brother said you

might be coming by." She headed to the interior of the apartment, leaving me standing in the doorway.

I closed the apartment door and followed Louise to the kitchen area where she'd dropped into a dinette chair and set her mug on the table. She crossed her arms and said, "What can I tell you that I haven't already told the police?" The aroma of coffee was stronger in the kitchen area. A coffee maker sat on the counter, the carafe one-third full. An overflowing trash can, with an aluminum tray sticking out, had been pushed against the wall in front of the oven. Dinner container?

"I don't know what you've told the police. I'd like to go over the events of last night with you, though, so I can get your perspective. May I sit down?"

She pushed a chair out with her foot, causing it to scrape on the vinyl floor. "Be my guest."

I sat down and put my shoulder bag on the table to my left. Could she be more hostile? Wondering that made me wonder whether her defensiveness had anything to do with something she had done or failed to do, or something she had known or should have known. I'd soon find out. I hoped. "Well, as I said, my name is Mavis Davis. I'm a private investigator." I took a card out of my pocket and pushed it across the table at her.

"I know all that. My brother told me." Her words were a bit slurred. She sipped from her mug and crossed her arms again.

"Would you mind going over with me exactly what you remember from last night?" I was assuming she wasn't drinking last night. No one had mentioned that. And then, I got to wondering, are evangelical people supposed to drink? Don't they have a thing about not taking foreign substances into their bodies? Or is that Baptists? Or both?

"I mind, but my brother has insisted. Since I rely on him for things when I'm in a fix, I have to do what he wants. Most of the time, anyway." She combed her hair with her fingers.

"Let's start with when you picked up the babies."

"I didn't pick them up. They dropped them off. Dave hooked up the car seats in my car. I always have a hard time getting those weird car seats for little babies connected right. They're so clumsy." She smirked. "I guess I'm clumsy, too."

"They dropped them off, hooked up the car seats, put the kids in them, gave you the diaper bags with the supplies in them, and left to go on their date?"

"That's right. We met outside in the parking lot. I left right away. I mean, I had to, I couldn't go back inside my apartment and leave the twins in the car, right?"

Rhetorical question. "What happened when you reached the church?"

"I managed to get each baby unlatched from their seat and carried them both inside, one in each arm. Believe me, it wasn't easy opening that back door, but I did it. Then I walked down the hall to the nursery and asked Laura Kate to go get the diaper bags out of my car."

"While she did that, what did you do?"

"I laid each baby in a separate baby bed."

"Were they crying or anything? Were they okay with all that activity? I don't know much about babies, so you'll have to tell me if I'm missing something."

"They were okay. They're really good babies. Like little dolls, perfect little dolls. Anyone would love them. They fussed a little, but that's all. I figured they might be hungry or wet."

"Laura Kate came back in with the diaper bags? Was anyone else around?"

"Nope." She took another swig and coughed, choking a little. After clearing her throat, she said, "Just us. When I walked past the kitchen, I saw her mother."

"Amy, her stepmother, you mean?"

"Yeah. My friend Amy. She was putting the coffee things out."

"Then what did you do?"

"I checked each baby to see if he or she needed a new diaper.

Then I got the bottles out, and since they were still warm, I told Laura Kate they wouldn't need heating up."

"Laura Kate understood you wanted the babies to be fed?"

She nodded. "Yeah. Laura Kate's pretty smart. She's good with kids. She said she'd feed them and rock them if they hadn't fallen asleep while taking the bottles."

"And you left?"

"I went into the sanctuary."

"Then what happened?"

"We always have opening words and a reading and a hymn—they call it praise, and a prayer and the sermon. Pastor Markham was in the middle of the sermon when we heard a scream."

"Did you know it came from Laura Kate?"

She shook her head. "No. I only knew it came from the back of the building. As far as I knew, she was the only one there. So I ran back there. The usher, Darrell, beat me to the nursery. Laura Kate was screaming bloody murder."

"And—"

"The usher grabbed her by the shoulders and asked, 'What's wrong?' She pointed behind her. 'The twins!' she said. And when I looked, I could see they weren't there, weren't in the beds." Louise grabbed her head, her elbows on the table, and howled.

I gazed around her apartment while she continued making that noise. I couldn't tell how large an apartment she had but doubted it was a two-bedroom as it had a smallish living room area. Usually, the ones with two bedrooms have a larger living room and dining area. The dinette room we sat in was rather small. Only a four-person dinette table would fit. I got up and stretched and rolled my shoulders. I checked my cell phone, but there were no messages.

Finally, Louise calmed down. I grabbed some paper towels from the holder attached under a cabinet and gave them to her. She rubbed her face and took a deep breath and sighed. Her expression was not very pleasant, as if what had happened was my fault.

"Sorry." She sniffed. "What else do you want to know?" She swallowed from her mug again and looked into it like she thought she might need a refill.

"I understand someone called the police."

"I think it was Pastor Markham, but I'm not sure. We got Laura Kate settled down. Oh, yeah, Amy was there, too, about the same time I was. A few minutes later, the pastor told everyone they could leave, and they started to just as the cops arrived and told them they couldn't. Everyone went back into the sanctuary and sat down."

"Did the police talk to everyone?"

"No. They talked to Laura Kate and me, and the usher, the pastor, and Amy, I think. The pastor told them he would give them a list of the members and that everyone who was there was on the list. I think the cops took down everyone's name anyway. One cop went out into the parking lot to look inside every car and truck. Then they let people go but said to be available in case they were needed."

"All right. And then?"

"Umm, I think they finally said we could go home. I'd told them about Dave and Connie, and they said they'd go out to their house and talk to them."

"Dave and Connie told me you didn't call them when this happened. Why did you wait until they came home?"

Her eyes traveled all over but wouldn't meet mine. "I don't know. It sounds crazy, but with the cops and everyone all around, I didn't really think about it until I was in my car on the way to their house."

"You could have called them from your car."

"I guess I could have, but by then I thought I might as well wait until I got there." Her face, which had been red, grew pasty white. She swallowed more of whatever that mixture was she was drinking.

"Louise, I've been wondering something. You said no one was in the back of the church when you brought the babies in, right?"

"Uh-huh, yes. Just me, Laura Kate, and Amy."

"And the pastor."

"Oh, yeah, I forgot. He was in his office. He's always in there getting ready for his sermon."

"Okay, and as I understand it, your brother called you on Sunday and asked you on that day if you'd babysit on Wednesday so they could have a date night?"

"Right. That's right."

"I forgot to ask them why they chose Wednesday instead of Monday or Tuesday for you to take care of the kids. Do you know?"

"Dave teaches on Monday and Tuesday nights."

"That makes sense. He called you on Sunday night, and you agreed to babysit the babies if it would be okay to take them to church with you?"

"Right."

"He and Connie aren't members of your church, are they?"

"God, no." She clapped her hand on her mouth. "They don't believe in anything."

"But they've been to the church?"

"Once or twice."

"Met some of the other people who go there, your friends?"

"Yeah. They know some of the people. They've met the pastor."

"As I understand it, you're best friends with Amy, Laura Kate's stepmother, and a woman named Carmen?"

Her eyes flitted around the room. "Um hmmm."

"The Wites know them?"

"Yeah. Yes."

"And both Amy and Carmen were at church last night?"

She pulled her hands under the table. "Just Amy. Carmen didn't attend. Have you met Carmen yet?"

"No, I haven't. Should I?"

She shook her head. "I was just wondering."

"Did you tell anyone you were going to be bringing your brother's twins to church on Wednesday night? I mean, he called you on Sunday. You must have talked to someone between Sunday and Wednesday night. Surely you told someone what you would be doing on Wednesday night."

"Everybody knows I go to church on Wednesday night, even the people at work."

"Which is where? I failed to ask you where you work."

"For the county. In the clerk's office. The county clerk."

"I have a friend in the district clerk's office. I don't believe I know anyone in the county clerk's office, although I've been there, naturally."

"You know they're two separate offices."

I nodded "Of course. Did you go to work on Monday, Tuesday, and Wednesday?"

"Sure. I work every day."

"Could you have mentioned to someone that you were babysitting your brother's twins on Wednesday night and would be taking them to church with you?"

She grew quiet. She rubbed a knuckle across her lips. Her eyes came up to meet mine. "I guess I must have. I'm kind of a blabbermouth sometimes. I didn't think anything of it."

"So, you may have told several people?"

She squeezed her eyes shut. "Oh my God." She clapped a hand over her mouth. "Yeah. And people could have overheard me talking. And now you're wondering whether those people could have told other people, and somebody could have decided they wanted those babies, right?"

"Yep. That's what I'm wondering. Didn't the police ask you about that?"

Shaking her head, "No. One of the cops was kind of—of boorish. The other was full of energy and talking to several people. I suppose they'll think of it soon and be back. You think so?"

"I'm not concerned with that. They probably will. But could you make a list of the people you think you told and anyone who could have overheard your conversations?"

"Oh God bless me. Of course. It's all my fault, isn't it? That someone took my niece and nephew. I'm responsible." She howled like she had before.

I looked away. I couldn't stand the howling, and anger filled me like a building fire. How could she have been so stupid? She worked at the courthouse? She must know what kind of characters are out in the world and all the stuff that's going on, yet she was apparently unaware of the dangers of giving out information about little children, just like the people who put their childrens' full names on the internet. Stupid. Stupid. Stupid.

"Louise, I need you to calm down. Please. It's late. I'm tired. I'm sure you're tired, too. Let me ask you this, did you tell your friend Carmen? Because I've already talked to Amy and logically, Carmen would be the next person for me to talk to. I still need to talk to Darrell, but just being the usher doesn't mean he knew anything about the actual kidnapping. I understand he ran into the parking lot but didn't see anything."

She dried her face. "Of course, I told Carmen. She's one of my best friends. She knows all about me and my problems."

"So, this is what I'm going to do. I'm going to go home and get some rest and hope my cold will be completely gone by tomorrow morning. In the meantime, before you go to bed tonight and before you go to work tomorrow morning, you're going to work on that list of people, okay?"

She nodded, looking like one of the most miserable people I'd ever seen. Her eyes still brimmed with tears. Her face remained discolored.

"Tomorrow morning, I'm going to find Carmen and talk to her. Then I'll talk to Darrell, the usher. Then, if it's okay, I'll swing by your office and pick up the list from you. I'll need those peoples' full names and phone numbers, and addresses if you have them."

"I can do that. Wait until Dave finds out about this. He's going to kill me."

"You can't worry about that right now. Focus on what you need to do." I started for the door. "I forgot to ask. Where does Carmen work? I can see her first thing tomorrow at her work, if I can't catch her at her home address."

"She's a detention worker at the county jail. They'll probably let you talk to her if you tell them what it's about." She followed me to the door.

I didn't see getting inside the jail as a problem. I'd been there before. Not always on the outside. Anyway, I had a plan. I needed to get some sleep, then start all over in the morning interviewing people. I just hoped Carmen hadn't blabbed about the babies to anyone. For that matter, the same for all those other people who would be on Louise's list.

CHAPTER

# TEN

T had called Carmen before I went to bed, but she didn't answer. I didn't blame her, I don't like to answer calls from numbers I don't recognize either. I left a message on her voicemail that I'd like to talk to her before she went to work or on her break about anything that Louise had told her. Then I fell into bed, feeling like I'd accomplished a lot, as well as like I had overcome my cold.

I awoke several times during the night, processing the case in my head and in my dreams. All the possible scenarios my brain could come up with floated through and woke me. I should have called someone, Margaret, maybe, and talked things over with her before I'd slept, but I'd been too tired. And didn't want to hear anything else about the Barry situation which, knowing her as well as I do, would come up. Sometimes in the past, I'd talk to Ben, but there was no Ben right now. He had his own problems. I did speak with Candy, giving her the information she'd need to try to talk to Laura Kate, but otherwise, didn't go into the details of the case.

Carmen did not call me back. When I tried her cell number again in the morning, she still didn't answer. I wondered whether Louise had told her what I wanted. I could've called Louise and asked her to call Carmen and tell her it was okay to talk to me. I didn't do that, however. I showered, dressed, swallowed some oatmeal and an apple almost whole, and drove to Carmen's home address.

Carmen lived in a rather large and well-populated trailer park a few miles out of downtown. Or, I should say, mobile home park. I thought if I got out there early enough, I could catch her before she went to work. The park looked like a pretty good place to live, though the lots left barely any room for someone to have outside living space. Residents would have to be careful about spitting. They might hit their neighbor's window.

A lot of mobile home parks had cropped up lately, because apartments had gotten so expensive, and buying a house was out of reach for so many people. I'd assumed Carmen was single, so only one person to pay all the bills. Ergo, the trailer.

I found the office and asked an irritated woman, who complained about having been disturbed so early, if she could point me to Carmen's residence. She grudgingly complied. The location was far into the back, so I had to drive to it. Carmen's home looked like the latest model. In her small plot, she'd planted a flower garden and positioned a plastic bistro table and two chairs away from the little road that ran around inside the park. There was a semblance of a pad for parking her vehicle, but no vehicle. I exited my car and knocked anyway. You never know. Her car could be in the shop, or she could have loaned it to someone. Alas, no one responded to my knock, and no sounds came from within the trailer.

I went back and disturbed the manager again, to which she didn't respond too kindly. "Ma'am, no one is at Carmen Garcia's trailer. Have you seen her today?"

"Nope. What else do you want?"

"Did you see her last night?"

"I don't see people unless they knock on my door, or I'm making a round just to check on things, which is what my husband usually does."

"So, that would be no, you didn't see her last night."

"That would be correct."

It had just occurred to me that Carmen might work shift work. They must have shift work hours in the jail. "I apologize for disturbing you, but just a couple of more questions. Do you know whether she works days or nights or whether there are three shifts at the jail?"

Her eyes examined something in the air above my head, then she said, "I believe they work twelve-hour shifts, but don't quote me."

"That makes sense. Just one more thing, what kind of car does Carmen drive, if you know?"

"I do know. She's a little Latina woman driving a blue extended cab truck, which makes no sense to me."

I wasn't going to ask her what shade of blue. I didn't want to press my luck.

"She can hardly see over the steering wheel. Maybe she has a booster seat in the cab." She chuckled at her little joke. "I don't know, ma'am, any more than that. She keeps to herself mostly."

"Thank you so much for answering my questions." I shook her dangling hand before she had a chance to pull it back.

From there, I drove to the county jail facility in downtown Houston. The Harris County Jail houses around nine thousand people and is the largest jail in Texas, almost the largest in the U.S. The sheriff runs the jail, so that makes Carmen a deputy sheriff. Or maybe they call them detention officers. Wasn't that what Louise had said? I think of women jailers as matrons, which is what they were called eons ago.

The cold front that had blown in had dropped the temperature, but the sky was clear, so the sun made it a comfortable walk from the parking lot to the office. I wanted to get a message to Carmen, or at least get someone to tell me when Carmen worked, or, if she was working that day, whether they'd communicate said message to her. I identified myself to the dispatch-type person and asked her to tell Carmen I would like to speak to her for a few minutes. She came back and said she'd checked. Carmen was on days, but she had called in sick.

As I walked back to my car, enjoying the fine weather, I had to force myself to unclench my jaw. It would be no exaggeration for me to say something was not right about Carmen being unavailable. She could really be ill, but somehow, I doubted that, especially since she was not at home. I tried her number again and left another message. Whatever was going on with her could be totally unrelated to the missing Wite children. I knew that.

Calming my angst, I climbed inside my SUV and unfolded the list of members, locating the name and address of the church usher, Darrell Warburton. I suspected he had nothing to do with the whole situation, but I had no clue what else to do. Though it was still not anywhere near lunch time, I thought I could ask him to meet me later for lunch if he worked someplace not too inconvenient.

While I was sitting in my vehicle, a police car drove down the street in front of the parking lot. I could've sworn my significant other, Ben, was inside. He was supposed to be out of town at his mother's funeral. I was sure it was him, but it was weird that he would be there outside the jail. He was usually in the office. What was he doing there, and why hadn't he called me when he came back to town? My stomach spun like a dog chasing its tail. Maybe it wasn't Ben who I'd seen. Maybe the stress of the Wite situation was already getting to me. I couldn't worry about it right then. I had a job to do.

I punched Mr. Warburton's number into my cell phone.

"Bank of the Gulf Coast," a female monotone voice said.

No one told me he was a banker, or even that he worked at a bank. Not that it amounted to a hill of beans. "May I speak with Darrell Warburton, please."

"Hold, please."

I watched the street to see whether Ben passed by again.

"This is Darrell Warburton," a deep voice said. "How may I help you?"

"I'm Mavis Davis, Mr. Warburton, a private investigator hired by

Dave and Connie Wite to help find their babies who were taken Wednesday night from the church." As if he didn't know they had been kidnapped, right? "I understand you were the usher volunteering on Wednesday at the church when they went missing."

"What did you say your name is again?"

"Mavis Davis. You can Google me in case you think I'm playing a joke or something. I can't help what my mother named me."

"Right now is not a good time to talk, Miss Davis. Is it something simple you'd like to know?"

"I'd like to go over the events of the evening with you, sir. I could come out to wherever your bank is situated at lunch time if that would be better. How about if I buy you lunch?"

He snorted into the phone. "Private investigators must get paid pretty well to afford to buy lunches. That would be okay, I guess, so long as you don't mind coming all the way down here."

"Where is 'here'?"

"A little town called La Marque in Galveston County."

"Oh, I know where that is. I've spent a considerable amount of time in and around Galveston. What time will you be available to meet me?"

"Eleven-thirty. We could meet at a little family-owned Mexican food restaurant I know of. The food's good and not that expensive. How about if I text the address to you? Give me your number. I'm on a landline, and it doesn't show the numbers."

Mexican food worked for me. I recited my number, and we concluded the call. About two minutes later, the text came in. Good. At least I would have made some progress before the end of the day.

I sat for a few minutes and watched the street while I decided what else I could do. A couple of people walking from their cars stared at me as they passed by. I supposed someone sitting in a parking lot across from the jail would be suspect. I might be waiting for someone to come out, though. I couldn't worry about it.

Anyway, tracking down Carmen was my number one priority after talking to Darrell. I just wanted to be sure there was no reason to suspect her of anything, but I couldn't do that if I couldn't talk to her. I punched in her phone number again and let it ring until it went to voicemail again and left another message.

I still had some time before I needed to get on the interstate and head south, so I called Louise on her cell. I didn't want to call her during the workday. I was just going to swing by there and pick up the list she should have ready for me, but I wasn't going to trek to the clerk's office if she hadn't finished with it. When she answered, I said in my calmest voice, "Louise, this is Mavis Davis. Did I catch you at a bad time? Are you at work?"

"I stayed home today. I called in sick." There were voices in the background, but I figured the TV was on.

That was inconvenient. "I was going to go by your office and get that list of people you told about the babies going with you to church on Wednesday. Have you finished with that?"

"I don't know, Miss Davis. I don't know who all could have heard me talking. I've done the best I can."

"That's okay. That'll give me some names to start with. Can you scan the list with your phone and send it to my phone, so I don't have to go out to your apartment? Or, you could drop it by my office if you're going to be out and about. I could get it when I go to my office this afternoon."

"I don't know how to scan with my phone. What if I take a picture of it and send it that way? Would that work?"

"Okay, do that when we hang up. I want to talk to some of those people this afternoon or evening, if I can. Before I hang up, Louise, I'm wondering whether you've spoken to Carmen. I can't get ahold of her."

"Did you call her cell? That's the only phone she has. The number should be on that church list you have."

"I've called it a bunch of times, and she never answers, and I leave messages, and she hasn't called me back. Did you call her and tell her I'd be looking for her?"

"No, I swear. Did you try her at the jail?"

"I'm at the jail now. Or I was. I'm sitting in the parking lot. They said she called in sick. Y'all didn't plan together to call in sick, did you?"

"Oh, God, no. I would have gone to work, but I keep crying every time I think about those babies. I can't work like that."

"I went out to her trailer, and she's not there either. At least she wasn't when I got there early this morning. I thought I'd missed her before she went to work, but apparently not."

"I don't know, Miss Davis. Now you've got me worried. If I hear from her, I'll be sure to let you know."

"Go ahead and send me that list now. I need to get on the road to meet someone for lunch." I disconnected and wrapped my arms around the steering wheel, resting my forehead on it for a few minutes. When my phone dinged, I checked it. Louise had sure enough sent a picture, but it was so small I couldn't make it out even when I spread two fingers across it.

Rather than deal with her again right then, I'd figure out something later. Candy was an expert in all that modern technical stuff, as was Margaret, mostly. I started my SUV and moseyed to the parking lot exit. Just as I began to pull out, a police car passed in front of my vehicle. Ben was in the passenger seat and made eye contact with me. So, he *was* watching me. I wondered why.

# ELEVEN

C andy dressed in a sweater over a long-sleeved flannel shirt and jeans and went to the office on Friday morning, pleased with herself for having served the problem woman the night before. After she parked her Moped in front of their office and before she went inside, she called Child Protection Services to report the drug dealers. She figured they'd know what to do with the information. When Margaret drove by to park in the back, Candy waved and continued the call. She explained about the family living next door to what looked like a drug house, as well as what could be going on inside. The person who took the call said they'd see what they could do about being sure the drug people were told it wasn't their neighbor lady who placed the call. Candy said, "Thank you. I guess I'm also worried about the baby I heard crying being trafficked."

"Don't worry, ma'am. We'll check into that, too."

Relieved, and pleased to be called 'ma'am,' Candy unlocked the front door and went inside, meeting Margaret in the hallway. "You get that woman served or not?" Margaret wore a fluffy fuchsia jacket over a red turtleneck and a pair of black slacks.

"It was kind of late last night, but I did! She was a nice lady with two little kids. I felt sorry for her."

Margaret put away her things. "I know what you mean. Sometimes I've felt that way, too. I'm going to the kitchen. Want some coffee or tea?"

"Coffee, please, with cake." Candy glanced at Margaret to see how she responded to the mention of cake. She didn't. "I'm going to look on my desk to see if Mavis left me any instructions. I didn't come back here before I went home last night. When I talked to her, she was pretty tired."

"I know she'll be happy about that service. The attorney for the husband is sometimes not very nice."

"As soon as I have my coffee, I'll go to the courthouse to file the returns and then Mavis gave me a job to do."

"Oh yeah? Having to do with what?"

"The kidnapping. You know about that, right? She wants me to see if I can get the babysitter to talk to me."

"I thought she was going to talk to the girl and her family yesterday."

"She did, but she thinks the girl is not telling everything she knows. She gave me this assignment, and I think I know how I'm going to get it done." Her grin stretched wide. "I didn't want to tell y'all, in case I can't, but Mavis gave me some info on the girl's school and her home address. I'm going to try to find her at her school, or go to her house this afternoon. I'm leaving as soon as you get the coffee made and wrap up a piece of cake to take with me."

Margaret stepped into the kitchen. When Candy didn't find anything on her desk from Mavis, she went into Mavis' office where she found a photograph and a scribbled note lying on one of the client chairs, with the description of the girl's car.

"*Candy, this picture is of the members of that church. I circled Laura Kate Allison, so you'll know what she looks like. Hope you can talk to her (but not if her parents are there) M.*"

The eight by ten photograph was a group picture. Mavis had

circled a girl standing on the end of the second row. She was a blonde with long hair. Candy grabbed Margaret as she came out of the kitchen. "You have a magnifying glass?"

"What for?"

"I want to see this girl better." Candy held up the picture and pointed to the girl in the circle. "I can't see her face very well."

"Follow me." Margaret dug around in the bottom drawer of the four-drawer filing cabinet in Candy's office. "We're hoping to fill up this drawer someday." She found a black, Naugahyde-covered magnifying glass and gave it to Candy.

"This thing is huge, what, four or five inches in circumference?"

"Yeah. I got it at an estate sale. The man who died was almost completely blind."

"It could come in handy for a lot of stuff."

"It has. Put it back when you're through." Margaret circled around to the kitchen. The smell of coffee floated in the air.

Candy studied the girl. She looked like other blond chicks, but maybe Candy could pick her out of a group. She knew the school. One of her friends had attended there. Mavis had said the girl had lunch privileges, which meant she could go home for lunch. Candy was going to wait outside the main door of the school and catch her if she could.

She went to fetch her coffee. "I like when Mavis asks me to do something other than serve papers. This kidnapping is a big thing, isn't it?"

Margaret nodded and poured a cup of coffee for herself. "What I want to know is what whoever it was plans to do with the kids."

"Maybe it was someone who doesn't have kids and wants some."

"Or knows someone who can't have kids and is going to give them to that person. I read in the paper not too long ago there's a shortage of babies for adoption in the U.S." Margaret leaned against the counter and watched Candy.

"That Supreme Court Justice said that I think. Wasn't that one of the reasons he gave for overturning Roe v. Wade?" Candy pulled a to-go cup from the cupboard and filled it.

"Well, it was one of those judges, if not him. That's a terrible reason to throw out that law."

"Have there been more missing children since that happened? You know, people could be stealing babies and giving them to people to adopt. I read where after Russia attacked Ukraine the Russians stole Ukrainian children and gave them to Russian families to adopt."

Margaret's features drew together into a scowl. "That's awful."

"You're on WebDetectives, aren't you? Have there been more postings of missing babies?"

"I didn't think of that. I'll look. I'd hate to think someone in this country wanted a baby bad enough to kidnap one, though it happens. They could get an older kid through the foster care system. Mavis knows all about that, by the way, from before she became a P.I."

"People don't want kids with problems. I've seen on TV where someone's taken kids. You probably have, too. Heck, there've been movies. I watch true crime shows, too. And my mother—"

"You're speaking to your mother now?"

Candy flicked her fingers at Margaret. "This was a while back. Anyway, she was telling me one of the women who lives in our neighborhood had her kids taken away from her and eventually adopted. One of them was a baby."

"I'm not surprised with where you live. That had to be CPS that did that."

"Yeah, I know. There was another woman, though, who used to live near us, who was in jail and someone tried to get her to give up her baby, but she wouldn't do it. The people were even going to give her money."

"That's illegal!"

"So's kidnapping! My mother told me the woman was so scared

that when she left the jail, she got her baby from her aunt who was taking care of it and moved out of town."

"Ugh. Listen, I've got some stuff to do."

"Yeah, me too. Have to go to the courthouse. Maybe the traffic is better now."

"Sure, it is." Margaret left the kitchen.

Candy topped-off her cup. She wrapped a piece of cake in plastic and stuck it in her pocket. When she stepped outside with her backpack, a police car drove up and double-parked in the street. An ugly cop crawled out and eyeballed her. She eyeballed him right back.

"Mavis Davis in there?" His tone wasn't all that friendly.

She shook her head. "She hasn't come in yet."

"Oh yeah? I'm gonna go look for myself." He gave her the stink eye.

She didn't do anything to deserve his being rude to her. She followed him back into the office in case Margaret needed her. He let go of the door when he went through it, forcing Candy to catch it with one hand while trying not to drop her coffee and backpack.

Margaret said, "Good morning. How may I help you?"

Candy knew Margaret's tone of voice and could tell Margaret was apprehensive. Maybe she knew the cop. They all knew Ben, and he wasn't Ben. In fact, now that Candy thought about it, Ben hadn't been by lately. Hmm.

"Mavis Davis here?" He stopped in front of Margaret's desk, which separated the space at the front of the office from the door.

"I already told him she's not here," Candy said.

He turned and looked at her. "I thought you was leaving."

"I will when you do. Mavis is *not* here. I told you that."

"She's not here, Officer Tyler," Margaret said. "I don't know when she'll be in. Have you tried calling her about whatever it is you want?"

So, this piggish-looking cop was the creepy Lon Tyler. Candy had never seen him before, much less met him. She'd heard about him, though. Several times.

"You and I both know she ain't going to take a call from me," Tyler said.

Margaret shrugged and arched one eyebrow, her eyes going to Candy's. "I don't know anything of the sort. You want to leave her a note?"

"You sure she's not back there? I'll go look."

Candy stepped in front of him. "No, you won't. That is, unless you have some kind of a warrant." Her heart beat like a kettle drum. She'd never stood up to a cop before, but she didn't like bullies.

He stopped and looked her over head to toe. He didn't try to shove past her. Maybe he figured if someone as young as her had the guts to stand up to him, she'd also file a complaint if he got out of line. She would, too, and realized now that her body language was understood by some people.

"Let me ask you this," Tyler said. "Has the Wites or anyone asked her to go snooping around in a kidnapping case?"

"We couldn't tell you that even if we knew," Margaret said. She stood and crossed her arms. "Now is there anything else you want to know? Because if not, we have work to do. We can't stand around here all day chatting with you."

Candy withheld a laugh. Now was not the time.

Tyler's neck grew red splotches. His breath came out in a rush. "Well, you can't stop me from driving around back and seeing if her car is parked back there."

"Be our guest," Margaret said.

Candy opened the front door for him. "After you."

He trod out and stood on the sidewalk for a minute. Candy let the door close. "I'm not leaving until I know he's gone."

"Thanks," Margaret said. "I wonder what he wants."

"Probably to tell her to stop something she's doing, like looking into the kidnapping case. She's said he likes to try to intimidate her."

Tyler climbed back into the police car and did a U-turn, circling around to the drive leading to the back of their office.

Candy drank her coffee and watched out the door until he drove away into traffic. Her inclination had been to give him a common gesture with one finger, but she knew Mavis would frown on that if she found out.

"Just need to put my cup in the kitchen, and I'm out of here," Candy said.

"I was worried you were going to try to drive your Moped with one hand and drink your coffee with the other."

"Nah, I wouldn't do that." She'd already tried driving one-handed, and it hadn't worked well. "You going to call Mavis and tell her about Officer Tyler?"

Margaret shook her head. "I'll wait until she comes in. You go on now and get those returns filed and go find that Laura Kate girl."

# TWELVE

T raffic heading south out of Houston before the middle of the afternoon was never as atrocious as heading north in the early morning, but it still took me a good hour to get to the restaurant Mr. Warburton had recommended. Thankfully, the SUV had a navigation system. La Marque streets are not as logically set out as, say, a county seat where a tourist can rely on the court-house square as a point of reference. Still, I found the hole-in-the-wall Mexican restaurant, arriving close to the agreed-upon hour. On both sides of a wide, paved street were a strip of outdated buildings that housed a variety of businesses. The restaurant was bookended by two worn-looking enterprises, a pawn shop on one side and a jewelry store and repair shop on the other. A similar place in the strip across the street was boarded up. A modern bank building stood on the corner a block away. I suspected that was Mr. Warburton's place of employment.

I like mom-and-pop restaurants, which is what this one appeared to be. The food is often old family recipes rather than chain-restaurant, cookie-cutter fare. When I entered, I was hit with the aromas of cumin, grilling onions and beef, corn, and something burning in the oven.

The place wasn't buzzing with activity, though it was still early. Decorating the walls were piñatas and velvet paintings that brought back memories of our travels to Mexico when I was a child.

At one table sat two suited businessmen. At another were a woman and a young child. One of the booths in the row against the far wall held a man who looked up as I entered and stood as I grew close, holding out his hand. Balding, square-jawed, and stocky, he wore a grayish suit, glasses, and a pleasant smile. We shook, and I slid into the booth opposite him. His handshake was warm and dry. No tells there.

After exchanging our names, I said, "What do you recommend here?"

A waiter came and took our drink order. "I'll be back in a moment with your drinks and glasses of water and to take your food order."

"The enchiladas are always good, but the burritos are, too."

I unrolled the white paper napkin and spread it on my lap. Mr. Warburton did the same.

"This always feels awkward," I said, "having a meal with someone I don't know."

"For me, too. But it's awkward to have any personal conversations in our little bank. If you close the door to your office people stare and become suspicious. Everyone knows everyone else's business in this town."

"Do you live here in La Marque, Mr. Warburton?"

"No, but I go where they send me. I used to work at a branch in Pearland until they moved me here."

"So, you live in Houston?"

He nodded. "Not that far from the church. I want you to know right away, I'm not as—uh—" his lips and nose wiggled back and forth. "I guess you could say *devout* as some of the people there. I mean, I'm a Christian, don't get me wrong. I go to *that* church because my wife likes it."

"I didn't come here to be critical of your church."

The waiter returned with our drinks, and we placed our orders. I'd decided to try the bean burrito, a dish I hadn't eaten in a while.

"I know you didn't, Miss Davis. It's just, well, people are often critical of evangelicals. Anyway, you didn't come all the way down here to talk about that."

I mixed my iced tea with lemon and sweetener and took a sip. They definitely knew how to make a good tasting tea. I don't care what anyone says, all iced teas don't taste the same. Some are nasty. But I digress.

"Right. I'll get to it so we can enjoy our meal when it comes. Pastor Markham and Louise Wite both told me you were the first person to respond to Laura Kate's screams."

"I ran back there as soon as I heard her and then ran back into the sanctuary and beckoned to the pastor and then ran back to the nursery. Louise came. And Amy. Laura Kate was hysterical, waving her arms about and pointing to the baby beds."

"Where are you positioned when you serve as usher? Do you get to sit down anywhere you want or how does that work?"

"I stand at the back doors. If you were there, you saw we have a small church with double doors opening in the back that lead to a single aisle to the platform, the dais, at the front."

"Oh, so if you're always standing in front of those two doors, you're in the position of knowing who comes and goes during the service."

"I'm always standing there except when we pass the collection plate. Then one of the ladies passes a plate on one side, I pass the plate on the other side, then she gives me her plate, and I take them to the pastor's office and lock them up. So, I'm only away from my post for those periods of time."

"Okay, I get the picture." No one had mentioned all that before, but I had never asked either and didn't know if it had anything to do with anything.

"I can see and hear everything from back there." He wore a sheepish look. "At least I thought I could."

"On Wednesday night, were you doing your normal routine as you just described it?"

"Uh huh, sure. Wednesday was, in fact, just normal."

"Did anyone leave the sanctuary once the service started?"

"Amy Allison was the last person in. She was in charge of coffee that night. And no one went out, even when the collection basket was passed around."

Some people must avoid putting money in the basket by going to the restroom. Funny. I'd never thought of that. "No one went out to go to the restroom during any part of the service?"

He shook his head. "No one. No one came in late either, if you're wondering."

I wasn't, but good to know. "Mr. Warburton, can you hear anything that's going on in that little hallway at the back of the church when you're standing in front of the doors and the service is going on?"

"I could, if there was anything to hear. Every once in a while, if someone brings a young child or children and they're cutting up in the nursery, I hear them laughing or shrieking. You know how kids are."

"But there wasn't anything like that last Wednesday."

"No. Nothing."

"Can you hear if someone goes to the bathroom, closes or opens the door, flushes the commode, and washes their hands?"

He rolled his eyes. "Well, yes. It's not real loud, though. I don't think the people on the first row of chairs in the back can hear that, but I'm standing in front of the crack between the double doors."

"Would you have heard anyone who came into the church from the parking lot if they came in late?"

"Unless they tried hard to keep the door latch from clicking, yes. Not always. Some people are more considerate than others."

"But if the congregation was singing the hymn or praise or whatever it's called—I'm afraid I'm not conversant in evangelical terminology—would that cover any noise that might come from the hallway at the back of the church?"

A dark expression formed on his face, as if he'd stepped into a shadow. "I see what you're getting at."

Holding our orders by folded dishtowels, one in each hand, the waiter delivered our food. "Plates are hot," he said as he set them down in front of us. "If there's anything else I can get you folks just give me a shout."

I tried not to swoon when I cut into and tasted the first bite of my burrito. I was right. Way better than chain restaurant food. We ate for a few minutes, looking up briefly out of politeness.

When I had plowed about halfway through my meal, I asked Mr. Warburton, "On Wednesday night, after the service began, did you hear anyone come in through the back door?"

"No, I did not. But you're entirely right that someone could have come in during the singing, and I probably wouldn't have known it."

"Of course, it would have to be someone who knew generally how the service is normally conducted."

"I would assume so, but I can't imagine anyone in that church stealing those babies. Most churches have hymns." His face lit up. "Someone could have listened at the back door and waited until we started singing."

I stared at him and forked another bite into my mouth. *Unlikely*, I wanted to say. When I swallowed, I asked, "How often are you the usher?"

"Often. I don't mind doing it, so I volunteer. Gives me something to do to distract me from—from all the things that go on in there."

I wasn't going to go into what all went on, like speaking in tongues, I imagined.

"As I understand it, Laura Kate is usually the babysitter, right?"

"Yes. She has a friend that will substitute for her if she's sick or something, but she's almost always there."

"Does she usually use the restroom during the service? Have you heard her in the restroom?"

His face blanched. "I suppose I have. I never gave it much thought."

"Did you hear her go to the restroom on Wednesday night?"

He laid his fork down on his plate and rested the heels of his hands on the edge of the table like he was going to push back. He cleared his throat, and his head shook a little. He breathed out a long breath of air. "I suppose I did. I'm trying to remember for sure, but I think I did."

"Well, that confirms her story that she went to the restroom."

"That's what she said, so she must have gone to the restroom."

"So, you do recall that she went to the restroom?"

"I think so. Yes, I'm sure she did, because I remember thinking she was in there for a long time. I wondered whether she was okay. Oh my God." His fist hit the table. "I should have wondered about those babies being okay, too."

"You know she said she was only in there a couple of minutes."

He rocked forward. "If that's what she said, it's not true."

And that's what I had been hoping Candy would get Laura Kate to admit to. I knew people often took their phones in the restroom with them, as gross as that sounds, and checked their emails or played games or called someone. I had suspected that's what happened in this case, but Laura Kate was not going to admit it. Her being gone that long gave whoever it was the perfect opportunity.

"Mr. Warburton, can you recall whether Laura Kate has ever during other services stayed in the restroom longer than it would normally take to do her—her business?"

His brows drew together. "I believe so. Seems like it. I never really thought about it before."

"Is it possible that someone else would know that she did that? Any other parishioners or whatever you call people at that church?"

"I guess anything is possible, Miss Davis."

"Let me ask you something else. After the pastor and Louise came into the nursery, you ran out to the parking lot to see if anyone was out there, right? That's what the pastor and Louise told me. I think it was them."

"Yes. Yes, I did. I thought that if whoever had the twins was still out there, I could catch them."

"But no one was there?"

"No. Except for the one streetlight that shines over the lot, it was dark out there."

"You're positive about that? You didn't see anyone or anything?"

Again, he rested his weight on the heels of his hands. He appeared to be thinking, trying to remember. He closed his eyes and shook his head. "Just some taillights pulling out onto the road at the far end of our parking lot." He looked at me.

The food in my stomach tumbled like clothes in a dryer. "Could you tell what kind of vehicle?"

Strident lines appeared between his eyes. "Truck, I think. They were higher off the ground than a car's would have been. Maybe a large SUV."

"You couldn't see an outline or anything identifying the vehicle other than the lights?"

He shook his head. "I'm sorry."

So, a truck or a sport utility vehicle. How many people in Texas owned one of those? Only, no exaggeration, millions. Literally millions.

"You think that was them, don't you?" he asked, his face grayer than it had been when I arrived.

"Don't you?"

# CHAPTER
# THIRTEEN

The drive back was hazy. Not the sky. My vision. My brain. Why had Laura Kate lied? Did she really have no knowledge of who the culprit or culprits were? Was she an accomplice? Or had she been duped? What took her so long in the bathroom? Was she ill or was she talking to someone her parents disapproved of? Or just playing solitaire, maybe?

Thoughts flew everywhere. Darrell had seen taillights. Were they the taillights of the vehicle the perpetrator or perpetrators drove? Or was someone merely turning around in the driveway? If it was the perp, was it a truck or an SUV? Did he really not recognize the type of vehicle it was, or did he recognize it as one belonging to a member who hadn't been at the service Wednesday night?

My cell was hooked up to the Bluetooth in the car and began playing my favorite tune. I had different tunes for several different people, including Ben, which was Dragnet. For strangers, there was just one tune. The screen said UNKNOWN CALLER but a Houston area code. I didn't like to answer if I didn't know the number. I preferred business callers to call on the office line. But having begun a new case and having a list of folks who might be involved, I thought I should take all calls. Against my better judgment, I punched the symbol on my dashboard.

"Is this Mavis?" a female voice hollered into my face.

"Yes, it is. Who is this, and how may I help you?"

"Mavis, it's Connie Wite."

"Oh, hey, I was going to call you this evening and bring you up to date."

"No, no! Listen! I need your help. Dave has been out of his mind with worry, then a little while ago, Louise called him. She told him she had something she wanted to tell him. She has something she wants to get off her chest. Something about our babies."

Methinks Louise was going to tell him she blabbed about the twins. I didn't like the sound of that. "What was it?"

"She wouldn't tell him over the phone. He started yelling at her, insisting she tell him right away. I could hear her crying."

"What did she say it was?"

"She didn't. She kept refusing. She wasn't going to tell him if he didn't calm down, because, you see, he was yelling in his scariest way. He told her he was going over to her house, and she better be there and tell him what it was. She told him not to come until he calmed down."

"So, did he go?"

"Yes! Yes, Mavis. And he has a gun!"

If my stomach hadn't already been playing a game of Twister, it was now.

"He ran into the hallway and got a gun out of the top of the hall closet. I didn't even know we—he had a gun. He never mentioned it. Then he checked to be sure it was loaded." She coughed and sniffed, and I could picture her swollen face. "He pressed something, and a clip of bullets came out like you see on police shows on TV." She started talking faster and faster. "He pushed the clip back in, and then got another bunch of bullets out of a box and put them in his pocket. He put the gun in his pants behind his back and grabbed a jacket and ran out of the house."

"This doesn't sound good. He's headed to Louise's apartment?"

"For sure. He was so mad, he looked like he'd have a heart attack if he didn't settle down."

Now was not the time to get into whether he suffered from heart problems, so I didn't ask. "Would he shoot his own sister?"

"I don't know what he would do."

"Connie, did you call the police?"

She let out a yowl like an unhappy alley cat. "I didn't want him to get arrested."

"So, you didn't call the police."

"I thought if I called you, maybe you could do something. He has his cell phone on him. Could you call him, and see if you can get him to calm down?"

Moi? She was delusional if she thought little old me could get an angry man with a gun who I barely knew to regain control of himself. "Did you call him after he left to try to talk him out of it? Maybe he's calmed down since he left the house."

"I did, but he didn't pick up. Please, Mavis. Maybe he'll answer your call. Maybe if he knows it's you, he'll come to his senses. You could tell him you'd talk to Louise and find out what she wanted to tell him. Would you please try, Mavis?'

First of all, I was pretty sure I already knew what blabbermouth Louise was going to tell him. I'd been going over in my mind how I was going to phrase it tonight when I reported in. Secondly, he'd been kind of hostile when I'd been at their house. I doubted he'd respond to me. But I would try. "Okay, I'll give it a—I'll give him a call. What's the number?"

Connie recited it into the phone, and I repeated it several times before I disconnected. I asked Siri to place the call, and she did. Or it did. Or whatever Siri is, did. But he didn't pick up for me either. We tried a second time. And a third time.

I had a sneaking suspicion if I called Connie back, she was going to ask me to go to Louise's and see if I could get him not to do any harm to his sister. I called Connie, and that was exactly what she said. I didn't even have my own gun. I kept it locked in my safe at the office, not that I wanted to have a gun battle with Dave. I was a good shot at a target, but—wait a minute—why was I even thinking about that?

So, here I am tooling into Houston amidst increasingly congested traffic and meanwhile trying to decide whether *I* should call the police. I knew what Ben would say, but Ben was not present at the moment. After mulling it over for a few minutes, I decided I'd play it by ear. Anyway, I was far enough away that Dave was going to reach Louise's house way before I would. If he was going to do something, the deed would more than likely be done before I ever arrived.

So, I didn't call the police. I called Connie back to get the make and model of the vehicle Dave drove and made a mental note of it, keeping our call short for the simple reason that it's hard to drive if there's hysteria in one's ear.

When I reached Louise's apartment complex, Dave's truck wasn't there. Yes, another pickup truck to add to the four million plus that occupied Houston. Anyway, assuming he'd either been and gone or he parked in another area, I climbed out of my SUV and, ever on the alert, looked to my left and right, and jogged to Louise's apartment.

The door was closed. I put my ear up to it and heard nothing. No music. No TV. No crying. No voices. Not a thing. I took a chance and rang her doorbell. After a moment, Louise answered the door. She was dressed in a light blue tee shirt, tan capris, and flip flops. Her face was red, her eyes bloodshot, the same as the last time I'd been there.

"I suppose Connie called you," she said. "I know she did. She called me on my cell and when I didn't answer, she texted that she was going to call you."

"Are you going to let me in, or leave me outside on this cold landing where we can have the conversation we need to have so long as you don't mind your neighbors knowing any more of your business than they probably already know?" I drew a deep breath.

"Come in." She stepped back and pushed the door closed behind me.

I didn't smell alcohol, but her breath did smell of cigarettes. At least no alcohol was a good start. "Has your brother been here?"

She appeared awfully calm for a person whose life could have been recently threatened. I followed her to the dinette table, where we'd sat and talked before. She dropped into her favorite place. A pack of cigarettes and a plastic lighter lay next to an overflowing ashtray in front of her.

"I didn't know you smoked," I said as I sat in what was now becoming my favorite place, or at least my designated place.

"I don't. I didn't. I used to, but I quit, but then last night I couldn't help it, I went out and bought a couple of packs."

"I'm not here to judge you, but I do hope you'll consider quitting again. If nothing else, quitting will keep you from going bankrupt."

"Yeah, the price is out of sight." She stared at me, her lips turned down in a deep frown. "So, yes, my brother was here. I'm not stalling. I'm scared. I'm trying to decide if I should call the police."

"Why don't you tell me what's going on? Were you going to tell him about telling people the babies were going to be at the church on Wednesday? If so, I don't see him getting violent with you."

"Oh, Mavis, it's way worse than that. I should have told you or the police in the first place."

A shiver ran down my arms. "Well, as they say, why don't you start at the beginning. A very good place to start."

With shaking hands, Louise began to light a cigarette, but when she glanced at me before she flicked the lighter, I shook my head. She put them both down. "I'm just so nervous."

"Start with telling me why you called your brother."

"Okay." Her lips trembled. She took a deep breath. "I told him I thought I might know someone who might know what happened to the twins." When she stopped talking, she bit her lower lip so hard, I expected to see blood.

"Jiminy Christmas. Why didn't you say so in the first place? Like on Wednesday night?"

"I didn't really suspect she might have something to do with it until she called in sick and you couldn't find her. I had called her, and she didn't answer."

"So, you're talking about Carmen? You friend, Carmen?"

Her head flew up and down. "You want me to tell you why I think she had something to do with it?"

"Yes. Of course, I do."

"Well, she told me once that she helped this lawyer adopt babies."

"Handle private adoptions, you mean?"

"Yeah. Private adoptions. Kind of nothing to do with CPS."

"How exactly did she help this lawyer?"

"Carmen works in the jail with the female inmates. The lawyer would ask Carmen if she'd get the mother, whose baby the lawyer was going to get, to sign the papers giving up the child. Carmen is bilingual."

I had to think about what she said for a minute so I could understand. "Wouldn't the papers have to be notarized?"

"Carmen would talk to the mother who couldn't speak English and explain the papers to her and then take her to the notary in the sheriff's office and then interpret the papers in front of the notary and the woman would sign them."

"Why was Carmen telling you that? Was there something about it that she was uncomfortable with?" Of course, I was suspicious right off the bat. Always, right?

"The lawyer paid her to do it."

"Hmm. Why would a lawyer pay a jailor to do something she probably was supposed to do anyway? I'm thinking that if an inmate has to sign a document in front of a notary, the inmate will have to be taken out of her cell and into the notary's office for the signing." Being uneasy about what she'd told me, I started drumming my fingers on the table. And where was Dave, by the way? Had he gone to find Carmen? At least I knew from experience Carmen wasn't going to be that easy to find. "If the inmate was only Spanish speaking, someone would have to interpret. I don't see a problem with that. So, was the money the lawyer gave Carmen like a tip? I know in Mexico you give *propina* for everything."

"You also give bribes for everything. I started thinking, and I hate to say this because Carmen's my friend, that there was more to it than that. That the lawyer was bribing her for something."

"What kind of money are we talking about?"

"Did you see her trailer?"

"Oh, yeah, nice—for a trailer."

"Top of the line and brand new. She said she'd been saving up for it, but her truck is new, too."

That didn't sound good. "I get the feeling you're going to tell me this thing with inmates signing over babies has been a regular thing?"

Louise palmed her face. "I told her I didn't want to know, but she kept telling me little bits here and little bits there."

"But why would you think Carmen would steal the twins?"

"Once, she told me the lawyer complained that not many white women in the jail were willing to give their children up for adoption. She wanted Carmen to tell her if she found one who would."

"To meet a demand for white babies rather than brown or black babies?" Disgust swept over me.

She dropped her face onto the table, her forehead hitting it. "If the lawyer is selling babies and she wanted some white babies…. That's what I've been thinking."

"That Carmen could get the lawyer to give her a lot of money for the twins?" Oh, Holy Mother of God. Human trafficking by a member of the bar. Could it be true? Apparently so. "You told your brother all this?"

"Enough for him to take off like a bat-out-of-hell in a search for Carmen. I told him you'd been to her trailer and her work this morning, that she was nowhere around, but he said he would find her if it was the last thing he did and if he had to, beat the name of the lawyer out of her."

"Did you call and warn Carmen?"

"I texted her, but I haven't heard back."

"You know he has a gun?"

"Oh yeah. He pointed it at me. I wasn't going to tell him anything until he cooled off, but then he pointed the gun at me. I gave him her address. The gun's a big one, too."

"Let's hope that if he finds Carmen, he doesn't do more than just point it at her."

# CHAPTER
# FOURTEEN

At lunch time, Candy waited across the street from Laura Kate's high school. Memories of one of the first cases Mavis let Candy help with flooded over her. Mavis had to find some kids who had gone missing. Worse than that, Candy had actually convinced Mavis to take the case in the first place, so she'd felt responsible when they disappeared. Later, Mavis was arrested during the investigation. Candy carried that guilt around like a heavy rock, though she'd never told Mavis how she felt.

She'd known the Woodridge/Lawson kids and had questioned their friends about where they were when everyone thought they'd been kidnapped. Those were high school kids, though. Now they were dealing with little babies.

Everyone she'd known who attended Laura Kate's high school had graduated, so Candy had no contacts who could have helped her. Armed with the photo, which she'd enlarged on the copier, she eyeballed kids as they began to leave the building and crossed campus to their cars in the student parking lot. Margaret had texted her with the description of the cars Laura Kate's parents owned. She didn't know which one Laura Kate drove.

When the flow of kids increased, Candy decided to take a chance and cross the street onto the campus to see if any of them would talk to her, to see if any of them knew Laura Kate. A security guard wasn't anywhere around, so she jogged over to a boy who was climbing into his truck.

"Hey, could I talk to you for a minute?" she asked the boy.

He slammed the door in her face, barely giving her a glance. He shook his head and started his truck. Candy stepped out of his way. She didn't want to be run over. He drove off with no hesitation, almost like he'd never seen her.

A girl came out of the school and crossed on the grass instead of using the sidewalk. Candy approached her. "I know you're going to lunch, but could you stop for a moment for me to ask you a question?

The girl, tall and gangly, looked like a basketball player. "Yeah. Just for a sec. My mother's waiting on me."

Candy held out the picture. "Do you know this girl?"

"Yeah. No. Our school has around four thousand kids. Sorry." She shrugged and strode away.

"Thanks anyway," Candy called after her.

Another girl who pulled on a windbreaker when she came around the corner at the end of the block, appeared to be in a major hurry because she started out jogging then slowed to a walk. When the girl got close, Candy stepped in front of her.

"Can I ask you a question real quick?"

The girl didn't stop, so Candy walked beside her and held up the picture. "Do you know this girl?"

"Nuh-uh," the girl said.

"You didn't even look at the picture. Could you just look at the picture for a moment? Look at the girl who is circled?"

"Why would I want to do that?" She panted like a dog.

"I'm trying to find her. It's important." Candy knew she probably shouldn't, but she said, "It's about those twin babies who went missing on Wednesday night. You probably heard about that?"

The girl grabbed the picture. "She looks familiar, but there are tons of girls with blond hair like that in my school. I don't know her."

Candy snatched the picture back and stopped dead. "Well, okay."

Time was running out. The number of kids was thinning. There couldn't be very many who were allowed to leave campus for lunch, could there? Okay, if there were four thousand kids in the school, maybe close to a thousand would be seniors so, maybe so. She hurried to catch another boy. He had white-blond hair and wore a letter jacket—a football jacket.

"Hey, guy, could I talk to you for a minute?" Candy knew she didn't look like anyone a football player would hang out with, given her purple hair, but maybe he was one of the nice ones.

"Walk with me."

"Okay." She turned around and walked beside him. They were apparently headed for a small sports car.

"What do you want?"

She held up the photograph. "I'm looking for this girl. Do you know her?"

He stopped and looked at the picture. "Sure. Laura Kate."

"Have you seen her today? I need to speak with her."

He started walking again. "We just had a class together. She usually parks around the side. She goes out a different door."

Candy wanted to smack her forehead. Of course, there would be more than one exit. She had chosen the wrong one. "Thanks." He did, in fact, get into the sports car. Must be nice. At least she now drove her new Moped most of the time instead of that old clunker, though she still had the clunker. She was the proud owner of two vehicles. So, there.

Staying on the sidewalk so security couldn't get her for trespassing, Candy hurried around the side of the building in time to see a car pulling out into the street. It matched the description of one of the cars Margaret had sent her. She ran back to her Moped and did a U-turn. She wanted to catch Laura Kate before she got home and went into the house.

They didn't live that far away. Candy was able to follow the car, though at a distance. It wasn't like a car chase in a movie scene. Laura Kate wasn't driving like she was trying to escape. Candy had no problem keeping up. As soon as Laura Kate parked in front of her house, Candy pulled up behind her and hopped off her Moped.

She approached the driver's side of the car as Laura Kate put a foot out. "Hey, Laura Kate. I need to talk to you."

"Do I know you?" Laura Kate hooked her purse strap over her shoulder and closed the car door.

"No, you don't, but I really need to speak with you out here. Not in your house."

Laura Kate's nose wrinkled, and her brows drew together. "That doesn't sound good. What do you want?"

Candy started to remove her helmet but stopped because she didn't plan to be there long. "I work for Ms. Davis, who I know you spoke with yesterday."

Laura Kate backed away in the direction of the house. "I can't talk to you without my parents being around."

"Sure, you can. In fact, Mavis said she thought maybe you wanted to tell her something but didn't want to say it in front of them."

Laura Kate tossed her head and pushed some of her long blond hair behind her ears. She glanced over her shoulder at the house. "I don't want to get into trouble."

"I don't want to get you in trouble. Wouldn't it be better to tell me whatever it was you were keeping back than someone else? We won't tell anyone if we don't have to." Candy hoped that was true.

Laura Kate let out a long breath. "I don't know."

"With what Mavis has told me about what happened at the church, I think I know what you don't want to say. How about I ask you some questions and you can nod or shake your head?"

Laura Kate laughed. "I saw that in a movie once. All right."

Candy's nose was running from being out in the cold on her Moped. She pulled a tissue from her pocket and blew her nose while keeping her eyes on Laura Kate. "Okay. Were you in the church restroom longer than you said you were? Nod or shake your head."

The girl looked over her shoulder again. Her face had turned pink. She nodded.

"I'm thinking you were on your cell phone."

Laura Kate nodded again.

"I'm guessing you were talking to someone you don't want your parents to know about, right?"

Laura Kate cocked her head and shrugged.

"Like a boy?"

She nodded. "Please don't tell my parents. I feel so, so bad as it is, and they'll ground me for life."

Candy squeezed Laura Kate's forearm. "I get it. Thanks. We'll do everything we can to keep it to ourselves. We just need to know details like these to figure out what happened. By the way, my name's Candy Finklestein in case you want to get ahold of me. I work for Mavis, of course."

"I really need to get inside. My step-mother will be wondering what's taking me so long."

"I understand, and really, thank you so much." Candy walked back to her Moped, feeling like her success would raise Mavis' opinion of her another notch. She pulled away as Laura Kate went inside the house.

Chilled from being outside so much, she drove to the nearest coffee shop where she bought a tall latte and grabbed a table in a corner as soon as it was vacated. She tapped Mavis' number into her cell phone. Mavis preferred live phone calls as opposed to texts, so Candy accommodated her. Mavis was the boss lady.

Voicemail per usual. "Mavis, I caught Laura Kate at her house. I'll tell you what she said when I talk to you. I'm gonna call Margaret to see if we have anything to pick up at either of the clerks' offices. If so, I'll get those served and then go back to the office."

After she ended the call, Candy sat a few minutes sipping her latte. When she'd first started working for Mavis half a day when she was in high school, she'd thought she might want to be a private investigator. Now that she'd been around for a few years, she wasn't so sure. Taking classes at Houston Community College had opened her eyes to so many more things. She liked being around the courts, though, near the action.

She could become a paralegal and if she liked that, when she saved up some money, go to law school. Or she could be a court reporter. They sat in court every day and heard all those cases, taking down the testimony of lawyers, witnesses, and the judge. That would be cool. She could become a police officer or a deputy sheriff. Ben was a police officer, and he was mostly okay, except when he got on Mavis' last nerve. There were so many other things she could do, even in the courts. She had a lot to think about.

She tapped on the office number.

"Good afternoon, this is the office of Mavis Davis. How may I help you?"

You never knew how Margaret might answer the phone. Lately, she'd been fixated on what she'd recited that day. "Hey, Margaret, it's me. What's up?"

"Did you get a chance to talk to that girl?" Margaret alternated between being long-winded and getting right to the point.

"Yep. I caught her at her house before she went inside."

"Hey, that's great. Did you tell Mavis?"

"I left her a voicemail. What are you up to? Did that cop, Lon Tyler, come back?"

"Not so far. He makes me nervous. He can be so yucky."

"I wonder what he wanted Mavis for."

"No telling. I guess he'll eventually find her, and she'll tell us."

"Have there been any walk-ins? Any new clients?"

"No, but there're some documents at the County Clerk's Office you need to pick up and serve."

"Nothing upstairs?"

"Just one today. Can you get those done? Where are you now?"

"I stopped to get some coffee. I got cold running all around. I'm going to have to start wearing more layers or drive my clunker."

"Okay. Well, call me if you need me."

Candy finished her coffee and headed out. The sky was growing dark and threatened rain. She wanted to get the papers as soon as possible. This would be a good time to go home and get her car. She sure didn't want to be out on her Moped in a rainstorm.

She liked serving papers. She liked that they trusted her enough to pick them up at the courthouse, serve them, and file the returns. She'd been too young when she was in high school to serve them, though she learned about it, and lots of other things, from Mavis.

Now, Candy was happy. Mavis let her do it all the time. Well, most of the time, unless the neighborhood where the person had to be served was dangerous, or Mavis thought the person might be threatening. Candy liked meeting new people. Most of them were like that lady the other night, sad. Some of the men had given Candy a hard time, teasing her in a nasty kind of way, but mostly it was fun. She liked driving around town, too. Especially now that she had her Moped.

Since she'd staked out that woman and gotten her served, she hoped she'd proved to Mavis that she could do more. Maybe Mavis would give her something else to do on the baby kidnapping case. She could only hope.

# CHAPTER
# FIFTEEN

I high-tailed it out of Louise's apartment and called Carmen as soon as I hit the road in hopes of warning her about Dave looking for her. Again, she didn't pick up. I wasn't surprised since she hadn't replied to Louise's text. I left her a message and hoped she'd at least read them while she was on the run.

I tried to think of where I'd go if I knew someone like me was looking for me. She must know she'd been found out. Would she flee? Did she have enough money and credit to get out of town? Of course, credit cards left a trail, and if what she'd been involved in was illegal, she sure wouldn't want a trail that the authorities would be able to follow. So, what she needed was cash. She might pull money out of an ATM. Or, if she hadn't spent everything on her trailer and truck, she might have stored cash in a safe deposit box. She might have some cash stashed in her trailer.

I'd been outside her trailer earlier in the morning, but I hadn't been inside, so I couldn't have seen evidence of someone packing to get out of town. Maybe she had gone to do some other things, thinking she had time to pack later. What other things could she have done that early? Not go to the bank, it wouldn't have been open, though she could go to an ATM. What she could do was hit up the lawyer for some money. I could see that. Tell the lawyer she'd keep her mouth shut if the lawyer gave her enough money to get far away and start over.

While Louise had been talking, I wondered how extensive the baby thing was, and what else Carmen had done. But I could worry about that later. What I needed to do was stop Dave from committing any crimes. I should go back to the trailer and see if she was there. She wouldn't have gone to the jail. She wouldn't have gone to her best friends, Louise or Amy. I just hoped she hadn't packed up and left yet, though she'd had plenty of time.

When I pulled up to her trailer, a bright blue extended cab truck sat on the pad next to it. I touched the hood. Barely warm, which indicated to me she'd been back for a while. Why hadn't she left town?

I banged on the door a couple of times until she answered. She was a dark-haired, dark-eyed, petite, sturdily built woman dressed in canvas-colored slacks that bulged a bit at the waist, a red turtleneck, and running shoes. She held an ice bag to her cheek. "You've got to be that Mavis Davis."

"That would be me. What did you do to your face?"

"You might as well come in." She held the door wide so I could enter. The place smelled like she'd sprayed rose-scented air freshener around.

"Was that Dave? Dave Wite? Did he hit you? Did you call the police?"

We both perched on the built-in sofa. She exhaled a large sigh and shook her head. "Yes, he's been and gone. No, I didn't call the police. What was I going to tell them, the reason why he hit me?"

"Where's Dave now?"

"I'm not sure."

"Did you tell him the name of the lawyer you've been working for?"

"Louise tell you about that? She must have. She told Dave. She's got a big mouth."

"They're her niece and nephew. What would you expect?"

"Yeah, but they weren't going to be raised right. Those people don't believe in God. Louise told me."

"They're atheists."

"Yes. Isobel was going to place them with good Christian families with good Christian values."

Now I'd heard everything. Someone steals children so they can give them to Christian families? How Christian was that? To me, it was an excuse for criminal behavior. "You can't be serious. There's got to be more to this story."

There was blood on the ice bag when she switched it to her other hand and winced when she put it to her cheek. "I might as well tell you since Dave made me tell him."

"At gunpoint?"

"He hit me with his gun. I hope my cheekbone isn't broken. It hurts like nobody's business."

I didn't feel much sympathy for her. "Do you think he's going to go find that lawyer?"

"Yes, I do. She's in court just about every day, even on Fridays, that's when she does her adoptions. If she's not in court, she's in a bar having a *cocktail* on Friday afternoon to celebrate." She snorted. "That's what she calls it. Her *cocktail* hour."

"Have you called her and warned her?"

"She didn't answer. I left her a message saying it was extremely important that she call me back."

Fridays were apparently the days for messages. "So, you think she'd be at her office, or the courthouse, or at a bar?"

"Any of those."

I'd probably be engaged in a futile effort if I went searching for the lawyer, but I was going to have to do that to find Dave, who would be searching for her. "So, what is this attorney's name?"

She closed her eyes and shook her head. "I hate to get her into trouble."

"Lady, she's already in trouble up to her eyeballs. Now, what is her name?"

"If I tell you, will you help me if I get arrested?"

"If?" I couldn't believe she wanted to bargain.

"Okay, okay. Isobel Oliver."

"If I go to the courthouse, I can warn her. They won't let Dave in with a weapon."

"Thank God for that."

"If I went to the courthouse, how would I recognize her?"

"I don't know if she'll be there today."

"If she was there, where would I find her?"

"Well, first of all, she'd be in one particular family court."

"And what does she look like?"

"She's a white lady, a small blonde whose hair looks like it was fried."

"Frizzy, you mean?"

"Yeah. It's medium length and thin and curly but sticks out. She wears these pointed glasses, usually in a color matching her suit. She always wears a little suit, either pants or a skirt suit. And she wears really high heels because she's so short."

"Shorter than you?"

"About as short as me. And she carries an old leather briefcase—a satchel, kinda big—with some initials on it, but they're faded. You wouldn't be able to see them at any distance anyway. I've been to her office and seen it on her desk."

"What kind of car does she drive?"

"A Lexus. A shiny, black Lexus that she has detailed every two weeks, more often if it's rained. One of those low-to-the-ground sports models."

"Okay, so where exactly is her office?"

"Her office building has a parking garage across from it. I'll write the addresses and everything down for you."

Clearly she thought I might help her. Or maybe she was concerned about the lawyer. "I would appreciate it if you'd write down the name of the bar or bars she likes to go to, also. And her phone number."

"All right." She got up and went to a drawer where she pulled out a yellow pad of large post-it notes. "It's actually a bar inside a hotel restaurant downtown. Ritzy. I know because I met her there once. Not to eat or anything. She never wanted to be seen with me but to deliver some documents to her." Blood congealed around the nasty cut on her cheek.

"Some documents you had one of the mothers in the jail sign?"

"I know Louise told you about that."

"Louise told me what she knows. I suspect there's a lot more you could tell me. Like how long this has been going on. Who all is involved. That sort of thing."

"I only know what I did for Isobel and a few other little things."

"I need to get out of here and see if I can find Mr. Wite or at least find this Isobel person and warn her. Does Dave know all the places you've told me about?"

"He doesn't know about the bar. He didn't ask. I didn't tell him."

"Okay. I do want to talk to you some more later, but just a couple of questions now. One, why did you do it? Two, where are the babies?"

She had the good grace to look sheepish. "Detention officers don't make a lot of money. Isobel gave me a lot of money. At least to me it was a lot of money. She probably received a heck of a lot more."

"And where are the twins?"

She shook her head. "I don't know."

"You did take them Wednesday night?"

"Yeah. I grabbed them and got out of there. I took them straight to Isobel's office and dropped them off."

"Oh, man. So, no telling what she's done with them. Does she even have the ability to take care of babies?"

"She has a small room in her office complex that's like a nursery.

She has diapers and formula, and baby food and stuff like that. That's all I know."

"So, you wouldn't know where they went from her office?"

"No. I wish I did, but I don't. I never wanted to find out more than I had to know."

I went to the door and opened it. "Carmen, I'll be back to speak to you more another time, but I've got to tell you, you're in deep trouble." I knew I should call the police right then and there but decided to risk her running. I needed to talk to her some more and if she was arrested, that would put the kibosh on that.

Her head dropped to her chest, and she uttered, "I know. Believe me, I know."

"Will you be here when I return?"

Her brows drew together like she was thinking it over. She sighed. "If I run, I'll only get in worse trouble."

That was not really an answer to my question, but I didn't have time to quibble. Jumping in my SUV, I started it and pointed it to downtown Houston. I thought the best place to start would be the family court. If Isobel Oliver had only one adoption scheduled for that day, she could be gone. If she had more than one, she might still be there.

Though it was only midafternoon, the sky had grown dark. It would be just my luck to arrive at the parking lot in the pouring down rain with no umbrella. The wind had begun blowing. It was tumbleweed windy, except instead of tumbleweeds, trash blew across the Houston streets. I found the family court building, found the closest parking lot, and circled around before I parked, looking for Dave's truck. No luck. So, I parked. I could smell the rain, or whatever's in the air before it rains. Ben had told me what it was once, but I never remembered. And why did thoughts of Ben pop into my head?

I went inside to the court Carmen had said was the one Isobel Oliver always went to. I didn't stop to wonder how she managed to always have her cases end up in the same court.

The courtroom was empty, the lights off, and the door locked. After a little wrangling with courthouse personnel, I was able to get to the court coordinator's office through a different door. She looked at me, an indifferent expression on her face.

"I'm Mavis Davis, a private investigator hired on a case involving potential adoptive children. I wonder, could I talk to the judge for a few minutes?"

The nameplate said her name was Lynn Naylor. A brunette, with pale blue eyes, peered at me over the top of her glasses and cocked her head. "No, Miss Davis. The judge isn't here. He's left for the day, and if he was here, you wouldn't be allowed to speak with him."

"Oh. Even to ask about procedures?"

"You can ask me or one of the clerks. Or get a copy of the local rules from the District Clerk's Office."

"Okay, thanks, I'll do that. By the way, I saw the courtroom is dark. Could you tell me whether the judge heard any adoptions this afternoon?"

"Adoptions are confidential cases. I can't talk about them."

"I'm not asking you to do that. I'm just wondering whether Isobel Oliver has been here this afternoon. I should have said that in the first place."

"She had one scheduled, but I can't tell you more than that."

"When you say she had one scheduled, you mean it didn't get done?"

"Correct. She didn't show up and didn't call, so we rescheduled for next Friday. She likes hers to be heard on Fridays, and the judge always accommodates her."

I gave her my best grin. "Thank you very much, Ms. Naylor. If I have any further questions for you that the local rules don't answer, is it all right if I come back?" I would come back regardless, but I certainly wasn't going to say that.

"I guess so, though I can't think of why you'd need to." She picked up a pen and glanced at the paper in front of her. "You have a nice weekend."

"You too." I hurried out of there. I couldn't see outside to tell if the rain had started. I hoped to beat it to my car. I didn't. I imagined the rain wouldn't stop Dave from completing his mission. I couldn't let it defeat me, either. From a rack of throwaway newspapers, I took one and held it over my head as I ran for my car. Once inside, I blotted my body with tissues from a cube until I was not dry, but not unreasonably wet. I asked Siri for directions to the bar Ms. Oliver frequented. The place had to be downtown, somewhat close to the courthouse complex.

The rain let up enough that I could see fairly well, and Siri helped me locate the place. Of course, I had to find another place to park. I hated to even go into the bar, because I had a sneaking suspicion if she hadn't gone to court, she wasn't celebrating in her favorite bar. Also, I was conscious of the fact that the locale was where mostly one-percenters went, and I was not dressed like a one-percenter. Not even a wet one-percenter.

Still, I talked myself into it. Not so much to save Ms. Oliver from whatever was her destiny, but to stop Dave from ruining his life. Now that we knew who stole the babies, the Wites would be able to get them back. I hoped.

Shivering from the rain and wind outside, as well as the frigid air-conditioning in the bar/restaurant, I managed to flag down the Maître D' and, ignoring his snooty attitude, asked about Ms. Oliver. I figured if she was a regular, he'd know her. He said not only was she not there, he hadn't seen her that day.

So, I'm wondering whether Isobel Oliver had made herself scarce on purpose, or whether she had matters other than her adoption practice to attend to, or, well, I couldn't imagine what. I didn't want to imagine. I just wanted to find her.

Finally, I ran back through the rain, jumped in my car, and got Siri to direct me to Ms. Oliver's law office, which was about ten minutes away. By this time, it was getting late in the day. I suspected she wouldn't be in her office either.

But I was wrong. When I turned onto the street where her office was situated, police cars had blocked it off all across the building entrance. I backed up and pulled down the way a little, passing by a truck that matched the description of Dave Wite's truck. That didn't bode well.

I parked and jogged through the now-drizzle, still holding the now-soggy newspaper over my head. When I got close, a uniformed officer was walking a handcuffed Dave Wite to a police car. I was too late.

"Miss Davis," Dave hollered. "I didn't do it."

I approached the police cruiser. "Stay back, lady," the cop said.

I stopped where I was since I was close enough to hold a conversation with Dave. "Do what, Mr. Wite?"

"They're arresting me for killing the lawyer, that Isobel Oliver, but I didn't do it. She was dead when I got here."

The police officer opened the back door and, putting his hand on Dave's head, pushed him into the car. "Call Connie. Miss Davis, you have to call Connie and tell her what's going on, tell her I didn't do it."

The cop closed the door, cutting off anything else Dave said. I nodded at him. I'd call Connie soon, but I wanted to find out what I could first. As the cop drove away, I walked to the front of the building, shivering in the cold. There was a light at the entrance, but even in the dark, the light didn't help. I couldn't get by all the bystanders and police. The rain had stopped, just a mist filled the air. I rolled up the wet newspaper and searched around for a place to toss it.

I was about to walk down to the corner where the city had placed a decorative metal trash can when a deep voice I recognized said from behind me, "Fancy seeing you here." Turning, I came face to face with the love of my life, trite as that sounds, Lieutenant Ben Sorensen. I would have hugged him if we hadn't been at a murder scene.

# CHAPTER
# SIXTEEN

I brushed my hand against Ben's. I'd missed him. "I thought I saw you driving past the jail this morning. When did you get in?" He looked good, but tired, the lines in his face deep.

"This morning. I caught the earliest flight available." His eyes were fixed on the building doorway. An ambulance pulled up, sans lights or siren.

There must have been a good reason why he hadn't called me, but we couldn't get into it right then with all the cops and bystanders hanging around. "How was the funeral?"

"Pretty much standard Baptist funeral where the preacher talked about her, but you could tell he didn't really know her." He grimaced. "Too much impersonal religious stuff, but that's what she wanted."

"I'm sorry, babe. It must have been hard."

He shrugged. "I got out of there as fast as I could."

He leaned toward me, pressing his dry shoulder next to my wet one. We hadn't been intimate since his mother died. That could be remedied easily that evening.

"My sister's going to handle everything with the house and all. She'll call me if she needs me." He peered down at me, his face looking dewy in the mist. "So, what are you doing here? You know the killer?"

I stepped back. "The *alleged killer*, you mean? I'm assuming you're speaking of Mr. Wite."

"Okay. The alleged killer. The man who was standing over the body of a dead woman. The man with a gun tucked in the back of his pants when our boys showed up."

"You're full of assumptions, and you just got back in town. Do you even know what this is all about?"

"Do you know what it's all about?" He looked skeptical.

"As a matter of fact, I do. That is, if the dead woman is the lawyer, Isobel Oliver."

"She's been tentatively identified as Isobel Oliver by several people who have offices in that building."

I had been hired by the Wites, yes, but in this situation, were the circumstances of my hiring confidential? I hadn't been hired on a murder case—even one where the accused was my client in the other situation. It looked like Dave would be charged. Today I'd learned things I hadn't had time to discuss with the Wites. Was I free to talk about those things with the police, even a policeman with whom I was especially familiar? I'm not sure there's a rule in the Detective Handbook that covered the situation.

"I can see the gears and pulleys in your brain turning round and round."

"Ha. Ha. Here's the thing. I've been hired by Dave Wite, the alleged assailant, and his wife. I need to talk to my client, at least one of my clients, to see whether it's okay for me to reveal what I've learned. The other client y'all have just hauled off to jail."

"So, Mr. Wite is your client?"

"Tell you what, Ben, let me consult with my other client this afternoon." I glanced at my watch. "Well, this evening, and I'll call you. I guess you'll have some kind of supervisory role since this is a homicide now?"

"As opposed to what it was before he killed her?"

"*Allegedly* killed her. I was hired to help the police..." I said in my most teasing voice.

"To do what exactly?"

"Solve the kidnapping of baby twins."

"I heard about that almost before I hit town. You think somehow this murder is connected to the kidnapping?"

"Well, yeah, I do, since it was Mr. Wite's babies who were kidnapped."

He nodded as though the information I'd just given him confirmed something he already knew. "If he suspected the dead woman was involved in it, that's certainly a motive for murder."

"We can agree on that. Has anyone said anything about any children being in the office with the dead lawyer?"

"I went in briefly. She was the only one there. I looked in all the rooms. She had a nursery in the back office where her body is. I wondered why. I kind of figured she must bring her children to work sometimes."

"Huh. No one has said anything about her having any kids, but I just found out about her today, so what do I know? Okay, I'm cold. I've got to get out of these wet clothes and go see my other client. I'll get back to you later. Promise." I squeezed his forearm and whispered. "Maybe we can get together tonight at my house?"

His eyes flared. "We'll see."

I flipped my hair, which flopped against my neck more than flipped, and walked back to my car, tossing the throwaway newspaper into the trash barrel as I went. My phone rang with Candy's film noir tone as I climbed inside.

"What's up, Candy?"

"Did you get my message? I talked to Laura Kate, even though she looked scared to talk to me. I promised we wouldn't tell what she said unless we absolutely had to. I'm right about that, aren't I?"

"You're not talking on your phone while you're driving that scooter, are you?"

"*No, mother dear.*" She snickered. "I'm in my car, anyway. I was afraid of getting rained on. And I'm, like, in the driveway of an abandoned building. Really, so don't give me the third degree. I honestly do know how to drive safely."

"I'm glad you managed to speak with her. I bet she told you she was in the restroom longer than she's said?"

"How'd you know?"

"Long story, which I'll fill you and Margaret in on later. Go back to the office and see if Margaret has something else for you to do—I'm assuming you've taken care of any service that came in today—and I'll be there later this evening. I have to take care of several things, including changing into something dry."

"I went home and changed vehicles after I picked up the service. I do have to serve a couple of people, so if I can catch them, I'll meet you at the office." She clicked off.

Plugging in my phone to charge on the way home, I drove to my house and changed into some dry jeans, a sweater, and a jacket, then combed my wet hair and put it in a ponytail. I texted Connie that I was coming over to her house in a few minutes and to please be at home. There was no way I was going to tell Connie on the phone that her husband had been arrested for murder.

Connie answered the door so fast I thought she might have been watching for me from a window. Her face was white. Her eyes red. Her hair mussed. She wore a pair of black jeans and a sweatshirt. She held a balled-up tissue in one hand.

I took her by the arm. "I guess you've heard, huh?"

She nodded. "Dave called me from the police station. They let him have one phone call." She put her hands over her face and wept. I led her into their den, a large room with a sectional sofa facing a fireplace with a big flat screen TV hanging above it. We sat for a minute or so until she could get ahold of herself.

"He told you he was arrested for killing Isobel Oliver?"

She nodded again. "They didn't give him enough time to explain what happened. He said he just wanted me to know where he was, and he didn't do it and to ask you to help him."

"I will, Connie. I'll tell you everything I've learned, and you might think this rude, but could I have something warm to drink?"

She eased off the sofa. "Of course. Come into the kitchen and you can talk to me while I'm making it. What do you like? Tea? Hot chocolate?"

"Tea would be good. Anything at this point. I was caught in the rain going from place to place and finally had to put on some dry clothes before I came here. Otherwise, I'd have arrived earlier."

She filled a kettle and put it on the stove. My mother used to do that. I had, too, but finally bought an electric one that turned itself off when it boiled. I'd almost set my kitchen on fire once when I forgot the kettle was on the stove and went off for a shower. I didn't think I was old enough to forget stuff like that, but my brain gets overloaded sometimes.

She leaned against the counter next to the stove. I leaned against the one opposite to her. "Give me a second," I said. "My head is spinning, figuratively, of course." I couldn't muster the energy to laugh at my own joke.

While I thought about it, Connie retrieved a mug from a cabinet and a teabag from a decorative storage tin on the counter and rested against the counter again.

"Okay, here's the people I've spoken to and what I found out today. First, you may know I saw Louise last night?"

"Yes." She gritted her teeth. "And I could—I could—"

"Slap the snot out of her?"

"Uh-huh. I'm so mad at her."

"Try to let that go right now. We'll talk about it later. Louise told me what she had done and pretty much pointed the finger at Carmen." I continued talking, summarizing what I'd done all day.

"Carmen was supposed to be Louise's friend. How could she do this? How could she steal Louise's niece and nephew?" Her cheeks were red with fury.

"We'll get to that. The kettle's boiling, by the way."

Connie turned off the fire and poured the water over the teabag. Her hands shook.

"Connie, try to calm yourself. I'm going to help you all I can."

"I know. I'm just so worried—about Dave and the babies."

"We're going to find the babies. I'm real close to that, and I'll tell you about that in a minute." I took the cup and started for the den. "Let's sit down and I'll finish telling you what I know, and we can go from there."

She rubbed her chin on the shoulder of her sweatshirt to catch a tear that had glided down her face. "Okay. I trust you, Mavis."

I took a sip of tea and put the cup on a coaster on the coffee table. We sat down, our knees pointing at each other. I told her about lunch with Mr. Warburton. "I managed to find out from him that Laura Kate lied about the amount of time she was in the bathroom."

"I figured that. It would have taken longer than Laura Kate said for a person to have gotten in and out of the church with the babies."

I held up a hand to stop her. "He also did see something in the parking lot. He saw some taillights he thought were of a truck."

"Carmen drives a truck."

"On my way back is when you called about Dave. I went to Louise's to catch Dave, but he'd been and gone."

She nodded and covered her mouth, stopping herself from saying anything.

"Louise told me a whole lot more than she did the first time. Dave got the story out of her before he left. So, I went in search of Dave. He had a good head start on me."

"I hope he didn't hurt Louise. I'm mad at her, but I wouldn't want him to hurt her."

"He pointed his gun at her to get her to tell him what she knew, but otherwise, he didn't do anything. I went back to Carmen's. Dave had been there, and he did hurt her, but not critically."

"Oh my God." She put her face into her hands. "He's not a violent person. He's usually so laid back and calm."

"Yeah, well... Carmen told him she had taken the children and given them to this lawyer, Isobel Oliver."

"That's why they think he killed her?"

"Yes. Long story short, I went to the courthouse and a bar she frequents, but she hadn't been at either place. When I arrived at her office, the police were hauling Dave away."

"So, Mavis, she really is dead?" She slapped her own cheek and leaned her face on her hand. "That was stupid. If she wasn't dead, they wouldn't have arrested him. Were you able to find out anything from the police?"

"She was lying on the floor of the nursery she had set up in the back office of her suite."

"Were the babies at her office?"

"No. No one was. I managed to exchange a few words with Dave before they took him away. I don't have all the facts. Neither do the police. It's early yet. No babies in her office, but I'm going to find them. I promise. We at least know now what was going on, what was going to happen with them."

Something light-colored stained Connie's sweatshirt about a third of the way down from her shoulders. Her boobs must be leaking milk. Poor lady. She wrapped her arms around herself and shook.

"What are we going to do, Mavis? Can you help Dave? What's going to happen with him?"

"They'll book him into the jail. They'll take him before a judge, and he'll have a bond set sometime, probably a high one. That's what they do nowadays. Once they set the amount of his bail, you'll be able to get him out of jail. I hope you have some money saved."

"Dave has always been frugal. He even already set up a college fund for the children."

They were probably going to need every bit of what they had. "He's going to need a lawyer, too. Do y'all have a lawyer? Have you ever needed a lawyer?"

She shook her head. "Why would we? Do you know of someone who would be good?"

"As a matter of fact, I do. There's a woman named Gillian Wright, who got me out of hot water one time. She practices criminal and family law. She's not cheap, but she's good. I liked her."

"If you recommend her, I'll call and see if I can hire her."

"I know she's still around, because we handle some of the document service on her cases." I retrieved my phone from my purse and scrolled to her name. "I'll share her contact info with you. Get your cell phone. It's Friday evening, but she might still be in her office. I'm giving you the whole contact, so you'll have her cell phone number, as well as her office number." I finished my tea and felt considerably better. I sent her Gillian's contact information.

"Thank you, Mavis. Thanks for all you've done. But you're not through with us, are you? We still need you to find our babies."

I hugged her. "Not through by any means. I'm going to get your twins back or die trying."

# CHAPTER
# SEVENTEEN

Even though I was pooped, I drove back to the office since I'd promised Candy I'd bring her and Margaret up to date. I would have loved to go home to rest for at least a little while. Not only did I hope wearing myself out wouldn't cause the cold virus to reverse course and return, but I was anticipating seeing Ben that night.

When I arrived, it was after five, but Candy and Margaret were both present. They'd locked the front door and were eating something at the table in the kitchen. Turned out to be more wedding cake. I'd eaten so much of it, I gagged at the thought of another bite.

I put my things in my office and took off my jacket and shoes. Walking in my socks, I went to the kitchen and sat down with them. Sighing, I shook my head and glanced from one to the other. "I don't know where to start."

"Before you do, Mavis, we wanted to tell you Lon Tyler was here this morning."

"Lon. What did he want?"

"We don't know. He wouldn't say. He just demanded to see you,"

Margaret said. She had a steaming cup of coffee in front of her and stirred it nonstop.

I put my hand on hers. "You nervous about something?"

"Just thinking." She laid the spoon on the table. "You should have seen Candy. Lon wanted to go look for you back here, but Candy wouldn't let him."

"Really?" I had to laugh. "Bet he didn't like that."

Candy said, "Nope. He sure didn't, but he knew he didn't have the right. I don't think he's used to people like me standing up to him." She shoved a bite of cake into her mouth.

"People like you?"

"Young women," she said through chews of cake. "Any women, probably." White frosting stuck to the corners of her mouth.

"Well, I'm proud of you. You were polite about it, weren't you?"

"Yes. I just told him he had to have a warrant," Candy said, beaming with pride.

Margaret said, "So he drove around back to see if your car was there and left."

"Guess we'll find out eventually what he wanted."

"Are you going to tell us what's been going on with the Wites?" Margaret asked.

"I am. So much has happened today that I've forgotten what you know and what you don't know. I guess I'll just tell you, but it may not be in the order it happened."

Candy bounced in her chair. "Well, go on, Mavis."

"Mr. Wite has been arrested for murder." I got up and looked in the refrigerator for something besides cake.

"What?" Margaret said.

"What? Who'd he kill?" Candy asked.

I found a cup of Greek yogurt and a spoon and sat down again. "I'm sure he didn't do it. None of our clients are ever guilty, right?"

Both of them nodded.

"Okay, here's what I've been able to find out. Carmen Garcia, who is a real good friend of Louise Wite, who is Dave Wite's sister, works in the jail with the female inmates. She also goes to that Holy Roller church where the babies were. A lawyer was paying her, she says to just get adoption papers signed by the women in the jail who were giving their kids up for adoption, but I think it was more than that." I was able to peel back the cover on the yogurt and take a bite while both of their mouths dropped open.

"Don't stop, Mavis," Candy said, looking at Margaret for support.

"Hold your horses. I'm hungry." I took another bite. "Apparently evangelicals don't think much of atheists."

"What's that got to do with anything?" Margaret popped a bite of cake into her mouth.

"The Wites are atheists."

Margaret swallowed and asked, "Did this Carmen person take the babies?"

"I haven't quite figured out why she thought that just because they had no religion, she could take the twins. The lawyer had placed a lot of babies from the jail for adoption, mostly Latino and black. The lawyer said she had clients, I've found out now they were customers, not just clients, who wanted white babies. Very few white babies come up for adoption out of the jail. Or maybe just not enough to fill the demand. Right now, I don't know how many babies we're even talking about, much less what color, shape, and size they were."

"Carmen whoever took the twins because they're white and gave them to the lawyer to put them up for adoption with white people? Is that what you're saying?" Candy's face wore a blanched, stunned expression. "How do you even do that with all the paperwork that goes into adopting a kid?"

"I haven't figured out how she got away with it yet. My main concern at this point is to find out what she did with them, where she placed those twins, and get them back."

"So, you're telling us Mr. Wite somehow figured out that Louise's friend Carmen took the babies and gave them to the lawyer on Wednesday night?" Margaret said.

"Yes. Wait a minute. Margaret, you're eating that cake? What happened to you being on that health-nut kick? I thought you weren't eating white flour and white sugar?"

"It's my wedding cake. I can eat it if I want to."

"I'm not challenging that, Margaret. You keep giving Candy and me grief about what we eat..."

She waved her arms in the air. "Back off, Mavis. I'm eating my wedding cake this one time—or rather, for a couple of days—I can do that if I want to. As soon as it's gone, I'm going back to eating healthily. Okay?"

Her response astounded me. Canceling the wedding must have had a really traumatic effect. More than she let on. "Okay, Margaret. You're right. You can eat whatever you want." I knew then that once we got the twins back and everything calmed down, Margaret and I needed to have a heart-to-heart about what happened with Barry. But right now, we had to focus on the Wite case.

"I'm sorry to spout off. Can you just tell us how Mr. Wite figured out what had happened?"

"Louise was the key to his finding out about Carmen. And sometime or another we'll probably figure out exactly how Carmen accomplished getting in and out of there, but right now that's not the most important thing. Although I'm sure Pastor Markham will want to know in order to improve security at his little church, assuming his congregation amounts to anything once they find out what happened. But that's neither here nor there."

Candy stood behind her chair and waved her hands as though demonstrating a point. "The lawyer must have been waiting outside when that Carmen person took the kids. Carmen snuck inside the church, I guess because she wasn't attending that night, and got the kids while Laura Kate was in the bathroom. That's why you wanted to know whether Laura Kate had lied about the amount of time she was in there."

"I went to lunch with the man who was the usher that night. They only have one usher at a time, apparently, because it's such a small church. The usher stands in the back in front of the doors to the sanctuary all during the service. I finally pulled it out of him that he could hear when someone went to the bathroom, when they flushed, whether they washed their hands, and when they went back out. Eventually, with my prodding, he realized Laura Kate had been in there longer than normal. And he even said he realized now that she had done it other times. I figure she was either playing games on her phone—"

Margaret said, "I hate it when people do that in public restrooms and you're standing out there waiting to go."

"Or she was having a conversation with someone she didn't want anyone to know about."

"She was talking to her boyfriend," Candy said. "And her parents don't know she has a boyfriend."

"Huh. Just what I thought. Anyway, I also found out that Carmen took the babies to the lawyer's office."

"She must have had help," Margaret said.

I shrugged. "I guess. But to get back to the murder of this lawyer. Louise realized last night that she had blabbed about how she was going to babysit the babies on Wednesday night and take them to church. She apparently not only told Carmen, but she talked about it at her office. She works in the county clerk's office."

Candy waved her arms in the air. "I was there today."

"Then after thinking it over all night, she thought she should tell Dave. I was already going to go out and talk to Carmen since Carmen was one of her very best friends and Carmen wasn't answering her phone and didn't show up for work."

"So, Louise told Dave what she thought had happened and Dave somehow found out about the lawyer and shot her?" Margaret patted at her lips with a napkin.

"He didn't shoot anybody. Dave went to see Carmen. When Carmen wouldn't tell him who it was, he busted her in the face and threatened to shoot her. So she told him. And he went looking for the lawyer. I was more than a few minutes behind him. Carmen told me what happened, so I went looking for the lawyer and Dave. I went several places and finally when I arrived at her office, they had cuffed Dave and were putting him in a police car to take him downtown and charge him with murder."

"Wow," Candy said.

"Yeah," Margaret said. "But if this lawyer was selling his babies, I could see why he killed her."

"He says he didn't do it. I don't know the whole story, but I intend to find out."

"No sign of the kids though?" Margaret asked.

"Nope. I'm going to ask Ben if they can get a court order to look in Ms. Oliver's files and see if they can find where she placed them. She sure placed them in a hurry, if that's in fact what she did. No telling. She could have given them to someone to babysit temporarily."

"What a mess," Margaret said. "Wait, Ben? When did he get back?"

"Early this morning. He was at the murder scene. We didn't get to talk much."

"Is he going to be working this case?"

"Probably. Or at least supervising it. I don't think they knew the murder could be related to the kidnapping. In fact, he didn't know anything about the kidnapping, but, of course, he had just come home."

"This is tough," Candy said.

My cell phone began signaling someone was trying to call me, but it was my "unknown caller" ring. I was tired and tempted to let it go.

"I'll get it." Candy ran into my office. After a moment, she yelled, "It's Gillian Wright. Wasn't she your lawyer when you got arrested?"

"Is she hanging on? Bring me the phone."

Candy's eyes danced when she crossed back into the kitchen. I figured she was remembering the case where I got thrown in jail.

Candy was the one who had gotten me involved in the first place. "Give me that phone, you," I said and snatched it from her, chuckling at her delight at the memory of my arrest. "Gillian," I said into the phone.

"Mavis! Y'all having fun over there? I heard you laughing."

"Candy was sort of reminding me of when you—when I was in jail, and you helped me out."

"Yeah, I remember that. Wasn't that long ago."

"My memory doesn't need refreshing. Are you calling me about Dave Wite?"

"Sure am. Thanks for the referral. I'm assuming they can pay me, or you wouldn't have given Mrs. Wite my contact information, right?"

"Right. They paid me some good money—cash—to help them find their kids. You're going to represent Dave?"

"I told her I probably would, but I want to talk to him. I think she said you said Isobel Oliver was shot?"

"No. He had a gun, but he didn't shoot her. She was dead when he got there. They let him call Connie when they were booking him in. Did you know Isobel Oliver?"

"I knew her in passing. She wasn't a friend or anything. She did a lot of adoptions here and in several other counties from what I understand."

"Yeah, Gillian, and it sounds like she was buying and selling children."

"You know, there had been a rumor to that effect some time ago. I don't know if anyone ever found out whether it was true. If she was in the baby selling business, someone other than Dave might easily have shot her. You're sure that's how she was killed?"

"No, no, no. She wasn't shot. They didn't have a cause of death when I was there. She was just found in the back of her office suite. Ben told me she'd been found lying on the floor in a nursery she'd set up back there. You remember Ben, don't you? I don't know much more than when the police arrived, they found Dave in there with her. And Dave says it wasn't him. Dave did have a gun. His wife told me, but no one was shot."

"Hmm. So, someone knew she was dead and called 911?"

"Must have. We'll have to figure that out."

"Where are you with the kidnapping?"

"We now know who took them, although I'm going to want to talk to that woman, Carmen, again and see what else she can tell me. I was in kind of a hurry when I spoke to her earlier today. And I'm going to try to get someone to let me go into Ms. Oliver's files and see if I can find out who has those kids."

"You're going to have to get a court order. Confidentiality and all. Listen, Mavis, since these cases involve the same people, we need to share information. In fact, I want you to be my investigator on the murder case. I'll get the Wites to agree to that. They'll pay me, and I'll pay you for work on the murder part. You can continue to work off what they've already given you on the kidnapping part. It'll be confusing, but keep your time on both. I'll talk to Dave Wite tomorrow morning at the jail and get back to you."

"Sounds good. I feel so sorry for these people. They seem like good folks. I hope Dave really didn't do it."

"Well, if he *did* kill the person who was responsible for the kidnapping of his children, in my opinion, it would be a defensible murder."

# CHAPTER

# EIGHTEEN

"Y'all," I said to the girls when I got off the phone, "why don't you go ahead and go home? It's Friday night. You have a life. So do I."

Margaret said, "You're right. I'm going home. Before you do, though, there're some little things that need attention. I left notes on your desk." She went to the front, packed up, and made a quick exit out the back.

"Good night," I called after her. "What about you, Candy?"

"Are you sure you don't want me to stay and help with something?" She stood, also, and pushed her chair under the table. She picked up their plates and forks and rinsed them and covered the cake and put it in the refrigerator. I imagined the Houston humidity was about to cause mold to bloom on it. Maybe on Monday Margaret would be okay with throwing it out.

"I'm good. I'm going to call Ben and see if he wants to catch some dinner in a little while."

Candy patted my shoulder as she walked behind me, and said, "Okay. I'll just get my stuff. Have a good weekend and, if you need me, you know where I am."

"I do. Thanks." In a matter of minutes, with both of them cleared out, I was alone with my overloaded brain. I finished my yogurt and rinsed my spoon and the plastic container, tossing it into the recycling bin. Before I left for the night, I wanted to make a list of what I needed to do. The list would unmuddle my brain.

I turned off the light in the kitchen and locked the back door. Even though I'd be leaving soon, I didn't feel safe being alone in the office at night. People had walked in on me from that back door in the past.

Grabbing a legal pad from the supply cabinet, I sat at my desk to make the list.

1. Make a note of what Gillian had said and what she wanted me to do. Confirm it with an email or a text.

2. Go back to talk to Carmen and find out what else she knew about the whole adoption business with Ms. Oliver. Should I tell the police about her and have her arrested for kidnapping? Yes. But talk to her first before they lock her up.

3. Figure out how the whole adoption process works normally, who all the players would be: Go online and look up the law on adoption; Ask Gillian to outline the normal process; Find out the names of the people who participated in Oliver's adoptions; Talk to my contact at Children's Protective Services, especially about the children of the people in the jail; Find someone in the clerk's office who will tell me what the process is in their office.

4. See Dave during visitation time in the jail and hear his story.

5. Figure out who called 911.

6. Talk to anyone else in that building who may have seen or heard something.

7. Check out businesses in the neighborhood to see if anyone saw or heard anything.

8. Find out cause of death.

9. When autopsy comes in, get a copy.

10. Ask Gillian to get a court order, if possible, to access Oliver's

files and find out where the babies are. MOVE THIS TO NUMBER TWO.

My head ached. When I spoke to Gillian, I'd go over my list and see if there was anything else she could think of that I needed to do.

It occurred to me that Dave's truck was parked on the street next to Isobel Oliver's office. I called Connie. "Hey, Connie, I just thought of something you need to do."

Her voice was deep and raspy. I imagined she was tearful again, or still. "I'll do whatever I can to get my husband and kids back. I talked to the lawyer."

"Yes, she called me. Is there an extra key to Dave's truck lying around anywhere? You need to get someone to go with you and bring Dave's truck home. If you don't have anyone, I can do it, though I'd prefer to do it tomorrow. It can't be left on the street for very long, not only might it be burglarized when someone thinks it's abandoned, but it could be towed. You don't need that."

"Okay, Mavis. Thanks for thinking of that. I'll get a friend to help me tonight. You don't need to worry about it. Tomorrow morning, I'm going to see if I can visit Dave in the jail."

"Good. That'll help his spirits, which I'm sure are pretty low right now. I'm going to try to see him sometime this weekend, as well. I know Gillian is, too, but lawyers can get in to see their clients outside of regular visitation hours, so she won't be there when you are."

"I have an appointment with her on Monday. I'm going to ask her if she can do anything about finding out where that Oliver woman put my kids."

"She will. I'm pretty sure she'll have to file for a court order to get into Ms. Oliver's office and files, but Gillian will work on that. All the legal stuff, all the cases Ms. Oliver is—was—involved in will have to be taken care of by someone. It's not going to be easy."

"I know. I'm trying to be patient. This is a terrible thing to say, but at least with her being dead she won't be able to finalize the adoption of my children."

"I thought of that, too. I can't imagine her having placed them with people who won't take care of them. Whoever they're with has to be well off to be able to afford to adopt. It's expensive."

"You know, I'm not a praying person, but I'm—uh—asking my higher power to look out for the children."

I wasn't planning on telling her what Carmen had said about them being atheists. It wouldn't serve any purpose, though it might eventually come out. "Okay, well, I'm headed home tonight to get some rest. I'll talk to you over the weekend. I'm going back to Carmen Garcia's again tomorrow and see if she's still there or if she's run for it. If she's there, I'll see what other information I can get out of her. I suspect she knows a lot more than she told me. I don't think she knows who Ms. Oliver planned to give the babies to, but I'm going to pin her down on that and whether she knows what the process is that Ms. Oliver goes through. She's already said she doesn't, but Carmen works in the jail, she's been around the courts, she has to know more than she let on."

"You'll let me know if you find out anything?"

"Of course. Try to get some sleep."

I packed my things into a tote bag, including the legal pad with the list on it, and turned out the lights except for the one we always left burning inside. The backyard light was solar, so it only came on at night anyway. A half-moon lit up our parking places. Paranoid as I am, I always look around me before I lock the door in case I need to escape back inside. No one was there.

Ben called as I pulled out onto the street. I was glad he hadn't forgotten about me. Not that he would for long. I wouldn't let him.

"Hey Mavis, I have a bag with your name on it sitting on the seat next to me. It contains Pad Thai." His voice sounded happy, as opposed to mad or sad, which I'd heard in the past.

My stomach growled in response. We both loved Pad Thai. It had been a while since I'd had any, so this would be a treat. Heck, just being with him would be a real treat. "Is the bag headed toward my house?"

"Nope. I thought for once you could come to my place. I don't think you've seen the new furniture I bought. I'm almost to my apartment now. I hope you don't mind."

"I'll be there before you can get the table set." I disconnected and turned the car toward the little apartment complex on the edge of the Heights where Ben lived. I didn't mind going to his place, ever. It just didn't seem to come up.

As soon as I knocked, Ben opened the door and swept me into his arms in a bear hug, kicking the door closed behind me. I'd missed his hugs. Then he laid a kiss on me that communicated that he'd missed me, as well. I felt my energy returning in anticipation of the Pad Thai dinner and then dessert.

"Am I glad to see you up close and personal," he said when he released me.

"Ditto. I was surprised to see you this morning. Let me put my things down. I probably shouldn't have, but I brought a couple of things from the office. I might have some questions to ask you."

"We're off duty."

"Yeah, when are we ever off duty? Are you going to offer me something to drink?" I went into his living room to drop off my purse and tote bag. "Wow. You really did buy new furniture. Makes your apartment look brand new." He'd purchased a large flat screen TV the year before, but that had been the extent of his redecorating that I knew of. Now, the worn-out sofa had been replaced with a matching sofa and loveseat in a solid gray. His cracked leather recliner was gone, an overstuffed recliner in a blue and gray print had taken its place. The orange crate he'd covered with a towel to use as a coffee table was gone, and in its place was a faux wood rectangular table and matching accent tables. They looked like good quality faux wood. "Nice job." I kind of figured a salesperson had helped him pick it out because it matched so well, but there was nothing wrong with that.

"You like it? I couldn't stand that old sofa and that recliner another minute. Lieutenant's pay is somewhat better than sergeant's. That helped."

I sat on the sofa to test it out. "You've been a lieutenant for a while now."

"I wanted to wait until I had enough money to buy the furniture outright. I don't want any more debt than what she stuck me with in the divorce."

Ben had been divorced for quite some time, but he'd had to pay the lion's share of their joint debts. His ex's lawyer had been better than Ben's. I ran my hand over the sofa. "Nice fabric."

He pointed to the wall behind the sofa. "I bought some prints for the walls, too. I like them."

One of them was a large flowery thing that coordinated with the furniture. The other was a movie poster. Both framed. I hugged him. "I'm very happy for you."

"Let's have dinner." I followed him to the dinette and kitchen area.

"Don't say anything about my dinette set. I know you hate it. I'll get a better one when I have the money for that."

"I wasn't going to say a word. I'm just hungry and glad to see you and hope we can have a nice conversation about what's been going on over the last week since you've been gone."

He handed me a glass of wine. "Go sit down. I'll bring the food to the table."

I didn't know what kind of wine it was and didn't care. It was white and wet. I was just happy to be there, to have some time together. He'd set the table and filled water glasses. I took the chair the farthest from the kitchen, so he'd be able to serve comfortably. "This is great, Ben."

"You're great, Mavis." His face lit up with a broad smile as he brought the containers of food to the table. He pulled out the chair adjacent to me and leaned over and kissed my cheek. "I mean it. I didn't think I'd miss you as much as I did, but I did."

I refrained from bouncing in my chair. "Let's not get into our mutual admiration society bit again. But really, it's so good to see you, too, and to be here. I think a week is maybe the longest time we've had apart since we've been together."

"I think so. Let me serve you."

*Let me serve you?* Was he up to something or was this foreplay? "I could get used to this." I grinned at him and took a sip of the wine. Not bad.

We spent the next thirty minutes bringing each other up to date. He told me more details about his mother's funeral than he'd said when I'd seen him earlier. His sister and he had planned a reception at his mother's house for afterward, his sister taking charge, him following her directions. They'd met with a lawyer to have the will probated. Since his sister wanted to administer the estate, he'd handed it all over to her and returned home. I hoped to meet his sister one day.

I told him what I thought would be okay about the kidnapping, without breaking any confidences, or naming names.

"You know who the kidnapper was? The actual person who took the kids, not the lawyer?"

"Yeah, I do. I know what you're going to say. I need to tell you or someone who it was, and I will. I need to talk to her some more first."

"Mavis, you're involved in an active police investigation again. You realize that, don't you?"

"Ah," I said. "But now I've been engaged by an attorney as the investigator on the murder case. That's different."

"David Wite already has a lawyer? That was quick."

"Yes. And she hired me to be the investigator, since I already know so much about what's happened in the last few days, know some of the people, etcetera."

He crossed his arms. I could see he wasn't happy about the situation, but for once, I had the authority to do what I needed to do. So long as I stayed within the bounds of the law, that is. And, of course, I always did that.

"Are you at least going to give me the name of the kidnapper?"

"Tomorrow. Or, since you're in homicide, who should I report the person to?"

"The officers on the scene were—"

"That has to be why Lon Tyler came to my office this morning. He was the one who caught the call on Wednesday night."

"He and another officer. He was just going to find out how much you knew."

"Connie Wite told me, or somebody did. I'll have to check my notes. But just because they caught the call, that doesn't mean they're involved in the active investigation, right? I won't have to call Lon, will I? Wouldn't it be turned over to someone with some—" I was going to say sense. "A detective? Someone senior to him, them?"

He chuckled out of the side of his mouth. Was there a note of sarcasm there? "I'll find out who it is, and you can call him or her if you're determined not to tell me the culprit's name. I just hope they don't flee overnight. Or, we could go to their house together—like now."

"No. I have other things to do with you tonight."

He flashed his eyebrows like Groucho Marx. "I'm not going to argue with you. Not right now, anyway." He picked up our plates and said, "Ready for dessert?"

# CHAPTER

# NINETEEN

In the wee hours of Saturday morning, I tiptoed out of Ben's apartment and drove home to shower and change. I hadn't expressed to Ben that I was worried Carmen might run, but I was. I hoped she wouldn't since she'd already been identified and since she had a law enforcement background. She knew things would go worse for her when she was caught.

I pulled on some clean cargo pants, a black turtleneck, and a jacket. The temperature had dropped during the night. The end of fall was nigh. Winter was on its way. When I arrived at Carmen's trailer, her truck wasn't on its parking pad. If she had run, I'd be in deep stuff with the police, again. No lights were on when I banged on the door. Twice. Three times.

When she pushed the outer door open, she stood there in a fluffy, red, velour robe and thick mismatched socks. Her eye was swollen. The black and blue bruise on her cheek under a bandage was the size of a man's fist, running down her face a couple of inches. "I knew it had to be you. Unless it was the police. I've been expecting to be arrested any minute."

"I thought you might not be here, since your truck isn't."

"It's across the street behind the gas station. I hurt too much last night to make the effort and couldn't even think of where to go. I was hoping if no one saw it, they would think I was gone." She shrugged, followed by a wince.

"You going to let me in?" I took hold of the door handle.

"I'll make some coffee."

I never really cared for coffee, which had created minor problems my whole life. I ought to carry teabags in my pockets. "I don't suppose you have any tea?"

"Sure." She moved slowly. I could imagine why, starting with not being quite awake to hurting from being punched in the face. She hadn't said if Dave had done anything else to her, but he may have. "There's a little metal canister in the closet that's my pantry." She pointed to a cabinet. "Ever lived in a mobile home? Everything is smaller. More compact."

"I've been lucky. I've had apartments, and when my mother passed away, I inherited her house. It's not huge, but it's comfortable." I found the teabags and took a mug from the shelf where she'd gotten her coffee cup. I looked over her head into the body of the trailer. It was nice and neat and well kept. A suitcase sat open on the floor next to the bed in the back bedroom. So, she had planned to leave. I wouldn't turn my back on her.

"You can heat up the water in the microwave unless you want me to get a pot and fill it with water." She saw where I was looking. "Okay, I did think about it."

"Microwave is fine." I thought microwaved water tasted different from boiled water, but everyone I told that to thought I was off my nut.

After heating up the water, we took our mugs—hers with coffee and mine with tea—to her small dinette table and had a seat. "I can give you a minute if you want to wash your face or something."

"Are the police coming to get me? Is that why you're here, to tell me?"

"My clients could have told the police about you. I haven't. But,

Carmen, don't you think it's best if you turn yourself in today so you're not embarrassed by them coming out here and arresting you?"

"I was thinking about that. Maybe you could take me down there?"

"To the police department?" That would be a new one. Me taking the criminal to the police? "Hmm. We'll see. But first, Carmen, I have some follow-up questions I want to ask while I still have the opportunity to talk to you. First, you know about the murder, right?"

She nodded but didn't look the least bit sad. "Ms. Oliver? Amy called me and told me last night. Louise called her and told her. Amy said Louise wasn't speaking to me right now."

"Can you blame her?"

"No. I did a terrible thing. I've done some other terrible things for that woman. I must have lost my mind. It was like I woke up yesterday when Mr. Wite came here and yelled at me and all. I thought he was going to shoot me."

I sipped my tea and studied her face. Since she wanted to talk, I wasn't going to stop her.

She looked at me. "You must think I'm a terrible person."

I didn't answer.

"You have to understand, I grew up with nothing. I was the first person in my family to finish high school, much less go to community college. Then I had a hard time finding a job until the sheriff gave me a chance."

"When was that?"

"Five years ago. I was going to work my way up from detention officer to a real deputy, to work on the street, drive a sheriff's car, maybe eventually become somebody."

"Sounds like a good plan."

"Well, it was, but detention officers, or 'matrons' some people call us, don't get paid a whole lot. I was doing okay, just okay. I give my mother money every payday. She barely speaks English. Her knees gave out, so she can't clean rooms anymore."

"Where does she live?"

"In the projects. But I didn't want to live there, so I bought my first trailer the year I got the job and started living here. It wasn't much, but it was mine."

"If you were doing okay, how did you get mixed up with Isobel Oliver?"

"Yeah, you would ask me that." She took a deep breath and dropped her shoulders. "Ms. Oliver—well, when one of the women before me quit, Ms. Oliver approached me and asked me if I could use some extra money."

"Who was the woman who quit? Did she work with or for Ms. Oliver, too? Were you taking her place?"

"I don't want to say. I don't want to get her in trouble. She's an old lady, retired."

I decided not to press her. I was sure someone else would once she was arrested. "Ms. Oliver asked you to do what, precisely?"

She stared into her coffee cup. "At first, she asked me if I would interpret the papers if any of the mothers were signing over their children. I could do that. I'm bilingual, no problem. There was no reason for her to give me any money. It's part of my job. We have a lot of Spanish speaking women who show up in the jail for one reason or another. But Ms. Oliver would give me a little money, kind of like a tip. Fifty dollars here or there."

Quite a tip. "Were you the only one doing this?"

She shrugged. "I don't know. No one in the jail talked about it."

"How did that work, exactly? Would she bring the documents to the jail and give them to you? And how did you get them back to her?"

"At first, yeah, she would bring the papers to the jail and give them to the front desk who would give them to me to explain to the mother. Then I'd take the mother to the notary up front. Then one day she, Ms. Oliver, asked me to run them over to the clerk's office for her so she wouldn't have to come back down to the jail. I said I would.

"And then, one day she asked me if I would talk to the women and find out which ones of them had children, especially young ones, babies. And she wasn't just talking about Mexicans, she was talking about black and white, too. Well, I talked to the women all the time, so that wasn't a problem. Some of their kids were in foster care. Some were with relatives."

"I can see that. And I guess some of them weren't getting out of jail any time soon? Like maybe they'd been involved in a serious crime?"

"Yeah, like that. And, of course, she wanted me to come back and tell her what I found out from the women. And then she wanted me to talk to them to see if any of them would be interested in giving up their kid for adoption. See, it was a progressive thing. She would talk to me about how much better off those kids would be in a good home rather than being in foster care until the mother got out of jail or prison. Maybe the kid would be stuck staying with a poor relative or with someone who didn't want them. Well, that made sense."

"I guess it would depend on the situation."

"You see how it was, don't you?" She began pacing the small kitchen space. "Eventually, she asked me to talk to this one woman, to talk her into giving up her baby. I don't know exactly how Ms. Oliver knew what the living situations were for these kids. Somehow, she did, though."

I wondered if Isobel had contacts in other departments or agencies. "And she kept giving you more and more money for doing the things she asked?"

"Yes, ma'am. And not just fifty dollars at a time, either. You see this new trailer? How do you think I could afford to buy a new mobile home on a detention officer's salary? Especially one as big as this?"

"I don't know what they cost, so I wouldn't know."

"Once I had a little money saved, I went to a bank to see if I could get a loan to buy a new trailer. I thought they'd have a better interest rate than the places where you buy these things."

"So you financed this?"

"I could only claim what my detention officer pay was, I couldn't tell them about what Ms. Oliver was giving me. I knew it wasn't right. I just didn't know how wrong it was." She sat back down and picked up her coffee cup, looking into it as if she were reading coffee grounds. "The bank said I didn't make enough money for me to be a good risk. I thought it might be because I'm Mexican, too."

I grimaced. I wouldn't have been at all surprised. "So, the mobile home company financed this?"

She shook her head. "No. I told Ms. Oliver that I was trying to buy a new mobile home, but I couldn't get the loan approved, so she co-signed for it." She slapped her forehead. "I don't know what I was thinking. The same thing happened with my truck. She co-signed for it."

Clearly, Ms. Oliver wasn't a stupid person. "After that, you were obligated to her, to do what she wanted."

She got up and poured herself another cup of coffee. "I couldn't even think about telling her no to anything, could I? When she started becoming more and more demanding, I wanted to quit, but I was stuck. If I tried to talk to her about it, she would say little things like, 'How are you enjoying your new truck?'"

I was glad I didn't have to ever meet Ms. Oliver. "Carmen, how many women did you talk into giving up their children for adoption over the last five years?"

"I have no idea. I didn't keep track."

"You didn't keep any records?"

"No. I didn't want to know. I just did my part and put it out of my mind until the next one."

"Somehow you went from just talking to Latina women to talking to every woman with children?"

"Oh, yeah. Practically right away. And what got so bad is when she would pressure me to pressure them. Like when she had someone who wanted a certain kind of baby."

"A certain kind? Like age or sex?"

"Well, that, but color. There weren't as many white babies lately."

So that's how it happened. Carmen saw her chance to make Ms. Oliver happy by finding some white babies.

"Are you telling me Ms. Oliver was pressuring you to find her some white children?"

"Yes, ma'am." She patted away the sweat beads on her forehead with a paper napkin. "And then Louise was complaining about having to babysit her niece and nephew. Well, not exactly complaining, but telling me about it, about how it was harder babysitting two babies at one time than one baby. And Louise and I had talked before about her brother and sister-in-law and how they don't believe in God. I happened to mention what Louise had told me to Ms. Oliver last Monday. She said it was a shame little babies like that would be brought up by nonbelievers when there were so many God-fearing childless couples who could do a better job of raising them."

I kept my poker face. "Did she promise you something extra for two babies at one time? Or was she getting two for the price of one?"

"I told her I couldn't take those babies, that kidnapping was a serious offense. I could go to jail for a long time. I refused to do it. At first. Then she talked about how she had these couples who had beautiful homes and lots of money and how well off the kids would be. They'd be able to go to private schools and have the best of everything. And besides, she'd pay off my trailer if I would do it."

"Okay, now you understand I'm not the police and I have no authority over you or anyone else, but I want to ask you a couple of more questions. Did anyone help you take those children? Anyone from the church? Like Laura Kate?"

"Goodness, no. I figured out how to do it because I knew Laura Kate's habit of spending a lot of the time in the bathroom talking to her boyfriend. One time I'd had to go and she kept me waiting for a long time. I could hear her on her phone. I took a chance that she would do it that night, and if she didn't then I just wouldn't be able to get the children."

"So, no one helped you. No one at all?"

She bit her lower lip. "I don't want to get anyone else into trouble."

"Well, let me ask you this. Would I be correct in surmising you sneaked into the back of the building after services started and hid out until Laura Kate did her thing and then took the children out the back door?"

"That's exactly what I did. When I got in, I unlocked the door at the back of the kitchen and waited. I figured if anyone saw me in there, I'd just tell them I was coming late to church."

"But there was someone waiting outside for you. There had to be."

"Miss Davis, there was, but I'm not ratting on them." She sighed and crossed her arms.

"It wasn't Ms. Oliver?"

She shook her head.

"Do you have any idea what or where or who has these children now? Did Ms. Oliver ever talk to you about how she went about placing the children?"

"Oh, she had a license. Whatever license you've got to have to be an adoption agency, she had one."

"Oh. Okay. I bet she had to file reports. I'll have to find out about that. I'll repeat my question. Do you have any idea—any clue, about where these kids are?"

"No. I really don't. The last time I saw Ms. Oliver before that night, the way she talked, it sounded like there was more than one couple. I think she was going to give one kid to one family and one kid to another family. Split them up."

Unbelievably cruel. "What about other people's involvement with the children? Did you ever meet a social worker?"

"No, not for her. For the women whose kids were in foster care, sometimes a CPS worker would come to the jail and meet them. But I never heard of one on Ms. Oliver's cases."

"What about an attorney for the father or for the child? Did you ever meet another attorney who was involved?"

"No. I don't think she had anyone else working in her office—a lawyer, I mean. Just her and her secretary."

"But there would have to be a lawyer for the fathers. No other lawyers came to the jail to speak to the mothers about the fathers of the children?"

Her head wagged back and forth. "I never took one of the mothers to the visitation room to meet any other lawyers—except on their criminal cases."

I was getting mostly nowhere and feeling frustrated. "Do you know anyone else I could talk to who might know where the Wite twins are?"

"No, Miss Davis. I tried not to know more than I needed to know. I'm hungry. Are you? Want something to eat? A bowl of cereal?"

People amaze me, even after all these years. "No. You go ahead. And decide if you really want me to take you down to the police station."

She crept back to the cabinet and got out a bowl and picked up the spoon she'd used to stir her coffee. "I do, if you'll let me call my cousin to take care of my truck and trailer after I finish my cereal." Then she got a box of Froot Loops and a small jug of milk and came back to the table.

Could it have been her cousin who had waited outside the door of the church on Wednesday night? While she ate, I checked my messages. Ben had texted, *"You didn't kiss me goodbye. Where are you?"*

I texted back, *"If I was going to take a perpetrator to a police station for kidnapping, where exactly should I take her?"*

Dragnet began playing on my phone. I knew it was Ben, and I knew he'd yell at me, and then we'd make arrangements for Carmen Garcia. That's exactly what happened. I took her to a station. I didn't kiss her goodbye either.

# CHAPTER
# TWENTY

After I'd washed my hands of Carmen, the time was mid-
morning, so I phoned Gillian. "You want to meet me for
coffee, or do you have to do something this morning with
your kid or husband?"

"Good morning to you, too, Mavis. You up and at'em already?"

"Yeah, and I could do with some nourishment and could kill two
birds with one stone if we met for breakfast. I could eat and tell you
what's going on, and we can decide how we're going to handle
everything."

"That was a mouthful. I'm dressed anyway. I was going to my
office and then later to the jail, but that can wait awhile. Can you
meet me at the Denny's that's near the jail?"

"That's not the one where the sheriff's deputy and her husband
killed a man, is it?"

"Ha. Ha. You know that wasn't really in Houston, right? Do I need
to give you the address or do you think you can find it?"

"I'll be there in five." I hung up and went to my vehicle, all the
while talking to my stomach, telling it to be patient. But it was
growling to beat the band.

I arrived first, so, as rude as this might have been, I went ahead and ordered the special: bacon, sausage, eggs, hash browns, and pancakes, along with another cup of tea, though I told the waitress to bring a teapot full. I needed the caffeine to make it through the day. I'm afraid Ben and I stayed up too late, and I woke up too early.

Gillian looked just the same as the last time I'd seen her, when she helped me out of a legal predicament a year or so ago, except now she wore jeans, a sweater, and a jacket, a ginormous brown leather satchel slung over her shoulder, and a wide smile. Last I saw her, she wore more formal, lawyerly clothes. Though we served legal papers for her, we never saw her.

We air-kissed each other's cheeks. A glimmer floated in her eyes. "You look great," I said.

"As do you. Staying out of jail agrees with you."

"Actually, I was at the jail this morning."

Her eyebrows rose. "Oh, really?"

The waitress came and took Gillian's order and advised me that mine would be right out.

"I'm starving. I hope you don't mind. I went ahead and ordered."

"One thing I remember about you, Mavis, is you like to eat."

"Yes, that's me. Seems like I'm always hungry but don't get to eat regular meals. Think it has to do with the business I'm in."

"It would seem so." She kept smiling.

"Anyway, you'll find this as hard to believe as the cops and Ben did. I drove Carmen Garcia—she's the kidnapper of the Wite babies—to the police station and turned her in. I thought the guy at the front desk was going to fall down in amazement. He told me why I couldn't do that, and then put her in the lockup until they could get her sorted out."

"That's hilarious! You mean she didn't try to run on you?"

"Your client struck her in the face yesterday and may have otherwise done some damage to her, she didn't say, but she moved like she was in pain. She's a petite woman, who looks like hell, with her face being one big bruise. She said she just couldn't get up the energy to run and hide when she knew they'd eventually find her, and she'd be in worse trouble than she already was."

"How was it that you were in a place where you could get her to go with you?"

The waitress returned with my food and centered it in front of me. I smiled my thanks and chomped down on a piece of bacon.

"That's impressive," Gillian said, indicating the platter, not me eating the bacon.

"And I'll finish it, don't you worry." I scooped up some scrambled eggs and stuffed them in my mouth, chewed and swallowed, and said, "It's a long story, but I found her yesterday and she's the one who told me who the lawyer was and where I might find her." After a sip of tea, I asked, "Are you following this?"

She nodded. "I'll stop you if it becomes too confusing."

"Well, you know what happened." I wiped my mouth and took a deep breath. "Dave had already attacked or assaulted her or what-ever you want to call it. I'm talking about Carmen. I was so busy trying to find Ms. Oliver that I didn't call the police on Carmen when I knew what she had done. Last night I was too tired to go back to her place—I wanted to get her to answer some questions before she lawyered up." I wasn't about to tell her I'd been with Ben, either.

Gillian's eyes were smiling. "I've heard that term before. Go on."

"So, early this morning, I went back to her place. She had hidden her truck, but she answered the door, expecting it to be the police. We had a nice chat. She agreed to turn herself in if she could call her cousin to take care of her truck and trailer, and if I would drive her down there." The hashbrowns were cooked to perfection and so good with a dab of ketchup on them. I took a big bite, wiped my mouth again, and said, "Any questions?"

I think she wanted to laugh some more, but the waitress came with her order, and we both ate for a few minutes.

Finally pausing, she said, "Well, first, did she know where Mr. Wite's twins were taken?"

"No. She said she wasn't a part of that—the placing of the children."

"Too bad. Mrs. Wite is beside herself."

"I know, and here's what I was thinking. Since Ms. Oliver is dead, won't the court have to appoint someone to take over her cases? I heard of that being done before. You could do it. You do family law, too."

"Oh, no, not me. I already suspected she was toeing the line with the adoptions she was doing. She had so many of them. I think the court is going to have to appoint some kind of special master or something. I'm not sure what will happen."

"But could you at least file a motion so the judge will let you see her files? Maybe access her computer? There's got to be information somewhere about where the babies went."

"Let me think about that."

"This thing is such a mess. I've been trying to think of who all I should talk to about the babies and then the murder. If it wasn't Dave Wite, who was it? I made a list of things I need to do, but I'm sure there are other things that will have to be done that I can do while you're preparing Dave's defense."

"It won't happen all at once. I mean, I haven't even met him yet. He's been arrested but not charged, not indicted. No prosecutor has been appointed. We don't know what court he'll be in. Once he's charged, I'll file a discovery motion."

I held up my hand to stop her. "That's all your area. For me, I think the number one concern is the children. What do you think about me questioning Ms. Oliver's secretary on Monday? Assuming she goes to work. I mean, someone has to take charge of the office."

"It's a crime scene, but maybe they'll be through processing it by then. If so, and the secretary is there, that's a good idea. Now that I think of it, I wonder if that person even knows Ms. Oliver is dead?"

"Hmm. She might not. Was it on the news? I haven't watched the news or read the paper."

"I don't know. I haven't either. But anyway, assuming she—since most legal secretaries are women—goes to work on Monday morning, and she can get into the office, yes, I think that's one of the first things you should do."

"Okay. And while I'm thinking about it, can you give me something in writing? Something that can serve as an engagement letter, so I have something to show the police when they hassle me about poking around in an active police investigation? I'm correct in thinking I can legally do it if I'm your investigator, right?"

"Yes and yes. And they know that. At least most of them do."

We ate in silence some more. Then I asked her to outline the normal adoption process for me.

"Okay," she said. "I haven't done one in a long time, because there are so many problems with private adoptions, and I don't want the liability. But I have served as the lawyer or amicus for the child. You can read about this online."

"I intend to, but I want you to summarize it for me. I thought I could maybe talk to people who have been involved with her."

"Right, of course. Okay. There can be a combined termination and adoption suit filed especially where all the parties are in agreement. There will be a lawyer for the adoptive parents. If the mother voluntarily relinquishes the child, the papers are filed with the court and there is no lawyer for her. Same for the father, if he's the legal father."

"What do you mean legal?"

"A long time ago, mothers would give up their babies and say they didn't know who the father was. Like they were raped, whether or not they were, but no one ever said that word. Then the courts decided no, that wasn't going to cut it. You can't just terminate an unknown father if no one has even tried to find the father, although in years gone by that was done hundreds of times. Now, if the mother names the father, and he claims to be the legal father—maybe he's on the birth certificate—and he relinquishes, no lawyer is needed. But if the legal father says he's not the biological father, then someone needs to find the bio father and get him to sign a relinquishment, or if he's cited by publication, an attorney would be appointed for him."

I tried to keep my eyes from crossing while she recited all that. "This is way over my head, Gillian. Can you just tell me who all I should try to talk to that would be involved? I promise I will go online and read about adoptions, but right now I just want to plan who I need to talk to starting Monday morning in a case such as this."

"Let's see. The attorney for the adoptive parents."

"We don't know who they are, so we can't start there."

"Right. The attorney for the termination of parental rights, whoever filed that suit if it's a separate suit. Hey, we need to figure out exactly how she was working this."

I'm afraid I huffed out a breath. This whole thing was confusing. "Well, I'll talk to the secretary, that's for sure. And what about in the clerk's office where the papers are filed, do you think I should talk to the clerk?"

"That's a good idea. The files are confidential, but the clerk might tell you Ms. Oliver's way of doing things, her practice. I don't know whether there is one clerk, or more than one clerk assigned just for adoptions."

"I'm going to find out on Monday."

"I just thought of something. This isn't good, but we'll have to check it out. Ms. Oliver could have been doing adoptions in more than one county."

I slapped the table. "There needs to be several of me. Wouldn't I need to go to each county to see if she files suits there? And we're in a hurry to find the kids. How can I do that all at once?"

"Just start with Harris County. Maybe you could have your staff call the surrounding counties, the clerks, and ask whether Ms. Oliver did adoptions there. They can call and say the reason they're calling is because she was killed on Friday and they're trying to find out who all needs to be notified."

"Excellent idea. That's why you went to law school, because you have a superior brain. I'll put Margaret on that first thing Monday morning. And I was thinking since these days Candy is the one who handles most of the service for us, maybe she could go up to our clerk's office here and ask around about who would be handling adoptions. Then when I go up there, I can ask for that person. Candy will have kind of primed the pump, though not really. But with her you never know. People like her."

"So, you'll start with the legal secretary. Margaret will call the surrounding counties. And Candy will try to find out what clerk handles adoptions here. In the meantime, I'll meet with Dave Wite today at the jail. You're going to meet with him sometime, too?"

"That's my plan. I'll have to do it at official visitation time, I guess. I want to find out exactly what was said at Carmen's and exactly what happened when he arrived at Ms. Oliver's office. Also, who may have seen him at her office. I'd like to talk to them."

"And anyone else in that office building who may have seen or heard anything inside or outside the building. So, we have a plan. Let's touch base daily, at least by text, if not by phone. And maybe more than once if we need to."

"Got it." We both had our work cut out for us. As soon as I finished my breakfast, I was headed over to that office building. Maybe someone who had been working on Friday would have come in on Saturday, too, and have some information.

# CHAPTER
# TWENTY-ONE

When I arrived at the building that housed Ms. Oliver's law office or adoption agency or whatever she'd been calling it at the time of her death, I was glad to see Dave's truck had been retrieved. The neighborhood wasn't necessarily crime-ridden, but it was Houston, Texas. I happened to know full size trucks were one of the most popular vehicles stolen.

The rectangular building was a modern gray brick with a lovely atrium in the center of the first floor that held a Ficus tree, some fake poinsettias, as well as some real flowers I couldn't identify. A wide circular staircase with tinsel decorated iron rails and granite steps started at the atrium and wound around to the second floor.

Several offices occupied the spaces on each of the four sides. Each individual office had a solid door embossed with numbers, and some held nameplates. Alongside each door was a floor to ceiling pane of glass where one could look inside the reception area if the glass wasn't covered. The floors were good quality indoor-outdoor carpeting. My business would never bring in enough money to pay rent in a place like that. Still, I could admire from afar.

Right inside the double doors at the entrance to the building, a directory was fixed to the wall. There were all kinds of offices in that building, including two other lawyers' offices, a dentist, and a photography studio. I wondered whether the lawyers would know anything about what went on at Ms. Oliver's office. I shot a photo of the directory with my phone, so I could study it later. Ms. Oliver's office was on the first floor. Turned out to be to the right of the entrance, which I saw as soon as I turned the corner. Crime scene tape had become part of the decor. The blinds covering the glass next to the door had been left open. The lights were off, but from the fluorescent lights and the holiday lights in the atrium, I was able to see into her office.

A Danish modern oak desk was centered in the reception area. A matching credenza, with a small artificial Christmas tree on the top shelf, was behind the desk. A tall bookcase stood to one side, and, of course, there was a secretarial chair, several client chairs, a large computer with a flat screen, and various other assistant's or secretarial materials on the desk surface.

A hall ran down one side. I could barely see an opening that must lead to the first office, but the hallway was long enough that I could imagine there were several other offices—including the nursery—and, of course, a restroom and probably a break area. Nice work if you could get it. The door handle didn't budge.

The office next to hers was also dark, as was the one after that. The third one after, though, had some lights shining from the back. There was a number on the door, but no sign to indicate what it was. The reception area held plain brown chairs and a coffee table with magazines fanned across it. That door was locked, too. Okay, it was Saturday, but some people work on Saturday. I pressed a buzzer, which I heard in the distance. I banged on the door and waited a minute. Then again. Then on the glass with my ring.

Finally, a woman in pink scrubs came to the door. "Do you have an appointment?" she asked without opening the door. Her voice was not difficult to hear, surprisingly enough.

"No, ma'am. My name is Mavis Davis. I'm a private investigator." I showed her my ID. "I'd like to speak to you about the murder that happened here yesterday."

She shook her head. "Don't know anything about it."

As she started to turn away, I said, "Please, there may be some other information you could give me, maybe about the other tenants in this building? I promise I won't take more than a minute of your time."

She looked skeptical, but a key turned in the lock, and she opened the door. "You can come in, but just for a few minutes."

"Thank you." I held out my hand to shake hers, but she just looked at it and locked the door behind me.

"What is it you want to know?" She backed a few steps away. She was a short blonde with green eyes behind pink large-lensed glasses. I put her at about thirty-five years old. I towered over her. Although she wore scrubs, she wore no name tag. I still had no idea what went on in that office.

I inclined my head toward the chairs. "May I sit down?"

"Sure, I'm sorry. I'm being rude. It's just that I'm really busy today."

"Well, I'll try not to be too long. What is it y'all do here anyway? There was no indication on the door."

"That's because what we do is of such a personal nature. People wouldn't want to be seen coming and going through our doors."

"My curiosity is piqued."

"I can understand that. DNA testing, urine analysis, things like that."

"Like crime stuff?"

"No, we could, but not usually. The DNA to determine parentage. Urine for job applicants. Other reasons, too. A few other tests."

"So, you've got some kind of lab back there?"

"Um hum, yes. So, how can I help you? I really know nothing about what happened. It was Ms. Oliver, right? She was killed?"

"Yes." I looked out the glass. "You can't really see her office from here."

"I'm usually in the back anyway. Everything we do is by appointment only. It's rare that I see anyone unless I go out in the middle of the day for some reason."

"You work here alone?"

"That's another reason I keep the door locked. I have a partner, but she's really the money behind this business. She's not here often. I have the expertise."

"Did you know Ms. Oliver?"

"Only a little. She came to me a couple of times to handle some testing for a case or some cases. I'm trying to remember. But it was a long time ago."

"No recent contact?"

"No, I'm sorry."

"By the way, what's your name, if you don't mind telling me?"

"Wendy Blackburn."

"Did you ever see Ms. Oliver with any children, any young children or babies, Wendy?"

"Hmm, I did, once. I get here really early, and she arrived at the same time one morning. She was carrying a baby."

"Was that recently?"

"No, a few years back."

Which at least partially confirmed Carmen's story that Ms. Oliver had been in the baby business for years. "Wendy, what do you know about the other tenants in this building? Anything?"

"There's a couple of other law offices. One is upstairs and the other is in that far corner." She pointed to an area I couldn't see from there. "I'm not sure how many lawyers work in each office, or if there's even more than one." She put her hand up to her mouth, brushing her upper lip with a knuckle. "There's an insurance agent. I think there's a kickboxing studio upstairs, the farthest from the front doors. Sometimes you can hear some pounding like someone is bouncing around. A small real estate outfit is upstairs. A photo studio. Oh, a veterans' organization is also up there. I forget which one."

"Do you know any of these people?"

"Not really. Also, there's the management office for this building. They manage one down the next block, too. I guess you'd have to look at the directory to see what else there is."

"Have you ever heard of any of the people who occupy these offices having a grudge against each other, any feuds?" I was into my murder investigator mode now.

"You know, as far as I know, most of the people don't even know each other, much less socialize. Of course, like I said, I spend most of my time drawing blood and all. I'm not wandering around the building."

"And you didn't see anything on Friday or hear anything?"

"Sorry. I wish I could be more help." She shrugged. "If that's all, I need to get back to work. I'm expecting some clients in a few minutes. They wouldn't want to see you. Most people who come here want everything to be confidential."

I walked to the door. "Well, thanks for taking the time. You've given me some helpful information."

Wendy unlocked the door and let me out. "You're welcome. Good luck."

I wandered around the rest of the first floor, looking into offices to see what I could see, which was next to nothing and no one else. Then I climbed the stairs. The upstairs was laid out like the downstairs with a railing around the atrium area. A rather feeble red and silver garland had been wrapped around the railing as well as a string of lights. I found the kickboxing studio that advertised martial arts for all ages. I passed by the law office and the photo studio.

All the offices were closed. On one side, a short, stocky Hispanic man began running a carpet cleaning machine. He wore a black jumpsuit with a company name embossed over the left breast and dirty black tennis shoes—what these days passed as the cleaning person's uniform. I doubted he would know anything, but nevertheless it wouldn't hurt to ask. He saw me approaching and cut the machine off. "Can I help you, miss?" His voice was heavily accented but easily understood.

"Yes, sir. My name is Mavis Davis. I'm a private investigator." I showed him my ID and returned it to my back pocket and held out my hand to shake his. He actually did shake my hand. His was larger than I thought it would be and leathery.

"Are you looking for someone?"

"Well, not really. I'm kind of checking out the layout of this place. I'm involved in the investigation of the murder that took place yesterday."

"I heard about that. That lawyer in the first office was killed by a man who was mad at her about something to do with his children. Am I right?"

"He's alleged to have killed her." I smiled at him. "We're innocent until proven guilty, right?"

"Correct, but he was pretty mad."

I perked up. "Did you see him?"

"No, but I heard them fighting. It was pretty loud."

"Where were you? What were you doing here?"

"Oh, I wear many hats. I'm the maintenance man, the janitor, the gardener, sometimes the plumber, the repairman. Since Covid, people quit and I kept taking on more work."

"I hope they gave you more money. Not that what you make is any of my business or has anything to do with what I'm doing here. So, what were you doing yesterday?"

"I was gardening." He grinned. "I was picking up the leaves the Ficus dropped, and I took out one of the little bushes, a shrub that died, and put in another one. That kind of thing."

"And you could hear an argument from the atrium to her office, Ms. Oliver's office?"

"Yes, no problem if it's loud enough, and it was."

"But you didn't see the man."

"No. I picked up my things and left because I didn't think they would want to know I was out here and could hear them yelling. It would have been embarrassing."

I wasn't sure if this was good or bad news for us, but it was information that might prove useful. "What time was this?"

He stared at the ceiling. "Um, three something? I'll have to think about it."

"Sir, may I have your name?"

"Allen Perez. You want my phone number?"

"Please." I handed him my phone with the notebook app pulled up and he typed in his name and phone number. "Thank you. Mr. Perez, I may have to speak with you again. Oh, I just thought of something. Apparently, you're here at odd hours. Like today is Saturday and you're here. Does that apply to nights too?"

"It can. You never know when you will find me here."

"Were you here on Wednesday night?"

"No, I wasn't."

"Mr. Perez, were you acquainted with Ms. Oliver enough that you would recognize her on sight?"

"Oh, sure, sure."

"Did you ever see her with any children, toddlers, or babies during the time you worked here?"

"I have worked here for a long time. And the answer to your question is yes. And I have heard crying, a child crying sometimes. Twice I watched when some people went into her office and came out carrying a baby."

"Wow. How long have you worked here?"

"Ten years? Something like that."

"What about Ms. Oliver, how long did she have her office here?"

"Not that long. Maybe she came a year or so after me."

"Did you know her personally?"

"Oh no. She knew who I was because they had to call me if they needed anything. Hey, I just thought. I'm going to be the one who has to clean that office before they can rent that space again. Wonder when that will be."

What a thing for him to have thought up. Pragmatic man. "It's going to be a while before that space is vacated."

"I may even have to replace the carpet if she's had children running around back there with food. I need to talk to management."

"Okay, Mr. Perez. You've been a big help. I sure appreciate you taking the time to speak with me."

"Anytime. I always like to talk to pretty ladies."

I chuckled and waved at him, taking the stairs to the first floor. I was about halfway down the stairs when Mr. Perez leaned over the banister and said, "Miss Davis, do you want to know about the other times I heard a man and Ms. Oliver yelling at each other?"

"Wait, what?" I turned around and jogged back up. "You heard arguments previously to yesterday?" This may sound melodramatic, but my heart pounded.

"One or two times, yes."

"When was this? Recently?"

"A long time ago and then recently."

"Was it the same man as you heard on Friday?" Anticipation filled me with adrenaline.

"I'm not sure, but it could have been."

"When was the last time before Friday?"

"Thursday."

Holy cow. "Okay, now, Mr. Perez, please think hard about this. Was the voice you heard on Thursday the same as the one you heard on Friday?"

He rubbed two fingers across his lips. He shook his head slowly. "I'm just not sure, ma'am. I'm sorry."

"Had you ever heard that man's voice before, other than maybe those times in the past?"

"So hard to tell with a man's deep voice. I could have. The voice could have sounded familiar." He shrugged. "I talk to so many people."

I stared at him, hoping he'd say more about the voice, but he shook his head again.

"If you remember or can think of anything else, please call me." I handed him a card and patted his arm. "Thanks for all your help."

My brain raced with all the possibilities. Had Ms. Oliver teed off someone besides Dave lately? Could be a real possibility, but who?

## CHAPTER

# TWENTY-TWO

Out on the street in my vehicle, as soon as I hung up from leaving a voicemail message for Gillian about what Mr. Perez said, I made another call.

"Margaret, I had a brilliant idea just now," I said into my dashboard receptor, receiver, or whatever it's called.

"You realize it's Saturday." Margaret's voice was more sarcastic than whiny. I'd known her for years and could recognize her moods and attitudes.

"Yes. But this is something you can do from home on your computer. Your computer's in working order, right?"

"Always...well, most of the time. Well, always since I bought the new one."

"Whatever. So, here's what I was thinking."

"Uh-oh."

"Come on, now. It's nothing hard or scary or dangerous. You're on that neighborhood group thing on the Internet, right? Where people in your neighborhood talk to each other about problems and stuff?"

"Yeah. Nextdoor. I put it on your computer and your phone, too. Don't you see it? It's a green icon thingy on your phone."

"Okay, well, I'll give it a look. But here's my idea. If you and Candy and I all go on Nextdoor and put something about the twins, maybe someone will know something. It's a possibility."

"We could do that. We live in different areas so different people are our *neighbors* on the site. Of course, Houston and Harris County are so huge, the chances are slim to none that anyone will see it or reply."

"I know, but it's worth a shot. Would you do that please? What I want it to say is something like: *Hey, neighbors, you may have heard that the lawyer Ms. Isobel Oliver was killed on Friday. Ms. Oliver also ran a child placing agency, placing children for adoption. We're trying to get the word out that everyone with a child placed by Ms. Oliver that hasn't been finalized please contact our office so the matter can be taken care of.*"

"Why don't I just say, *Hey, someone kidnapped a set of twins last Wednesday. If you have any friends or neighbors who had a baby placed with them for adoption late last week or maybe two babies and they're...*what color hair do they have, or do they even have any hair?"

"Oh. Let me call Connie, and I'll call you back." I disconnected. All I knew about the babies is that they were fraternal, a boy and a girl, and six weeks old.

I immediately called Connie. "Hey, this is Mavis. I have an idea and I need a description of the babies."

"What? Hi Mavis. I'm at the jail, waiting to see Dave. What do you need a description of the twins for? I mean, they're babies."

"Yeah, I know they're white babies about six weeks old, but do they have any hair, and, if so, what color is it? I'm assuming their eyes are blue? I always heard that all babies have blue eyes until they change colors."

"I don't know about that, but yes, their eyes are blue. And they have wispy blond hair." She let out a small sob. "I'm sorry. I don't know what else to tell you about them. So, what is this for?"

"The Internet on that Nextdoor thing, and I'm thinking we

should put out something on Facebook, too. Don't you think that's a good idea?"

"I guess so. It wouldn't hurt. But, Mavis, if somebody has them and they see that, might they just hide them or something?"

"They could, but that's not the only avenue we're pursuing. I think this is worth a chance. I really believe that eventually we'll find them. It may take longer than you'd like."

"It already has! I hate that word *eventually*. But I trust you. So, let me know if anyone contacts you. Should I do that myself? Should I ask Louise, even though I'm not speaking to her, to do it, too? And any of my friends?"

"I don't see why not. You never know. Let's do it. Today. Wish I'd thought of it yesterday or Thursday. You take care now." I disconnected.

I called Margaret back. "Okay, Margaret, the twins have wispy blond hair and blue eyes. They're six weeks old. They could have been placed separately. In fact, Carmen Garcia said she thought Ms. Oliver was going to do that."

"That's mean. They would grow up not even knowing they had a twin."

"Yep. Also, after you put this on Nextdoor, go ahead and put it on Facebook and I will, too. If you're on anything else—there's so many now—that a lot of people might see, will you put it on there too?"

"You want me to call you and read to you what I intend to put up there?"

Should I trust her or not? "What you said earlier is a lot more direct than I was being. Go ahead and use your judgment about what to write, but make sure you list our phone number and the name of the office."

"They might contact me directly."

"That would be great. We can only hope. Thanks, Margaret. Have a good weekend. Are you and Barry doing anything, by the way?"

"He's here now. We're going to lunch and then might do other things."

I wasn't even going to ask. "Talk to you later."

I called Candy and asked her to do the same thing. She wasn't on Nextdoor. I asked her to join it and put the message as her introductory message if she could. She said she'd hate to think anyone in her neighborhood would adopt babies when most of them didn't even have a job. Me too. I had an additional request for her

"So, Candy, I have something else I'd like you to do. This would be on Monday."

"Whatever you want, Mavis."

"You know how you've become the main one to pick up and serve and return the service the lawyers hire us on?"

"Yes. I know that."

"I'm wondering whether you've made friends with any of the clerks. You go there often enough."

"I'm pretty friendly with a couple of them. Sometimes, if they're not too busy, we talk and maybe go down to the break area and have a soda."

"Here's what I'm thinking. As I'm sure you know, adoptions are confidential cases that no one can look at besides the judge, the lawyers, and the clerks. Could you go to the district clerk's office and find out which clerk or clerks handle adoption cases? Also, I'm wondering whether private adoptions are handled differently than those involving children in foster care."

"I could do that. You want me to see what information I can get from my friend about the procedure they follow in those kinds of cases? I don't think their procedures would be confidential."

"Well, if you can get it, sure. And if you can get anything about Ms. Oliver specifically and how she handled things, that would be great. I want to find out as much as I can about the legal aspects of this. Gillian Wright's going to see what's going to go on with Oliver's practice. Maybe even get permission to look in her files."

"Yeah, I bet that doesn't happen."

"I don't know how the court handles things when a lawyer dies.

Gillian isn't familiar with it either. She's at least going to find that out."

"You want me to see what I can find out about Ms. Oliver's cases?"

"Yes, but the entire procedures she follows. Also, maybe you can find out if there's a specific clerk assigned to her cases and what attorneys have been appointed to represent the absent parent and the child."

"No problem, babe."

"Babe? What?"

"I heard Ben call you that one time, so I thought I'd try it out."

"No. Just use my name, thanks. So, go over there first thing Monday and get back to me ASAP."

"Roger that." Candy disconnected.

I shook my head and smiled. She couldn't see me, so it was okay for me to smile. I had to keep somewhat of a tight rein on her.

I called Margaret back for one more thing.

"What, Mavis?"

"I hope I didn't interrupt anything important."

"Just tell me what you want, so I can get on with my life."

"You don't have to get all huffy about it."

"Mavis..."

"Okay, on Monday, I want you to call the district clerk's office for all the counties that surround Harris County and speak to the clerk in charge of adoptions, if you can."

"And what do you want me to talk to them about?"

"First, tell them Ms. Oliver is dead. Then tell them we're charged with finding out what counties she practiced in and whether she handled adoptions in their county. Then, if so, anything they're willing to divulge about her."

"Got it. Anything else?"

"You don't have to run by me what you're going to say. I think you can handle this."

"Mavis..."

170

"Just kidding. Goodbye."

While I was running around getting things done, I thought I might as well go visit Dave at the jail. I knew Connie was lined up to visit him when I spoke to her a few minutes ago. I would probably see her there. I wondered if she took anyone with her. Connie didn't strike me as the sort of person who would know someone who has visited the jail in the past. That sounds discriminatory but, as far as I knew, she had no experience with the criminal element and their families.

I drove to the facility, went in, requested to see Dave Wite, and was instantly rebuffed. I wasn't a family member or a lawyer. No go. I needed to get that authorization form from Gillian ASAP before I ran into any more brick walls.

"If I bring a letter from the attorney representing Mr. Wite that says I've been hired to be the investigator on the case, will you let me in to see him?"

"More than likely." The woman behind the window smiled and popped her gum at me. "Step away, so I can take care of the next request."

"Just a minute. As the investigator, will I be able to see Dave during hours that are not open for regular visitation? Like a lawyer would?"

"I'll have to ask. Or you can call ahead. Now step away. Please."

Well, I guess she put me in my place. Humph. I still had a good part of the day before me so I decided to contact Angela Strickmeier, who was a supervisor at Children's Protective Services. We'd worked together when I was a social worker way back when.

"Angela," I said into the phone in my most cheerful voice.

"Oh, God, it's Mavis. I haven't heard from you in so long. First, are you calling me in an emergency?"

"No, I—"

"Okay then, how are you and what do you want? I never hear from you unless you want something."

"That's kind of rude, don't you think? No. No emergency. I'm fine. And it's not true that you never hear from me unless I want something. We had lunch not long ago."

"Mavis, that was last year."

"Oh, well it seems like it was just a while ago. I bought you lunch at—"

"Whole Foods and we each paid for our own. I have no problem doing that again. You must want something, but you know I try not to bring my work home with me. How about we meet at Whole Foods Monday at straight-up noon?"

"You don't even want to know what it's about?"

"Not if it's not an emergency. My time with my family is valuable."

"Well, all right. What I have will keep until then. And I really will buy this time."

"Yes, you will. I'll make sure of that."

My Saturday night fate was decided. I headed home. Lucky for me, Ben called a few minutes later and asked if I wanted a replay of the night before, but at my house, and would a pizza be okay? He had really missed me.

# CHAPTER
# TWENTY-THREE

I woke up on Sunday morning in my warm, cozy queen-sized bed to the sound of rain pattering on the bedroom window and the smell of coffee and bacon floating in from my kitchen. Reaching out to the space beside me, I found it bare and only a little warm. Ben had been up for at least a few minutes. I opened the bedside drawer and took out the little clock I keep in there—I don't like ticking in my ear at night—and couldn't believe how late I'd slept. Eight-thirty? Late for me. Good thing it wasn't a workday morning. Yes, I did work some Sundays but tried not to make it a habit.

Ben's head appeared around the doorframe. "You up, sleepy-head?" He was wearing the blue flannel pajamas I had given him the Christmas before with the proviso that he leave them at my house for cold winter nights. Houston did get cold sometimes. In fact, only a few seasons ago, we had a days-long freeze.

"I must have been tired." I stretched and threw the covers back, unafraid for him to see me in my birthday suit. I exercised when I could and ate healthily now and again. I did feel his eyes on me, though.

"Breakfast is almost ready. I'll put the kettle on while you shower."

I swear we sounded more and more like an old married couple. I hurried to the bathroom to get cleaned up.

About fifteen minutes later, dressed in a pair of jeans, a pink sweater, and my pink fuzzy house shoes, my wet hair combed but dangling on my shoulders, I wandered into the dining room. Though my cottage was small, it did boast five rooms, not counting the bathrooms, of which I had one and a half. So, kitchen, petite dining room, living room-den combo (that's what I like to call it) and two bedrooms. One of my favorite spaces was the sixth room, the front porch. Though not screened in, which was a real bother when the mosquitos were swarming, the porch was deep enough for a couple of chairs, a small table, and plenty of porch sitting.

Ben had set the table. The newspaper, sans plastic wrapper, lay next to my plate. A cup of tea was brewing in my ginormous mug on the kitchen counter. Scrambled eggs were about done. Bacon drained on a paper towel-covered plate, and toast lay on a saucer. Ben sipped coffee from the mug with his name on it. I couldn't help but be on my guard. It wasn't that we hadn't cooked for each other before, but could something be up? Suspicion would be my middle name, if I had one.

He laid a juicy, coffee-tasting kiss on me. "Mmm," he murmured. "You brushed your teeth."

"You taste like coffee." I retrieved a teaspoon from the drawer and set about fixing my tea. "Thank you for doing all this. You're being so sweet, and you know how I feel about you, Ben, so don't get defensive, but what's up?"

He gave the eggs a stir and turned the fire off under the frying pan. Reaching me, he pulled me into a brief hug. "I had a lot of time to think when I went to the funeral. My sister and I had a reunion, along with Matt and the kids. It was good to see them. I looked around the room at the funeral proper, and I realized how mortal I am, we are."

"Scary?" I picked up my tea and leaned against the counter, facing him. "I think about that sometimes, too, especially when I'm in a jam."

"Our lives are complicated, but I want to spend more time together and be kinder. We get at odds too often. We could be a little nicer to each other.

"Is breakfast ready? I'm starved."

"You see what I mean?" He laughed and handed me a plate. "Mavis, it's hard for me to tell you these things."

"I know, and I do appreciate it. I was afraid you were going to propose again."

"Nope. If you ever want to get married, you're going to have to propose to me. So, let's eat."

We took our plates into the dining room and busied ourselves with eating for a few minutes. I glanced at the newspaper headlines. The usual political developments.

"What do you have planned today?" I asked between bites. "Umm, good."

"Have to go to the station in a little while. You?"

"Still trying to find the Wite babies. And, of course, help Gillian with the criminal case."

"We have that lawyer's laptop computer and phone. The techs are breaking into them to see what they can find."

"I wish I had her phone. I'd call every number until I got some information."

"Somebody will probably do that."

"I'm going to go online and read about adoptions, so I have a full understanding of how things are supposed to work. There're times I wish I'd gone to law school. Some of this stuff is so complicated. Family law is worse than criminal law."

"You're just used to criminal stuff."

"They both have more paperwork than I'd like to have to do. One of the things we're thinking is that lawyers who worked with her on the adoptions might know something."

He speared a piece of bacon and held it in front of his mouth. "If you're out there talking to people, and Lon shows up, try not to get into it with him. He's just trying to do his job." He bit off the end of the bacon.

I know I pulled a face. "Can't he be assigned to a desk job someplace?"

"Above my pay grade." Ben laughed. "It is weird that y'all end up in the same place sometimes when Houston is so big."

"I'm ill-fated when it comes to him. Anyway, let's not talk about Lon. I'll get indigestion. I want to ask you something." I was hoping he'd pass along what I was about to say.

"Whatever I can answer, I will." He took a large bite of toast and waited.

"If you were investigating this murder, and you were told the dead person had been arguing with a man a day or two before the defendant came in and allegedly killed her, wouldn't you look into it?"

His eyebrows shot up. "Who told you that?"

"The maintenance man. Do y'all have someone talking to people at that building to see if any of them know anything, or are you satisfied with arresting Dave Wite?"

"I'm sure a case is being built."

"This isn't your case? You're not supervising it? If not, why were you there?"

"I am, but no one has brought me that information. I'm sure when they think they have something, they'll tell me. I'll ask about it."

"So, y'all are looking to see if anyone else could have killed her?"

"He was found standing next to the body."

"Let me ask you this, who called 911? Someone did. How did they know she was dead?"

"You're starting to sound defensive, Mavis. We're not enemies here. This is what I'm talking about. Let's not get at odds with each other, especially not after the last two nights."

I exhaled a deep breath, trying to calm down. Ben waited and watched while I mulled things over and finished my breakfast. When I pushed my plate away, I said, "Okay. I'm with you on that. I don't want to fight. It's just there are two missing kids, and my client is in jail for a murder he says he didn't commit, and I believe him. He says he might have killed her if she didn't say where the kids were, but she was dead when he walked in."

"I got that. And I'll see if they're looking into the call and if they're interviewing other tenants of the building."

"Okay. I'm going to do that too, interview the tenants. Just don't know in what order I'm going to do things. The lawyers. The tenants. I wish I could find out what adoption cases she hasn't finished up with. She may have gotten crosswise with some of them, although if she controls how the case goes, I imagine they'd be really careful with her."

He nodded. "I would."

I was surprised he didn't ask me to be careful, but I think he's realized by now not to. "Ben, after talking to Carmen, I know Ms. Oliver was up to no good. It could involve more than the adoption stuff, but at least that."

"Carmen waived her right to a lawyer and gave a complete statement. We're well aware of what was going on. Some of it, anyway." He reached over and squeezed my forearm. "We're not enemies. We're on the same side. We have people trying to find those children. And I'll make sure the focus on the murder is not limited to Dave Wite."

"Okay. I'm going to do my job, though. And Lon better stay out of my way."

Ben laughed. "You and he are sometimes the bane of my existence."

"He's definitely the bane of mine. A real bane in my rear end."

"There's no one who doesn't know that. What else are you doing today?"

"I'm going to get better acquainted with social media. We're putting the word out about the babies. You never know when someone will see something, know something, right?"

"Since we know now it's not a ransom thing, the case has gone public. We're even thinking about Mrs. Wite doing a TV interview."

"Keep me posted on that?"

"Sure." He swallowed the rest of his coffee and rose from the table, plate in hand. "Glad we had this little chat." He laughed and kissed me on the cheek.

I got up, too, and followed him into the kitchen, admiring him for making such an effort. He could be a chauvinist sometimes, but I had to give him credit for trying to change.

# CHAPTER

# TWENTY-FOUR

Burdened by her winter jacket, her helmet, and her backpack, Candy entered the family section of the district clerk's office to pick up the papers Margaret had texted her about earlier. She craned her neck, searching for her friend Lorraine, hoping they could talk, that Lorraine could help her with Mavis' request. Lorraine, however, was nowhere to be found. A clerk she didn't know was staffing the front counter, so Candy asked for the service she was supposed to pick up. When she received the documents, she stuck them in her backpack. She also had some to pick up in the civil section, which luckily was in the same building. She hoped she'd see Shaun there.

Shaun, who was only a year older than Candy, was working the counter in civil. He rewarded her with a grin and shining dark blue eyes when she walked in. Shaun was taller than Candy, six feet, and wore his black hair in a crew cut. He was wearing a long-sleeved button-down navy blue and red plaid shirt. He was a runner, so he was thin. He'd been trying to get Candy to go jogging with him, but so far, he hadn't succeeded. She couldn't see any good reason to get that tired.

"Hey," he said, his dimples deep. "I have your service ready."

She wasn't sure how he knew what she was there to pick up, but no matter. "Okay. Thanks." She put those documents into her backpack with the others. "I was wondering, are you anywhere near your break time? I need your help on something and thought we could talk about it if you were going on your break in a few minutes."

He glanced at the clock on the wall. "Let me ask my supervisor. We're not that busy this morning." He circled around several desks and a corner. Candy tried not to think about him looking as good when he walked away as he did coming toward her. Did mature professional people think about stuff like that during office hours? Yeah, they probably did or else there wouldn't be all the office romance you hear about.

She stepped aside so other people could be served. She didn't have to worry about taking too much time or being late, since she was on a mission. Mavis had given her an important task.

A few minutes later, Shaun appeared in the hall and beckoned to her through the plate glass window. She followed him to the stairwell and down the stairs. "How long do you have?"

"Fifteen minutes. I'm glad you came by. I was wondering whether I'd see you this week."

They walked together to a break area where Shaun inclined his head at a corner table. He bought them both sodas and chips and joined her.

"These are the kind you like, right?"

"Thanks, yes. So, Shaun, I don't want to get you into trouble, but I need some information for my boss."

"And it's something I can get here in the courthouse?"

"In your office, I think. Do you know anything about adoptions and Children's Protective Services cases and lawyers who are appointed by the judges in that kind of case?"

He ran his hand over his clean-shaven cheek. "I worked in that section one summer when I was in high school, the family section. But I haven't spent any time there recently."

"Do you know any of the people who work in that section now, like Lorraine?"

"She's pretty cool. Is she a friend of yours, too?"

"I like her. She's always real friendly. Anyway, can you find out which clerks work on those kinds of cases? Mavis or I may want to talk to them. And I wonder, do you know who keeps the list of lawyers who the judges appoint on those kinds of cases? That's not confidential, is it?"

"Yeah. I don't think there's a problem with either of those. The list of lawyers is probably on the computer. The judge's court coordinators would have that list, so they can grab a name and fill in a blank quickly when the paperwork comes up. I think they notify the lawyers, too, though I'm not sure."

"You can find out though, right?"

"Oh, sure. What's this about?"

Candy didn't think there was any reason why she couldn't tell Shaun what they were working on. Especially if it would help her get the information she needed. "Did you hear about that lawyer who got shot last Friday?"

"Yeah. I knew her. She came around all the time when I was working in the family section. Is Mavis working on that case?"

"Kind of." She lowered her head and whispered, "Our client's twin babies were kidnapped last week and given to that lawyer, who was going to put them up for adoption."

"No way." He grabbed her forearm.

"Yes, way. Believe me. Pretty wild, huh? So, Mavis is trying to find the babies. She thinks if she can learn who all the lawyers are that were appointed on that dead lawyer's cases, they might know something. Like maybe that dead lawyer gives the kids to someone to take care of while she sets up the adoption or something like that."

"They could. I think if they represent the kid, they have to at least meet it or see it if it's a baby." Shaun had ambitions to be a paralegal or a lawyer, too, depending on how his finances played out. Candy and he had talked a lot about what they were going to do when they finished at community college. Shaun said, "So, yeah, I don't think the list is a secret. I'll find out how you can get a copy."

"Great. You're great." She put her hand over his.

He grinned. "Is there anything else? Maybe I could find out if she has any pending cases?"

"Is there a way you can find out without getting yourself in hot water?"

"I can at least find out if she has some active cases. Probably whether she has some with someone appointed temporary managing conservator."

"Wouldn't she be it since she's a licensed adoption agency?"

"Oh, yeah. It could be, or she could take the adoptive parents to court and get them appointed while they're waiting on the home study. I'm not sure how she does it." His eyes met hers. "How she did it."

"That's what we're trying to find out. But you couldn't find out the names of the adoptive parents or the names of the lawyers on those cases, could you?"

"I'm not sure what you need that for?"

"I'm not either. Maybe I don't—hey, what about if she filed new cases on Thursday or Friday after those babies were kidnapped?"

"That would be awfully fast."

"Yeah. I guess I don't know enough about how all this works to know what Mavis needs. Well, anyway, thanks for whatever you can do."

He squeezed her arm again and pulled his hand back. "You know, Candy, I was wondering, since you won't go running with me, you want to go to a movie sometime?"

"I thought you'd never ask."

He laughed. "You could have asked me, you know."

"Yeah, I could have, but I'm always afraid to."

"Yeah, me too. So, is that yes? I can check on Fandango and see what'll be on next weekend."

"Okay. If you want to get the tickets, I'll buy the popcorn and Cokes."

"Deal." He glanced at the clock on the wall. "Walk back up with me?"

She nodded. "Oh, let me share my contact info."

They bent their heads over their phones and shared each other's information. Tossing their trash on the way out of the break area, they walked arm in arm back to the stairwell and up the stairs.

"I'll text you as soon as I find out anything," Shaun said. "It's kind of exciting to be helping find those kids."

"Yeah, this kind of stuff is what I like, not just serving papers. I like it when Mavis gives me important stuff. Or even if she doesn't, but I get myself involved anyway. I'll have to tell you about that."

"I hope you'll be telling me a lot of things," he said just before he opened the door to the office and swung inside.

"Me, too."

CHAPTER

# TWENTY-FIVE

N ot wanting to keep Angela Strickmeier waiting, since she was doing me a favor, on Monday at straight-up noon, I stood just inside the doors of Whole Foods and scanned the parking lot. We'd been good friends when we both had worked at Children's Protective Services. She'd begun working there a year or maybe eighteen months before I left. I've missed her. Somehow my social circle had been reduced to Ben, Margaret, and Candy, though I received an occasional invitation to a holiday party, and if I went into my favorite bar, the owner and bartender recognized me, and we'd have a chat. That's how it goes in our modern world...of course, I'm not counting my five hundred or so Facebook friends. Would any of them come to my aid if I needed it?

A recent model gray and silver Prius cruised to a stop in front of the doors. Though Angela had changed her hairstyle, when she craned her neck, looking in, I recognized her and dashed outside to let her know I'd kept the date. When she saw me, she held up one finger and went to park.

Jumping out of her car, she hurried toward me. She wore a full-length tan trench coat over a black cardigan and matching shell tank top with black and green plaid pants. An oversized black leather bag hung off one shoulder. Her light brown hair now had blonde streaks and was in an upsweep, which was being down swept by the wind. She pulled off her sunglasses when she approached me, her chestnut eyes shining. I hugged her when she stepped inside. Being five-ten or thereabouts, I towered over her. She might be petite, but she radiated energy. She always had.

"How the heck are you, Mavis?" She led the way to the prepared food aisles where she snatched several items off the shelves. Clearly, she was a regular.

"Same as always. You? How's it going at CPS?" I picked up a salad and a bottle of green juice and followed her to the checkout line.

"I've been bumped up again. A little more money, but you know how lousy the pay is with the state. Plus, more work with so many people quitting."

"You get benefits, though, so that's helpful. How's Joel? How's the kid?" We were moving up in the line, so I pulled out my credit card.

"Both good. Joel's doing well in his law practice. He makes plenty of money, being a lawyer. You ought to get one of those." She laughed.

"What, a husband? A lawyer? I have a lawyer, but she's a woman and married."

"A personal injury lawyer. If they're pretty good, they make lots of money and you can do whatever you want."

"I do whatever I want now. I'm just pinching pennies all the time."

"Just teasing. You like where you are. I know that. I'm just so happy these days. I want to spread the joy." She turned away while the clerk rang up her food and moved to the aisle to wait for me.

I paid for both of us, as promised, then followed her once again. She'd spotted a table almost all the way to the end, which was okay with me. I wasn't especially eager to share information with the public. I slid onto a chair and took the top off the bottle of the green juice, taking a big swallow. I almost gagged. I was trying to eat healthier, well sometimes, but honestly, it could be agony. Still, I'd bought it. I was going to drink it.

"Do you like that stuff?" She'd spread her food out in front of her, roast chicken, mashed potatoes, corn, broccoli, and a fruit salad. And a chunk of garlic bread. Her co-workers were going to love that.

"God, no. We're supposed to try to eat healthier, right? Once a week or so, I do that even if I'm miserable during the meal. See, I have a salad, too."

"If I remember correctly, you'll find a sweet sometime this afternoon."

"If I can. So, tell me why you're so full of joy." I looked at her food. She ate a lot for a small person. "I think I know."

"I'm pregnant again." She stuffed some potatoes into her mouth.

"You're not even showing! How can that be?"

"I am though. I swear. Four months. I'll start showing soon. I won't be able to wear these wool pants with no stretchy waistband. I love these pants in cold weather."

"Congratulations. I wondered whether you and Joel were going to expand your family. That's great. Let me know if you have a baby shower and I'll come." It would give me a chance to socialize outside of the office and maybe see other people from CPS that I once worked with. I just hoped Mandy, the big boss at that office, wouldn't be there. But I couldn't worry about that just now.

"I will. I need to replenish my nursery. How about you? Are you going to settle down any time soon?"

I shook my head. "You know, Angela, I really like my life the way it is. I have my own house, thanks to my mother. I don't have anyone telling me what to do, keeping track of me, or looking over my shoulder. Except Ben."

"You're still with Ben?" She took an amazingly big bite of chicken.

"He knows if he wants to have kids, he'll have to look elsewhere.

And get this, he put a tracker on my phone! At first, I got angry about it, but then I thought maybe it was a good idea."

"Joel has one on mine, and I have one on his."

"I have one on Ben's, too. We had this huge discussion. I told him it was only fair, so he finally agreed. And then I went a step further and got Margaret and Candy to let me put one on theirs. We do get into scrapes sometimes."

"You always have. That's not a bad idea. When Willie gets a phone, we'll definitely put one on his. Anyway, why are we here?" She swallowed from her own juice and waited for me to finish my bite of salad so I could reply.

"You need to get back to work. Here's what's going on. Do you know the lawyer, Isobel Oliver?"

"Oh my God, you're not involved with her, are you? Wait, did I read in the Chronicle that she was killed?"

"No, I'm not, and yes, she was. Last Friday."

"But they arrested the guy, right?"

"Okay, this is complicated. She was found dead at her office on Friday. The man arrested is our client and didn't do it."

"Yeah, right."

"Wait, it's even more complicated than that. Dave Wite, the man who was arrested, and his wife are the parents of twins who were kidnapped on Wednesday night from a church."

"I didn't see that in the paper."

"They were trying to keep it quiet at first in case it was a ransom deal. But they hired me to assist the police in trying to find the kids. I've been searching for them ever since."

"Isobel took them?"

"Keep eating while I try to explain. I don't want you to be late for work."

She took another mouthful.

I summarized most of what had happened in the past few days. "Well, it turned out the kidnapper gave the babies to Isobel Oliver."

Angela choked. I had to get up and pound her on the back. Her eyes watered, and her mascara ran. "We've been looking into Isobel Oliver for a long time." She wiped her eyes with a napkin.

"CPS suspected she was doing something not quite legit?"

She nodded. "Received her license years ago and started out practicing law and placing a few children in private adoptions. That was way before my time. Then over the years, people got to wondering how exactly she was able to place so many children. Where did she get them?"

"How'd y'all find out what was going on?"

"Okay, you know all the CPS stuff is confidential. The clerk's files are confidential. All that stuff is confidential but not to us. Not long ago, there was a child who was in foster care. The agency had permanent managing conservatorship. We were looking for a permanent placement or adoption for him. The foster parents weren't interested."

"That's not uncommon if all they want to do is foster."

"Right. No problem there. But then, I'm trying to remember how we found this out, Isobel somehow got managing conservatorship in another county."

"What? How'd she do that?"

Angela scratched her ear with one hand and then her head with the other. The scenario must make her nervous. "As best we can figure out, she filed a termination and adoption suit in that county around the time we filed ours. She'd obtained a relinquishment from the mother as well as one from the father. She went to the court in that county and had the court terminate their rights and appoint her as managing conservator."

"Did y'all have relinquishments from the parents?"

"Not both. The mother relinquished. We cited the unknown father. The court here appointed one of those lawyers from the list, and when we had our hearing, our agency was appointed managing conservator."

"So dueling managing conservators. Huh. I wonder how she found the father."

"Yeah, we were wondering that, too. Oh, now I remember how we found out she was involved in the case. One day Isobel went to the foster parents and told them she was the managing conservator and that she was looking for an adoptive home for the boy. The foster parents called us. The kid was living in their home."

"Well, this certainly is a weird story. What happened in that case?"

"It's still pending. Competing lawsuits, too. The agency's lawyer is asking the judges to confer. It's going to be interesting now to see what's going to happen, with her being dead."

My brain was bursting. Isobel Oliver sure knew how to make a mess. "Here's something I just thought of. In the case you're talking about, is the mother in jail?"

Her eyes widened. "She sure was. She's in prison now."

"Well, have I got news for you." I told her what Carmen Garcia had told me. I thought Angela was going to choke again.

When I was through explaining, she said, "We wondered about that. Of course, we didn't know where the kids came from. We weren't allowed to see the confidential files we weren't involved in."

"Did that thing with dual managing conservatorships happen more than once?"

"I don't think so. I'll have to ask if it ever happened years ago. I do know there have been children we were going to file for who were placed with relatives or in a kinship placement without us having to get involved and who were later adopted by someone else. That was something we'd discussed more than once."

"If I recall, kinship placement is a person who has no legal relationship with the child but has had enough contact that they're like a relative?"

"Yeah, like the mom's best friend who loves the kid."

"Don't they usually keep the kid and get permanent custody or adopt them?"

"They have, but not always. Sometimes people change their minds after having the responsibilities of raising a child."

"You know what I think? If Isobel was paying Carmen, she was also paying the birth parents. In other words, buying children. I bet she charged the adoptive parents an arm and a leg. You hear all the time how expensive adoptions are."

Angela closed her eyes and shook her head. "It's a form of human trafficking, just not *coyotes* bringing the children across the border. So what do you want from me, Mavis? You've given me more information than I've given you."

"You said the courts appoint lawyers to represent the parents from a list, right? Is that also true for the children's lawyers—the ad litems? They're appointed from a list too?"

She nodded. "Yes. In every case."

I was trying to get it all organized in my mind. Gillian's information about criminal case procedures together with Angela's information about family case procedures threatened to overwhelm me.

Angela looked at her watch. "I'm going to have to go in a minute." She scraped the remainder of the potatoes onto her fork and stabbed the last bit of chicken.

"I'm just thinking about what I need to know from you, and here's what I'm thinking. I can probably get the list of court appointed attorneys from the clerk or the court. Do you think the courts use the same attorneys for private adoptions as they do for your agency's cases?"

"I have no way of knowing that. I could try to find out, though. Somebody else might know, like Mandy." She raised an eyebrow and smiled.

"Yeah, you're just mentioning Mandy because you know how we feel about each other. But however you can find out, please do. Can you find out who the lawyers are on that case in the other county?"

"I might."

"What about the social workers who do the home studies on private adoptions? Is there a list of those? I could sure use that. In fact, if you could find out if the court always uses someone from that list whether or not it's a private adoption, that would be great."

"You're thinking the social workers might have already done home studies on people who have hired Isobel to get them a baby? I see where you're going here."

"It's possible she had adoptive parents waiting in the wings for her to find just the right baby to fit their *order*. If I can get that list of social workers, I can contact them and maybe find the people who have the Wite babies. Because we know she had to put the kids somewhere when she got them on Wednesday night."

"Boy, this is complicated."

"Yeah, I could interview all the social workers and the lawyers who've been appointed on CPS cases and see if any of them have been on her private adoptions. If not, maybe they know who the court appoints. I have a list of questions I need answered."

"I bet you do." She grabbed her bag off the floor next to her, and we both stood. "I'll take my job any day." She reached up and hugged me. "I'll contact you as soon as I find out anything." And she was off.

I plopped back down, wondering what I was missing, if anything. One thing I was hoping Candy had found out was what adoption cases of Isobel Oliver's were still waiting to be finalized. And why they weren't completed. I also wanted to know how many thousands of dollars she got for selling a child.

# CHAPTER

# TWENTY-SIX

I walked out to my car and called Gillian at her office. I needed to bring her up to date.

When her secretary put me through, I said, "Hey, it's Mavis. We need to talk about some stuff."

"You can call me on my cell. You don't have to go through my secretary, especially since you *kind of* work for me now."

"*Kind of* is right. Like an independent contractor. That's good. Saves time. Anyway, I've been busy, and I'm sure you have, too. I tried to get in the jail to see Dave, but they wouldn't let me, because I wasn't family or his attorney. Can you help with that?"

"I can, but I'm not sure you need to talk to him."

That didn't sit well. "Why not?"

"I can tell you what he told me when I interviewed him. Why don't you come to the office? I don't like discussing the facts of cases on cell phones."

"Yeah, okay." She might be a little paranoid, but whatever. "While I'm there, can I pick up that engagement letter?"

"My secretary may have already sent it to your office, but we can give you another one. See you in a couple of minutes."

"It'll be more than a couple, but I'll be there." I'd rather talk in person, as well. I hated it when I'd get off the phone and then remember something I meant to ask about. I knew the way to her office, unfortunately, from past experience. Now, I'd be there in another capacity.

About twenty minutes after I left the Whole Foods parking lot, I pulled into the lot at Gillian's. Her office building was not nearly as impressive as Ms. Oliver's but was still a lot nicer than my own. Though her office was some distance from downtown, it still had to be pricey. No regular Joe could afford rent anywhere close to the courthouse.

I walked in and asked, "How's Dave doing? Have they set a bond for him? Did you ask him the details about when he arrived at her office?" The questions were out of my mouth before I seated myself.

She looked as professional as usual, in a dark gray pantsuit and mid-heel pumps. Her hair was shiny clean and a little windblown. "His bond is half a mil. I'm going to file to have it reduced. In fact, Perlita is working on that right now."

"That's a lot, isn't it? Do you think the judge will go for it?"

"Dave has a lot going for him. I don't see why the bond was set so high in the first place. The judge will probably cut it way down. Anyway, Dave said he walked into her office, and she was lying dead on the floor right in the nursery area. Imagine a lawyer having a nursery in her office. First I've heard of that."

"I've been to the building and saw the basic layout. I think the nursery was way in the back."

Her forehead wrinkled up. "Dave said she looked like she hadn't been there for long. And then the police came and yelled at him to stop whatever he was doing and hold his hands out and not to move. Dave had his gun, but said he never drew it. He had it tucked into the back of his pants under his shirt."

"Was he believable?"

"Yes, he was. He was distraught. He said he might have killed her if he'd asked to get his kids back and she refused, but he never had a chance to do that."

"So, the police arrived and arrested Dave, no questions asked?"

"Pretty much. He didn't try to resist or anything. He told them he had a gun. They pulled up his shirt. He was afraid if he reached back to get it they might shoot him."

"Yeah, good thinking. Who called the police?"

"Don't know, but I hope to find out."

"They didn't get the caller's name? They would have gotten their information."

"I'm planning on finding that out. I'll file a discovery motion as soon as he's indicted and assigned to a court. I should be able to get the caller's name then, if not before."

"I have a lot of questions. How did the 911 caller know about her?"

"That's what I want to know. I'm also going to ask for the autopsy. Whatever I can get them to give me. That'll take a while."

"I guess Dave told you about Carmen. Did he tell you he hit her? I think he may have hit her more than once."

"He feels badly about that. I doubt the police would charge him with assault, though."

"Not with her being a kidnapper. I wrung her out pretty hard. Ms. Oliver had a real racket going. She was kind of extorting or bribing or whatever you want to call it to get Carmen to do what she wanted. But the main thing is, Carmen claims she doesn't know what happens to the children or where Ms. Oliver stashes them once she gets them before she places them with the adoptive parents. She doesn't know any of that end of the case."

"They could be stashed with a babysitter somewhere right now."

"They could. Or she could have given them to the adoptive parents, if she'd had some waiting in the wings, and then have plans to go to the court this week and get temporary orders."

"How she could do that without parents relinquishing...don't say it. I know even as a lawyer, I can be naive. Someone could forge their signatures. On top of that, a notary would have to know that and be a part of things, don't you think?"

"I'm planning to find that out if I can. Back on the criminal side of things, I wanted to tell you, not that it's likely I would forget, what happened when I went to the office building on Saturday to see if I could find any witnesses. Most of the offices were locked up tight. The way the offices are set up, they have floor to ceiling glass next to the doors. You can see into some of them. Some of them have vertical blinds or curtains. Oliver's blinds were open. I could see all the way into the back. Several individual offices are in the suite. A fairly long hallway has to lead to where she'd keep the children."

"You got a feel for the venue."

"If you mean where the murder took place, yes." As if I didn't know what a venue was. "Anyway, her office is right inside the front door to the building so someone could get in and out fast though they'd have to risk being seen. But there could be lots of people coming and going. I need to see if there's a back door to the building. Wouldn't there have to be one?" Rhetorical question. "Did Dave say if he saw anyone leaving the building when he was entering?"

"No, but I didn't ask. Was anyone there on Saturday who might know something?"

I needed to go to the jail and speak with Dave. "Yes. First, I talked to a woman who owns a...fluid testing company, I guess that's what you call it. She didn't hear or see anything. Her office is in the back of the building."

"No one else was there?"

"I met the man who is the janitor—really a jack-of-all-trades. We had a nice chat. As I was leaving, he remembered to tell me he had heard an argument between Ms. Oliver and a man on Friday. Their voices were very loud."

"That's not good. He could identify Dave's voice? He could testify that it was Dave who was arguing with her?"

"He could, Gillian, if it was Dave. But get this: he'd heard her in arguments with someone before, a man, and not on Friday. He thought it was Thursday. That couldn't have been Dave."

"You're kidding. He can swear that the voice was the same on Friday as Thursday?"

"He's pretty sure. Unfortunately, not positive. And he couldn't tell what they were arguing about."

"That gives me some hope."

"I'm planning to go back there, maybe even this afternoon, to see if anyone else heard anything. I'll talk to Ms. Oliver's legal secretary if the police let her back in the office. Seems to me she'd be the one person in the world who would know the most about what Isobel had been doing in these adoptions all these years."

"She could even be the notary. There's so much we don't know."

"And Gillian, I was thinking, you really do need to go to one of those family court judges and talk to him or her about getting the clerk to bring up all Ms. Oliver's pending adoption cases. You do family law, too. Surely you know the judges?"

"Is there something specific you want to see in the court files? I mean, other than seeing if she's filed a case or cases in the last few days that might involve the Wite children?"

"I'm not sure, exactly, but I have my suspicions that if she was buying and selling babies, she could have been up to much, much more. Someone besides Dave could have been really angry with her. I want to see everything I can get my hands on." I could just imagine what a treasure trove we'd find.

"What else could she have been doing?" Gillian asked.

"That's a rhetorical question, I'm sure. But we need to know what she was up to. It could be key to Dave's defense." Just talking about it gave me an adrenaline spike.

Gillian started counting things off on her fingers: "Charging huge amounts of money for these babies, to start with. What if she has a fee schedule, which I doubt, and she lists what it will cost in terms of hospital costs for the expectant mother, attorney's fees for the ad litems, her own attorney fees, court costs. She could pad it with other costs."

"I've been wondering whether some of these adoptive parents even know where their kid came from. If they knew the mother was in jail, did Ms. Oliver ask them to pay for the mother's legal defense?" It could be just another rhetorical question, though both of us hoped Oliver wasn't in as deep as she could have been.

"That's not legal, but with what she's been doing, what would she care." Gillian said. "We're on the same wavelength. The adoptive parents would have no way of knowing whether that money went to the mother's defense or whether Isobel pocketed it."

"And wouldn't care. They'd get their baby. So many people will pay anything to get a baby. Gillian, I've been thinking of something else she might have done. You know how she co-signed for Carmen's truck and mobile home and then held that over her head?" I thought I'd told her about that, but maybe it had been Angela. So much info so fast. "What if Ms. Oliver had something to hold over the heads of these rich adoptive parents?"

"A form of blackmail. That could get her killed. I'd be interested in knowing how she would do that," Gillian said.

"That's another reason to see her office files and her court files. Here's my plan for the rest of today. I'm heading to Isobel Oliver's office. If her secretary is there, we're going to have a heart-to-heart, if you know what I mean. I want to see those files. I want to know everything that secretary knows. I want to find out if she knows of someplace where Isobel would leave the children after she got them and before she delivered them to the adoptive parents. I want to see her billing records and her bank accounts."

"Whoa, Mavis. You're setting out a tall order for yourself."

"I know, but Gillian, I've got to find those kids. That'll be the very first thing I'll lean on that secretary for. I have my fingers crossed that even if she's not involved in the illegal aspects of this baby buying business, she'll know enough that the kids can be found."

"After that—"

"After that, I'm really going to focus on finding out who, besides Dave Wite, might have had a reason to kill Isobel Oliver. I'll go at it from her law office side."

"I'll go at it from the court files side. There's one judge I'm pretty good friends with. If she's not in trial, if they're not picking a jury this afternoon, I'll have a good chance of talking to her. If anyone will get the clerk to pull those files, it will be her."

# CHAPTER
# TWENTY-SEVEN

I nside the office building in which Isobel Oliver's personal office was located, the crime scene tape lay across the floor in front of the door. Through the open blinds, which if I'd been the secretary I would have closed to exclude gawkers, I spotted a dishwater blonde, mid-twenties woman sitting behind the secretary's desk. Before I pushed inside, I noticed many of the office windows which had been covered on Saturday were now open. In fact, people upstairs and down watched me from them. When I gave them the beauty queen wave, they quit.

The woman behind the desk looked at me with a dazed expression when I entered Oliver's office, as if her mind were wandering, or she was daydreaming. Anyone might find it hard to focus if they came to work and found their boss had been murdered.

As tall as I am, I knew I could be intimidating, so instead of my normal ebullience I toned my voice down. "I'm Mavis Davis, a private investigator on the Wite case." Flashing my ID at her, I said, "I wonder whether I could ask you some questions?" I held out my hand.

The woman appeared to regain consciousness. Her dark eyes

focused on me, or at least appeared to. She wore a green polo-style shirt with World Con engraved on some kind of insignia above her left breast. I was pretty sure World Con was a sci-fi thing. Candy would know. Anyway, I wasn't there to discuss that. Long, dangly silver earrings hung from her ears, her short hair not quite long enough to cover them. Racks of bracelets ringed each arm. She looked at my outstretched hand and slipped her hand in and out of mine almost before I noticed. What I did feel were cold fingers.

"I'm Imogen Myers, but people call me Jean."

"Imogen, haven't heard that name in like, forever." I was hoping to warm her up.

She rolled her eyes. "My great-aunt's name. My mother's favorite aunt."

"Do you know about what happened to Ms. Oliver?"

She dragged her hands over her face and nodded. "I guess you do, too, or you wouldn't be asking."

"I do. That's why I'm here. May I sit down?"

"You can bring one of those chairs closer."

I did that. "So, Jean, do the police know the crime scene tape is down? That you've come in here, to a crime scene?"

She nodded, again. "I called them on my cell when I got here, and once they transferred me around about a jillion times, somebody came on and said I could take it down. I didn't know what to do with it, so I left it. Maybe they'll come and get it. I don't know. I'm babbling." She let out a big sigh. "I don't know what I'm supposed to be doing."

"I can imagine. How long did you work for Ms. Oliver?"

"Couple of years. I'm her—I was her secretary. I've been going to Lone Star College to get my associates as a paralegal. I'm close to finishing. Now I'll have to find a job in another law office. Oh!" She clapped a hand over her mouth. "Is it terrible for me to say that?"

"That's okay. Don't worry about it. Were you close to Ms. Oliver?"

"Not really. I mean, she was polite enough and all that, but she was kinda cold, if you know what I mean. Like, not the motherly type, and I'm young enough to be her daughter."

"So, just a purely business relationship?"

"Yes, like that. I aimed to just try to get in and out on time, especially when I had classes."

"Were you here on Friday?"

She shook her head. "No. I only work half-a-day on Fridays. When she hired me, she told me the routine would be Monday through Thursday eight-thirty to five and eight to twelve on Fridays, with the provision that if something came up on a Saturday, I'd run in here and get it done. She said that would only be once in a great while, which it turned out to be."

"Like what kind of stuff on Saturdays?"

"If she needed me to knock out some forms really quick, like if someone was coming unexpectedly and the paperwork wasn't prepared. She could do stuff on her computer, but all the official forms are on my computer. I didn't have to do it often."

"Do you have access to her computer? What'd she have, a laptop?"

"No, never did. The police took it anyway, and her cell phone. I searched this morning."

That confirmed what Ben had told me. "Back to Fridays, what would she do after you left, do you know?"

"I don't. I don't know if she went home too, or what."

"I heard of a judge once a long time ago who always let his staff go home at lunch on Fridays and it turned out he'd have booze and women up there for a little party every Friday afternoon."

Dimples appeared in her cheeks when she laughed. "Was that here in Houston?"

"No. One of the outlying counties. I don't know if it was true. I just had heard that."

"That's crazy."

She'd perked up at hearing my story. That's what I wanted. I wanted to make friends with her. "On a more serious note, how did you find out Ms. Oliver died?"

"The police called me. I guess they dug around and found my contact information."

"Hmm. Since y'all were strictly business, you may not know some of the info I need. Did you keep her calendar?"

"I did, in this computer here, but there was never anything on it for Friday afternoons. I didn't think that was weird or anything since she told me at the beginning I wouldn't be working then. I guess I thought she wouldn't either."

"There's no way you would know who might have come here after you left last Friday?"

She shook her head. "I have no idea. The police told me a man came in and killed her. That's all they told me. They said the office would be locked up and no one would be allowed inside until they'd cleared it. Are you working for the man who killed her?"

"He didn't kill her. He's accused of killing her. Does it bother you that I'm hired by his family?"

"Not especially. I figured lots of people would want to ask me questions, like they do on cop shows on TV."

"Anyone else been here today?"

"A man from an Internet news site and one from the Chronicle. Several people who have offices in this building have come by. Since I don't know much, I can't tell them much."

"Jean, are you a notary?"

"No, ma'am. Ms. Oliver had someone she used. I never had to get my notary thingy."

That answered another lingering question. "You know who it was?"

"It would be on copies of some of the papers in the files."

"Would you mind looking?" Having that information might not help me or Gillian, but it sure would be good for the authorities to know.

"Okay." She popped out of her chair and opened a file cabinet drawer. Rows of files with various color labels were clustered together.

"What do all those colors on the file tabs mean?"

"For different kinds of cases." She closed the top drawer and opened the one below it.

"Didn't she primarily do adoptions?"

Jean looked over her shoulder at me. "Some divorces and annulments and landlord-tenant stuff. She owned some apartment complexes, so she'd be her own lawyer on those cases."

"I didn't know that."

"Yeah. She was always kicking people out of her apartments," she said, her head shaking and her voice sounding shrill as she thumbed through the files. "I thought she was mean to some of those people, but I couldn't say anything."

"I wouldn't want rental property. I'd hate to evict someone."

"Me, too. Here's one." She pulled the file out and laid it on the desk.

I copied down the information. I'd never heard of the person, but there was no reason I should. There are tons of notaries. It's not hard to become one. Some people do it as a sideline, to make extra money. So many documents need to be notarized. "Thanks, Jean."

She put the file back and closed the drawer. "Why do you need the notary?" She sat back down and brushed her hair back and picked up a pen and twirled it in her fingers.

I studied her face, her demeanor. Could she have known about the businesses Oliver partook in? I was trying to decide what to tell her, what to ask her, and whether to even approach some of the subjects I wanted information about. I couldn't see how she would be involved if she wasn't the notary, what illegal acts she may have performed.

"Why are you looking at me like that?" she asked, twirling the pen faster.

I clasped my hands and leaned my arms on the desk. "I'm wondering about you."

"About me what? Did I do something wrong?"

"I don't know. Did you? Let me ask you this, did you agree with everything you observed Ms. Oliver do, besides the evictions?"

She cocked her head. "I don't know what you're getting at."

"I think you do. You're not in trouble or anything if you didn't participate in her activities, but if you know some things she did that she shouldn't have or something that may have gotten her killed, it would be helpful if you shared that information."

She sat mute.

"Jean, did you handle collections for her? By that I mean, did you do her billing? Did people come in and pay personally, and you gave them receipts?"

Her brows drew together. Her nose wrinkled. Her lips stretched across her teeth, fading to pink. I wasn't sure if she was going to scream at me or start crying.

"You can tell me, Jean. I'm not here to hurt you or anything. I'm trying to figure out what was going on with Isobel Oliver that might have gotten her killed by someone other than my client."

She let out an enormous sigh. "I was looking for another job. She didn't know that, but I was. I just hadn't found one yet. I wanted to get out of here."

"You did know she might be doing some things she shouldn't?"

"I did. Usually I never handled money, and she didn't really do billing. She had a management company that handled her rental property mostly, collecting rent and all that, though we did the legal papers, and she always made it her business to go to court on the evictions." She covered her mouth with her hand and paused as though wondering whether she should keep talking. I kept quiet. "I wrote letters and sent checks she wrote out to the lawyers who were the ad litems on the adoption cases, but otherwise, I didn't see any financial stuff. A couple of times when she was out of the office, some people dropped by and left checks for her."

"Did they ever pay in cash?"

She shook her head. "Not to me. No one paid with cash or a

credit card, at least not to me personally. Isobel collected when they were in her office. I know she took credit cards and checks, because she'd leave to go to the bank to make deposits sometimes."

"When they left checks with you, what were they for, do you know?"

"One of them had a notation on it. It was the name of the child they had adopted. At least, I thought they had adopted the baby, that the case was over, so why were they giving Isobel money?"

What I had been suspecting sounded likely to be true. Somehow, she was bleeding some people for money, though why, I didn't yet know. "She didn't require them to have their bill paid in full before she finalized the adoptions?"

"I thought she did. I thought when people came in here, they paid their fees up front. Sometimes I heard her on the phone telling someone that some things came up. They needed to send more money."

"Did you open the mail?"

She shook her head again. "I wasn't allowed to, except what looked like junk mail, or if something official came from a court or one of the clerks. Otherwise, I was instructed to put the mail on her desk for her to open."

"That included all her bills, as well?"

"Everything. I know there were envelopes from some of her clients."

"When those people gave you those checks, what were the amounts? I mean, were they for very much?"

"*Mucho* money. Thousands of dollars. I would just put the check on her desk. We never talked about it."

To me, that confirmed Isobel Oliver could have been getting more money from people than she should have. Enough to pay the mothers for the children? "How did the people act when they came by?"

"Okay, I guess. Some were friendly. One man, I remember, was angry, but he told me he wasn't angry at me, just the circumstances. I didn't know what that meant."

"You didn't ask?"

"I didn't ask. No way."

I chewed on my lower lip and contemplated the situation. What, if anything, was Isobel Oliver doing besides buying and selling babies? That was bad enough, but it sounded like she was up to something more. Jean didn't appear to know.

"Miss Davis, what should I do now that she's dead? She owes me my salary. How will I get paid?"

"That's a good question. The attorney I'm working for is going to ask a judge what the courts will do about Ms. Oliver's cases. I'm sure they'll have to appoint someone to wind things down. I'm not sure how that works. If I were a judge, I'd give that person the power to pay the bills. Your salary is a bill. So, if I were you, I'd keep working every day until I found out what was going to happen. And keep track of when you come and go."

She grimaced. "What if I never get paid?"

"I'll ask Ms. Wright, the attorney I work for, what she thinks and get back to you. I can't help but feel this office needs to remain open until everything is concluded. If not, what would the poor people do whose adoptions and other cases haven't been finalized?"

"I see what you mean. I don't know how many that is."

I licked my lips. My throat and mouth were dry. "Speaking of which, Jean, are all those files kept in the same place? Could you compile a list of them if you had to?"

"Sure, I guess."

"I wonder if you'd have a problem doing that for me?"

"I don't know. Would that be okay? I know they're confidential."

I had wondered whether she would pick up on that. "Yeah, that could be a problem. Okay, I have several questions for you. First, do you know whether Ms. Oliver placed any children last week?"

She shook her head. "Not that I know of. I didn't work up any petitions or anything."

So much for the Wite children. "Hey, I'm wondering, were there ever any children here, back in the nursery, when you were here?"

"Oh, sure. I don't know what you call it, a handover or something? But Isobel would come in with babies—little kids, sometimes, and then people would come get them. The new parents would come get them."

"Did that happen last week?"

"Not when I was here. Should it have?"

It sounded like she didn't know about the Wite babies, and I wasn't going to mention it. "I'm not sure. Okay, I'm wondering a couple of things. One, do you know if she had a babysitter who kids would be with before she brought them here?"

"I'm pretty sure there was somebody. There had to be, because she'd just show up with these kids. Not all the time, but occasionally. I always wondered where they had been before she got them."

"You never asked?"

"I didn't dare. She could be kind of scary."

"You don't know who would have been taking care of the kids before she brought them here?"

"No. Miss Davis, all this kind of stuff is why I was trying to find another job."

"I understand." I still thought an ad litem would have to know who that person was. And would the social worker who did the home study also have to know? I wasn't sure. "Would you be able to maybe give me the names and addresses of the lawyers who served as ad litems on her cases?"

"Hmm. I have the list the court is supposed to use on my computer, with the names and addresses. I'm not sure I should give you the names of the exact lawyers who have been on cases."

"Just the list would be helpful. I could contact them myself and see if they'd talk to me. That way, you wouldn't be placed in a bad position."

"Okay, yeah, I could do that. That's not confidential. I can print the list off my computer. Give me a few minutes."

207

"But you aren't comfortable with giving me a list of pending adoptions?"

She shook her head. "I'm sorry. I don't want to do anything that would cause me trouble in getting to be a licensed paralegal. Does that make sense?"

"Of course, no problem. While you're doing that, may I use the office restroom?"

"All the way down the hall, straight back." She turned to her computer and switched it on, which made me wonder what she'd been doing all day. Staring into space?

While I was really going to use the facilities, I took the opportunity to peek into each of the open doors on the way. One office, the first one, was quite opulent. Huge mahogany desk and credenza, Eames executive chair, and matching client chairs. Rows of books in tall bookcases. A variety of decorative items and oil paintings. No expense spared as far as I could see.

Another office was almost bare. Just a desk, a chair, client chairs, and a two-drawer file cabinet. Opposite it, a small kitchen with a table and chairs, refrigerator, microwave, and dishwasher. The third space down the row was the now-famous or infamous nursery. If I were ever to have children, which I wouldn't, they would be lucky to be raised in a place with such good quality baby furnishings and toys.

When I returned to the front of the office, Jean said, "Here's a list I printed out of the attorneys and their contact information." She handed me a manilla envelope.

"Jean, I want you to know how much I appreciate your cooperativeness. If it's okay with you, I'll speak with the attorney I'm working for to ask around about any open legal secretary or assistant positions. To put the word out for you."

"Could she call me a legal assistant?" She flashed another dimple-filled smile at me. "Thank you, Miss Davis. I'll take your advice, too, and keep coming in for at least this week or until I hear from someone who will tell me what I'm supposed to do."

"And when I talk to Gillian, I'll tell her your circumstances and see what she thinks can be done." I held out my hand again. This time she had a firm handshake. "Take care."

She nodded and came to the door, locking it behind me.

When I reached my SUV, I opened the envelope to see how long the list of attorneys was, so I'd be able to plot my time. If there were a lot of them, it could take me days to catch them in their offices and interview all of them. I was not happy to see quite a few pages. I thumbed through them, recognizing a few names of people we had served papers for. A couple of other names rang a bell, but I didn't recall at that moment from where. A separate list was behind the first one. That list contained the names, addresses, and contact information for Ms. Oliver's clients, the adoptive parents in pending cases.

# CHAPTER
# TWENTY-EIGHT

With the two crucial lists Jean had given me in hand, I swung by Gillian's office on my way back to my own. It was getting late, but I thought she'd be as excited about the information Jean had given me as I was. Unfortunately, her office was locked up tight. I didn't blame her one bit. I was pretty tired myself. It could wait a day.

Be that as it may, I drove back to my own office, where Margaret would be waiting. No way would she go home, not having heard what I'd discovered that day. I wanted to hear what she'd found as well.

When I drove by the front of the office on the way to park behind the building, there was a truck I didn't recognize parked smack dab in front of the sidewalk leading up to the door. A new client, maybe? Which got me to wondering whether there would be any time to work for a new client in the next few days, and secondly, did they have money to pay us? As always, we had bills to pay. We're holding our head above water, but sometimes just our noses, so we can breathe. Plus, the holidays were coming, and I liked to give "the girls" some kind of bonus. So far, each year they'd gotten something. Candy's Moped was parked in the back along with Margaret's car, so it was no surprise when I found both in the office.

When I entered through the back door, the aroma of something baking filled the air. I put my things on my desk before going into the kitchen, which was my usual practice, to get something to drink if I hadn't stopped for a bottle of water or tea somewhere. Lo and behold, a man sat at the table in a chair opposite from Margaret. Candy sat adjacent. Once I was in the kitchen, I identified the baking aroma. Chocolate chip cookies. Cookies? Not cake, the half-eaten wedding cake lay on the table, though it was destined for the trash bin that evening, even if no one but me knew that. Cookies, which indicated to me they were an offer of appeasement.

Margaret jumped up. She wore a nice pair of black slacks, a tan V-necked sweater over a black collared blouse, and some stacked heel shoes—something new for her. Candy had her usual Moped outfit, turtleneck sweater, jeans, and her pride-and-joy boots. The man, who had to be in his thirties, had white-blond hair in a crew cut, silvery blue eyes behind glasses, and a nice smile above a sweater over a turtleneck. I couldn't see below the table except for shoes, which appeared sensible.

"This is Barry," Margaret said, an expression on her face that begged me to be nice to the interloper.

I reached out to him. "Barry, nice to meet you."

He stood and shook my hand. I could see he was wearing a pair of dockers. The guy knew how to dress, unlike some she'd dragged in over the years.

"Glad to meet you, Ms. Davis." His handshake was warm and firm, his voice low and melodious. I could see why she was attracted to him.

"Mavis," I said, "if you please, Barry. And sit. What are y'all up to?" I wanted to get down to it with the girls, but not in front of Barry. I don't know how much Margaret shared with him, but he wasn't going to be privy to it in person. At least not from me. I opened the oven door and peeked in to see where the cookies were in the baking process.

"Mavis, if you'll sit down, I'll explain why Barry is here."

I was apprehensive but did as she asked. "Okay, but I really need to share a lot with y'all before you go home."

Margaret held up her hand. "Okay, but you've got to hear this."

"Yeah, Mavis, you won't believe what we've been doing."

"Lay it on me." I crossed my arms and waited for whatever wacky thing the girls had been up to that day.

"You know how you asked us to put stuff about the Wite twins on our social media?" Margaret asked.

"Yes, and y'all did that over the weekend, right?"

"Mavis, people have been calling like crazy," Candy said.

"Really?"

"So many calls that I asked Barry if he'd come over after work and help us return them this evening." Margaret glanced at Barry, who took her hand as it lay on the table.

"Really." I couldn't think of what else to say at that point.

"Really," they all said in unison.

"Some of them are crazy people," Margaret said. "I don't know, maybe I shouldn't have put my phone number on Nextdoor, but I did."

"I hate to tell you, when I went on there on Sunday afternoon, I put your number on Nextdoor, too, as well as the office number," I said.

"Well, that would explain people asking to speak to you. I didn't identify anyone but myself in what I put on there," Margaret said and glanced at Barry.

"I put my number and Margaret's and the office number," Candy said, leaning her elbows on the table.

"Barry," I said, "ordinarily I'd be upset that anyone in my office was sharing information about what we're working on without my consent, but it's a little too late for that. Suffice it to say, I appreciate your help."

"You're welcome," he said.

"So, Mavis, I printed out the written responses I received on the various Nextdoor and Facebook etcetera sites and recorded the phone numbers people left on the office answering machine." Margaret turned her attention toward Candy. "Candy printed out hers."

"And we have our own voicemails," Candy said, "so we started returning the calls. All three of us."

"And?"

"There are a lot of nutty people out there, Mavis," Candy said.

"No kidding. Any good results?"

"I've been making notes next to the printed messages," Barry said. "They've been returning their cell phone calls first. People have been reporting anyone in their neighborhood who has adopted a baby or any child."

"Nothing so far about twins," Candy said. "At least in my calls. I only have one or two left."

"So, there were a lot of them?"

"Well, they started coming in over the weekend after you told us to put that message out there. The calls continued today. Maybe some people don't look at their social media until they go back to work. So far on mine, there were a lot of nice people who said they'd be on the lookout."

"Mine, too," Candy said.

Barry nodded.

"But nothing concrete. Are there more still to be answered?"

"Yeah. But we also wanted to tell you what else we've been doing, if that's okay."

"Yeah, of course. But I could listen better if I had a nice warm cookie."

"They'll be ready in a few minutes." Margaret glanced at her watch.

She was wearing a new watch, which looked like those I'd been seeing a lot of in the past few years in ads. "Where did you get that?"

Margaret smiled at Barry. "Kind of an engagement gift from Barry."

Barry shrugged. "She wouldn't marry me the other day, so I thought we should have a long engagement. The ring is coming."

"Okay, y'all don't get all sappy on me. Barry, I'm suitably impressed."

"I was hoping you would be. I really care about this woman, and now that we've calmed down, I want things to go smoothly." His eyes widened with what I took to be hope.

Margaret's face grew red, and she stared at their clasped hands.

"Yeah, yeah, yeah. Like I said, don't get sappy." I couldn't help myself, I grinned at the two of them and caught Candy doing the same, her eyebrows raised in approval. "So, you first, Margaret."

"Well, in addition to all these calls we've been talking about, I did take care of other normal things including responding to calls for us to handle service, etcetera. Then I phoned the clerks in all the counties surrounding Harris County like you asked me to. Isobel Oliver has offices in two of them."

"Offices? So, she has law offices in three counties?"

"I looked her up, Mavis. She listed the offices on her website, so I went to Google Maps and zoomed in on them. They're little places like where you rent an office and the complex has one main person sort of directing traffic."

"Probably so she could meet clients there, I'm thinking."

"Yeah. Brazoria County and Montgomery County are where they're located. I talked to someone in each of the district clerks' offices. I was surprised they'd give me the information, but they did once I told them she was dead. One time I had to tell them she was murdered."

"They change their tone after that?"

Margaret gave a quiet little laugh. "Yeah. Of course, I didn't ask them any details about her, and that made it easier for them. I asked them if she practiced law in their county, particularly doing adoptions. Then I asked them if there were any that had not been finalized. And finally, I asked whether she'd filed anything late last week."

"Good going, Margaret. And what did you find out?"

"She has one pending in Montgomery County, nothing right now in Brazoria County, two in Galveston County, one in Waller County, and nothing in Liberty, Chambers, or Fort Bend Counties. They said she doesn't come to Liberty or Chambers."

Candy said, "She gets—got around."

"And what about filings last week?"

"None."

"Whew. Right now, we'll focus on Harris County and just proceed on the assumption that she hasn't yet filed anything on those twins. Unless you found that something was filed here last week, Candy?"

Candy rolled her eyes. "I haven't been able to get as much information as Margaret yet, but I have someone trying to get it for me. I did get some information late this afternoon. They emailed me that the procedure they follow is exactly as it's laid out in the family code and that one clerk and a backup handle those cases."

"Well, that's something. I did read the code over the weekend to get a better understanding of the process."

"Me too," Margaret said. "Complicated."

"Me too," Candy said, "and some of the articles on the Internet."

Barry said, "I didn't." Everyone laughed.

"I practically begged Gillian Wright to go see the friendliest judge and see if he or she would give her access to Ms. Oliver's files, the court files, to see what's been filed, what the orders say and all that. I've just been wondering whether Ms. Oliver, who was a terrible person, by the way, filed something prospectively for someone in hopes that Carmen Garcia would find her 'suitable' children soon."

"She'd have to make up facts," Candy said.

"She apparently had all kinds of—I don't know what to call it —scams going. Creating facts wouldn't be hard for her."

"No wonder someone killed her," Margaret said.

"I'm glad you didn't say Mr. Wite. Because I really believe he didn't do it. I think someone else, some other man, got so angry with her that he killed her with no advanced planning, if that makes sense. The janitor told me he heard arguments coming from her office more than once."

"That wouldn't be Dave Wite," Margaret said.

"Oh, I forgot," Candy said, "they also emailed me the list of lawyers who are ad litems on those cases."

I chuckled. "I got one, too, from Ms. Oliver's legal assistant."

"Gillian sent one over, too," Margaret said. "I printed it out."

We all laughed again.

"At least we won't need to make photocopies for each of us." I wasn't going to mention the adoptive parents' list in front of Barry. I didn't know him enough to trust him not to tell someone Jean gave me the list.

"I can compare them, make sure they're identical," Candy said. "Right now. Margaret, is your copy on your desk?"

"Mine's in an envelope in my bag." I remembered the other list. "Why don't I get it while you get the other two."

Margaret said, "While y'all run to do that, I'll get the cookies out of the oven."

Barry watched the three of us all run in different directions. From his expression, he appeared to be enjoying himself.

When we reconvened, Candy compared the three lists. "They're completely identical. I recognize some of the names of lawyers we've done business with on other types of cases."

"Okay, here's what I want y'all to do, at least Margaret and Candy, before you return any more of those calls you've received. You can continue to return those calls if you want, Barry. I don't know what you'd planned. This is awkward."

"I can do that," he said.

"So, what is it?" Margaret asked. She held a spatula and was removing cookies from the cookie sheet and placing them on a cooling rack.

I thought I would faint from the chocolate and sugary smell. I planned to ruin my dinner. "As soon as one's cool enough, could you hand a cookie over here?"

"God, Mavis, you're so impatient. Would you please tell me what you want me to do besides bake cookies?"

"I want you and Candy to call or email those lawyers and ask them if they have any idea where Ms. Oliver might have stashed the babies."

"Wow," Candy said.

"I can't think who else would know, except maybe the social worker. I haven't met her, or them, yet. There could be more than one. In fact, I need to identify who they are if we can't find the kids through the lawyers. I forgot to ask Ms. Oliver's assistant. I can call her back tomorrow."

"What if they know?"

"Then we find out if the babies are there and get the police and go get them. I'll touch base with Ben on exactly how we'd do that."

"Tomorrow soon enough?" Margaret laid the cookie sheet on top of the stove with the spatula.

"Yes. Try their office phones first and then their cells if they have one listed. Or you could email them tonight. Maybe they check their business emails, if they're separate from their personal ones. Y'all can divide the list in half."

"What are you going to be doing, Mavis?" Candy asked.

"I have a lead on some of the pending cases. I'm going to check them out." I wasn't going to say more than that in front of Barry. First thing the next morning, though, I planned to be at the door of the first set of adoptive parents on the list.

# CHAPTER
# TWENTY-NINE

Basically, I considered the task I had assigned myself to be a house-to-house search. I was going to try to set eyes on the children, find out the status of each case, find out if there was anything fishy about Ms. Oliver's dealings with the adoptive parents, and whether they knew where the child had been prior to their taking delivery, so to speak.

Tuesday morning, dressed in my best jean jacket, turtleneck sweater, and a pair of slacks, I headed out. I'd told the girls to let me know if they got any strange reactions from people they spoke with, and I would do the same. We'd check back with each other at lunch. With my list and my Google Maps printout in hand, and Siri on my phone, I found the first house.

Dennis and LaToya Coates lived in a mid-sized ranch style house in a middle-class neighborhood. When I arrived, there was a small blue sedan in the driveway with a car seat in the backseat. The yard was cut, and a few shrubs sat under the front windows. A Thanksgiving wreath still adorned the front door. I rang the bell and waited. A few moments later, a thirty-something fair-skinned black woman answered the door. She held a black child who looked like she was not quite a year.

Not to be presumptuous, but I suspected the twins weren't there. No matter. I identified myself, told her I was a private investigator working on the Oliver case, and asked if I could come inside.

She smiled and said, "I'm running a little late on my holiday decorating," and snatched the wreath off the door. "Come on in."

She led me to a tidy front living room and put the baby down on the carpet with a toy from the coffee table. "Now, what may I do for you, Miss Davis."

"You didn't flinch when I said I was working on the Oliver case. Do you know about Ms. Oliver?"

"Uh huh, yeah. Somebody killed her last week. Read it in the paper. So, you're looking for who did it?"

"Something like that. My client has been arrested for it, but we don't think he did it."

"We who?"

"His attorney and me."

"How can I help you?"

"As I understand it, Mrs. Coates, Ms. Oliver handled the adoption of little..."

"Cynthia."

"Little Cynthia. We have some questions about how she handled some of her adoption cases and wonder whether you would be willing to talk about how she treated your case."

"Sure. It was fine. We had heard about her, so we put in an application with her."

"Who did you hear about her from?"

"A woman who works at the car dealership where my husband works."

"You don't work, I take it? I mean, outside of the home."

"I'm planning on going back when Cyn is a year old."

"What do you do?"

"Used to sell cars, too, but when Dennis and I got the baby, I left that dealership. I have a job lined up at another one. The manager is friends with Dennis' manager."

"Okay, so here's what I'm wondering. Did you and Ms. Oliver get along okay? I mean, were there any problems with the adoption process?"

"It cost a lot of money. We had saved up and it took all our savings. But that's okay. We got just what we wanted. We can always get more money."

"Did you ever meet the birth mother?"

"We have an open adoption. We went to the hospital when she went into labor. The baby was given to us at the hospital. She signed the papers after a few days. It was easy, though with the social study and lawyers, like I said, it cost a lot of money."

"Was the total amount within the range she quoted y'all when you first met with her?"

"It was more, but not much more."

"But you're pleased with how things worked out? When I told you about Ms. Oliver a few minutes ago, you didn't appear to be upset at the idea that someone killed her."

"Miss Davis, she was a cold fish. She did a good job for us, but we didn't really like her, you know what I mean?"

"If you'd wanted to adopt another child, would you have gone through her agency?"

"We never wanted more than one."

"But if you had, would you?"

"If we couldn't get another agency to find a baby for us, but otherwise..." she shrugged.

I stood. "I'm assuming your case is finalized, right?"

"Oh, yeah. It has been for a long time."

"Did you know it doesn't appear the final order has been entered?"

"No way." Her body tensed. "Ms. Oliver gave us a copy for our records."

"I'm just telling you what's my understanding. Perhaps you should go to the courthouse and check it out."

"Thank you. I will. As soon as I can get a babysitter." She walked me to the door and let me out, shaking her head as she closed it.

I found no one at home at the second house and left my card with a notation on it asking them to call me.

No one was at home at the third house, either. I guessed people didn't always take a lot of time off after adopting a baby, though I had no clue how old either of the children would be or where in the process the cases were. The people could just be at the grocery store.

At the fourth house, a substantial home just on the fringes of the richest neighborhood in Houston, another thirty-something woman came to the door. This one was white, and her demeanor, though polite, gave me the impression she had a sense of entitlement. Again, I introduced myself. She didn't move from the entryway. At least not at first.

"I understand, Mrs. Miles...you are Mrs. Miles, correct?"

"Correct. Mrs. Wesley Miles. I'm wondering why a private investigator would be at my door."

"I'm getting to that. I'm investigating the Oliver case. Are you familiar with that, know what I'm talking about?"

"No. Don't believe I do. The only person I know named Oliver is Isobel Oliver, who is our attorney."

"May I come in, ma'am? I promise I'll take as little of your time as my business requires."

She looked over her shoulder, and at that point I heard a child crying. She said, "Okay, but I have to get Angela, my baby, up. She's finished her morning nap. Come in and close the door behind you."

"Yes, ma'am." I closed the door and followed her down the hall and up the stairs. Halfway up the stairs, she stopped and looked at me.

"I—I guess it's okay for you to come on up."

"Oh, I can wait downstairs. I wasn't sure what you wanted me to do."

"No, you're already here, so follow me." She led the way to the child's nursery, where a cherubic infant with fine red hairs standing up on her head was bawling. Her red face wasn't really tearful though she looked angry.

Mrs. Miles picked her up, and the baby stopped crying instantly. Mrs. Miles checked the child's diaper and changed her on a changing table that matched all the other baby furniture. She took off the little tee shirt the baby had been sleeping in and slipped a pink dress over the kid's head. "There, now." She kissed her on the cheek.

"Let's go back down, shall we?" She left the room, and I followed again.

"Just show me where you want me to go. I apologize for my bad timing."

'It's okay. Pretty much my life revolves around Angela now. There's always something to do regarding her care. Why don't you go into the den? I'll just warm up a bottle and be with you in two shakes." She turned the opposite way.

The den was about three times the size of Mrs. Coates', the previous mother I'd talked to, living room. A dark gray sectional sofa with a recliner at each end was centered in front of one of the biggest TVs I'd ever seen outside of an advertisement. I'd bet my retainer fee in the Wite case that Mr. Miles was a football fan in a big way. Maybe all the sports. The rest of the room paled in comparison to those hefty pieces of furniture—the coffee table, side tables, built in bookshelves with several group photographs prominently displayed, and a wet bar. I wasn't envious, but I did admire her furnishings. I was sure there was an equivalent room somewhere for Mrs. Miles to entertain in when Mr. Miles was otherwise tied up.

When Mrs. Miles returned, she had Angela cradled in her arms where the baby sucked at a bottle. I figured she was maybe six months old. Not that I'm any expert.

"Now, what's this about?" She settled in a chair opposite me.

"I guess you haven't heard the news about Ms. Oliver?"

She shook her head. "What about her?"

"Someone killed her last Friday."

Her eyes flared as she sprang to her feet, almost causing the baby to drop the bottle. "That can't be true. We were just in touch with her last week."

"I'm afraid it is true. The police report isn't back yet, but my guess is that someone strangled her."

She sat back down and pulled the baby closer. "But she's our adoption attorney. How are we going to finalize our adoption without an attorney?"

"Mrs. Miles, if I could be straight with you, Ms. Oliver was being investigated for some irregularities in her adoption practice. For example, she had someone working for her to procure children for adoption." That was about the nicest way I could think of to put it.

"Procure? That doesn't sound good."

"It wasn't. Let me ask you this, where did your baby come from? Did you meet the bio mother?"

"Angela was a foster child. A CPS baby. I'm not sure if there's a name for kids that are in the care of Children's Protective Services."

"You didn't meet the bio mother or father?"

"No. We read their pathetic histories."

She emphasized the word pathetic. "Well, it's good you got her that way. Some of the others...well, never mind. Let me ask you this, did you feel the fee she charged you was fair and reasonable?"

"Not really. It's not like we couldn't afford it, but it was more than we had thought it should be, considering that she didn't do the termination part, the state did. But we had been through in vitro several times and that's so expensive, we're just glad to finally get a baby." She kissed the top of Angela's head.

"And a very nice one with the loveliest hair."

Mrs. Miles chuckled. "You could be related with that red hair!"

"Maybe she's my sixth cousin or something." I laughed. "Anyway, let me ask you this, did Ms. Oliver quote you one fee and then later raise it for some reason?"

"Yes, she did. My husband was very angry about it. He felt she was taking advantage of us."

"In what way, if you don't mind telling me."

"We had Angela already for about three months before Ms. Oliver contacted us and apologized profusely but said she had somehow misquoted her fee, that we would have to give her several thousand dollars more before we could go to court and finalize the adoption."

"Did she say what it was that would cost more?"

"Not really. She said there were some bills that needed paying, some more paperwork that needed doing. We were scared because the way she phrased it, we thought she might come and get Angela if we didn't pay her."

That kind of behavior on the part of Isobel Oliver might very well be what got her killed. Someone lost his temper. "Y'all did pay her?"

"My husband took a check over there last week."

"When last week?"

She blinked several times. "You're not implying my husband—"

"No, no. Not at all, but he might be a witness if something was going on in her office that shouldn't have been."

Her forehead drew together in a frown. "Monday, I think."

"No worries. She was killed on Friday. What a mess this is. Well, let me just tell you this, Mrs. Miles, the court may appoint someone to take over Ms. Oliver's cases—to close her law practice, in fact, but that may take a while." I stood and walked to the door. Mrs. Miles followed. "My advice to you is that you and Mr. Miles find another family lawyer and ask her or him to immediately go down to the clerk's office to review your file. If everything's in order, you should be able to finalize your adoption."

"My husband is going to be so angry that we have to pay another lawyer."

"Can't be helped, but it shouldn't be much to conclude the case. And would you ask him to let me know if he observed anything odd when he was there last Monday? Anything, anything at all." I handed her a card and departed her house.

When I reached my car, I called and left a message for Gillian. "I'm pretty sure I know what got Isobel Oliver killed. Greed. Call me when you get a chance."

# CHAPTER

# THIRTY

T had worked up an appetite, driving around the city and talking to mothers, or at least knocking on doors. Thinking over what Mrs. Miles had told me made me wonder how many other people Isobel Oliver had treated that way, had somehow milked for money. The Miles family couldn't be the only one. The woman was buying and selling babies and extorting money from the adoptive parents. Those two things alone were enough to get a person killed.

I stopped at a very busy deli for a tuna salad sandwich with a diet drink and to speak with the girls to see how they were progressing with their phone calls. We were making progress, and though I knew time was of the essence, we were doing as much as we could. I wished I knew what the police were doing. I hadn't crossed paths with anyone working on the investigation. Wouldn't they have prioritized it?

"We've been hitting it hard," Candy said when she answered her cell phone. The office line was busy, and Margaret hadn't picked up her cell. "I've served a couple of people and called in-between."

"That's great. How are they responding?"

"The lawyers' secretaries I talked to said they'd give them the message. I talked to one lawyer who said he knew some of the others that did ad litem work and he'd tell them what was going on and give them your contact information."

"No replies to the emails? I was sure hoping we'd get some results. I find it hard to believe no one knows where the adoptees are before they're delivered. I'm afraid that sounds like delivering a package, but, well, that's kind of how they've been treated."

"Yeah. I'm headed to the clerk's office to see what my friend there says. I'll let you know if I hear anything."

Once that call disconnected, my cell rang. Margaret. "Hey, Margaret. So far, I haven't found the kids. What's going on with you?"

"There really are some crazy people on Nextdoor and Facebook. I'm kind of wishing we hadn't put that message out there. Now, some of the people are arguing with each other about adoption. Anyway, nothing from that end, and I've left messages for the lawyers on my list."

"I'm going back out there as soon as I finish my sandwich."

"Will you be back in the office this afternoon?"

"I don't know if I'll be back or not. Some people weren't home, but I was able to talk to some adoptive mothers. I'm thinking I'll aim for two more and leave my card at the ones who aren't home. If it doesn't get too late, I might swing by the first ones who weren't home and see if they've returned. That should take me a while. This is tiring stuff."

"Better you than me. I'm holding down the fort here."

"I know you are. Do me a favor, please. Call Connie Wite and bring her up to date on what we're doing. I don't want to get bogged down with a long conversation when I'm driving."

"Sure. I'll be here when you get back."

I'd tried to map out the route I would have to take so I wouldn't have to backtrack, but I wasn't completely successful. The first house I went to that afternoon was in the same neighborhood as the first one where no one was home.

The neighborhood was in an older part of a suburb of Houston, though many people considered it part of Houston. You could leave Houston and not even know you were in West University. Anyway, I drove past the million-dollar-and-up homes until I found the house I was looking for. To say I felt out of place even though I drove a relatively late model SUV, as compared with my classic Mustang, would be an understatement. I brushed off the arms of my jacket and pressed down the wrinkles in my slacks as I approached the house.

A middle-aged white woman, wearing an apron and with a dust cloth in her hand, answered the door. Over her shoulder, I could see gleaming wood floors and a wide staircase.

"Good afternoon, I'm looking for a Mrs. Jacobs. Would that be you?"

"Not by a long shot," the woman said with a small smile. "I'm the housekeeper. Can I tell her who wants her?" Her voice was gravelly like she was a smoker or getting over a cough. I hoped she didn't have Covid.

"Mavis Davis. I'm a private investigator. Could you tell her it's about Isobel Oliver, and I'd just like a few minutes of her time?"

"Why don't you come inside. I'll run and get her." She closed the door behind me, but I waited right next to it, afraid to venture into what might be out of bounds for a stranger.

A few moments later, the housekeeper returned. "Come with me." She beckoned, and I followed her into a sun porch, which could have been something out of a Better Homes and Gardens magazine: lots of healthy-looking potted plants, white wicker couch and several wicker chairs, dining table and six chairs, and so forth. But what had I expected in West University?

Anyway, a lovely woman with long black hair, hazel eyes, and olive skin came toward me. The aroma of her perfume smelled fresh like just-cut flowers. She wore what could have been a cashmere V-necked hot pink sweater over black corduroy slacks and ankle boots. A tiny gold chain with a tiny charm I couldn't make out encircled her neck. Gold bangles and a gold watch were on her right arm. The other, bare, but a wedding set with a diamond as big as my thumb-nail graced her left hand. Her well-manicured fingers clasped mine in a healthy grip.

"I'm Maria Jacobs," she said. "Won't you come in and have a seat?"

How welcoming was that? "Thanks so much." I did, on one of the overstuffed cushions on the white wicker rocker.

"Nora can get us something to drink. Would you like some coffee?"

"No, thank you. I'm good. But you go ahead."

"That's okay, Nora, I'll have mine after the baby wakes up from his nap."

Nora departed, leaving me alone with this beautiful, elegant woman. "Now, what's this about Isobel Oliver? I was disheartened to read that she had passed away. If you're asking about her, you prob-ably know we're adopting a baby."

"Yes, Mrs. Jacobs, I do. That's what it's about."

Her eyebrows shot up. "Oh dear. We discussed it and have an appointment with another lawyer to finish out our adoption. Is there something we should be concerned about?

"May I ask, what does your husband do?"

"He's a physician. Plastic surgery. And before you ask, I'm a lawyer. I used to do corporate law but took a leave of absence when we got Christopher."

"Which was when?"

"Umm, maybe seven months ago."

Seemed to me the adoption should have been finished by that point, but what did I know? I'd take a chance with this woman, since she had a legal background, and tell her what was going on. "Mrs. Jacobs, you did see that Ms. Oliver's death wasn't an accident. She was killed by someone."

"The newspaper did say they had a suspect in custody."

"Yes, and to be frank with you, I work for the lawyer who will be defending the suspect, but we're investigating an additional matter."

"Should I be talking to you?"

"I don't see why not, if you and your husband are in no way involved with Ms. Oliver's death."

Her face blanched. "We're not, believe me."

"Okay, well then, let me tell you what I'm up to. I'm trying to find a set of twins. We have reason to believe Ms. Oliver was involved in their kidnapping."

She gasped, her hand going to her chest. "There was something in the paper about that this morning, but I didn't see it was connected."

"The suspect in the murder case is the father of the missing children."

"He killed her because she took his kids?"

"Allegedly killed her. He didn't do it, and we're looking into that, but what we're first and foremost looking into is the missing children. They're only six weeks old."

"Oh my God. That poor mother."

"I know. Here's what I want to ask you about. Do you know who the bio mother of your baby is?"

"No. Neither of us wanted an open adoption, so the way Ms. Oliver handled our case was to do the termination separately."

"Do you know how Ms. Oliver came to know about the baby being available for adoption?"

"We assumed the mother contacted Ms. Oliver's agency. There's a website and, as I understand it, a yellow page ad in the past, though I don't know if with the Internet she kept that up."

"Is it safe to assume she charged you and your husband a great deal of money to handle this adoption?"

"Let me just say upwards of twenty-five thousand."

My sphincter muscles flexed. "Did you and your husband specify the age, sex, and race of the child you wanted when you met with Ms. Oliver at her agency?"

"Yes, we told her we wanted a baby. As close to newborn as she could find but not an open adoption. We didn't want to go to the hospital when the birth mother had our baby or anything."

"Did she ask you all to pay the medical fees for the birth mother?"

She nodded. "Yes. In addition to the agency fee, which I guess was her fee. The court costs were additional, also, but they're not much. The ad litem fees weren't either, but were more than I remembered them being when I did an internship with an attorney who handled some family law cases."

So that I wouldn't be confused, I asked, "To be clear, there was her fee, the ad litem's fee, the court costs, and the medical bills, right?

"Right. I believe that's all."

"Let me ask you this, when your baby was born, did Ms. Oliver take custody of the child until she could give the child to you?"

"She did. She said she didn't want to give us Christopher until the birth mother had signed the relinquishment, because she could change her mind and that would be painful for everyone."

"That's understandable. Do you know where the baby stayed until you got him?"

She rubbed her lips together, her hair swinging when she shook her head. "We never asked. She had told us she had a qualified caregiver." She eyed me for a few moments before she said, "You're thinking those missing twin babies might be with that caregiver, aren't you?"

"I sure am."

"I think you're probably right. She probably has used this person many times over the years. She was in business for a long time."

"Yes. Think back. Can you tell me anything about where the baby was?"

She rested her chin upon her fist for a few moments. "He was far enough away that she said it would take her an afternoon to go out there and back."

"So, not in Houston."

"Couldn't be. I wish I could help you, Miss Davis. That's so sad about those twins. If the caregiver doesn't know anything about who they are and what happened to Ms. Oliver, no telling what will happen to them."

I didn't think she knew anything else that might be of help. I didn't want to tell her that her baby may have come from the county jail. I had no way of knowing that. The medical bills they had given Ms. Oliver could very possibly have gone into Ms. Oliver's pocket, but I couldn't concern myself with that. "One more thing I just thought of. The ad litem who is on the adoption case, is that the same person who was appointed on the termination?"

"You're thinking he might know where she places the babies before they're placed with the adoptive parents, aren't you?"

"I am. Wouldn't you think they'd go out and see the baby before the termination? Even if the baby can't talk or anything, I would think the lawyer would want to make sure the baby was fine."

"I can give you his name and address," Mrs. Jacobs said.

"I have a list of who the court appoints in my bag. I'll just get it out and you can tell me which one it is. I already have my staff calling all of them and asking questions." I fumbled with the tote bag I was carrying that day until I found the list, which was already looking a little shopworn.

Mrs. Jacobs scanned it. Almost at the end was their ad litem. "He's a nice guy. I'm sure he'd tell you anything he knows."

I made a note. "We'll be asking. Well, that's all I have for now."

"Would you like to see Christopher before you leave? It's about time for him to wake up from his nap."

I nodded. "Sure would. I love babies." Well, that wasn't a complete lie. I just didn't want any. I followed her up the stairs and into a delightfully decorated nursery that was blue everything. She led me to the crib and a baby whose skin so closely matched hers that he could have been her biological child.

# CHAPTER
# THIRTY-ONE

After zig-zagging my way across Houston the rest of the afternoon and having no success in finding anyone home, I landed back at my office a little after five. Again, a strange vehicle had parked right in front, a big SUV. Of course, it's a public street, and someone could have gone shopping within a few blocks of us. Still, being the time of day it was, I would have been surprised.

I was even more surprised when I entered through the back door and though I didn't smell cookies baking, which told me Margaret didn't think she was guilty of anything, I did hear voices, including an unrecognizable male voice. After leaving my tote on my desk and dropping my purse in the bottom desk drawer where I kept it, I followed the voice to the front of the office. A man who was not Barry, and was way too old for Candy, sat in one of our reception area chairs. Margaret perched on the edge of her chair behind her desk. Candy sprawled in one of the other reception chairs.

The man, who was well over six feet tall with hair the color of the night, high cheekbones, and sea green eyes, leaped to his feet when I entered. He was dressed in a dark suit with a light blue button-down shirt and a tie loosened at the neck. A rain jacket laid over the arm of the chair next to him. He came forward and held out his hand. "Richard Alan Dunn."

I'd heard of women being called eye or arm candy. I don't know what men who were equally attractive were called, but this guy definitely would qualify. "Mavis Davis." His large hand would have dwarfed mine if I'd been a smaller woman. As it was, his cool, soft mitt did such a good job of covering mine I wouldn't have minded lingering.

"He's an ad litem, Mavis," Candy said. She had bounced out of her chair at the same time as Mr. Dunn. "He's on the list. He heard about what we're doing."

"I think he's old enough to speak for himself," I said, remembering Ben and pulling my hand away. "I take it what she says is correct?"

"Yes, ma'am. The word around the family courts is you're trying to find out who Ms. Oliver would have left some children with?"

"He's quite far down my half of the list, Mavis," Margaret said. "I wasn't far from his name, though I think I did email him..."

"That's fine, Margaret. Mr. Dunn, you must have some information, or you wouldn't be here. Would you like to come into my office?" I led the way down the hall. "Would you like something to drink? Coffee or a glass of water? We may have a soft drink in the refrigerator."

"No, ma'am. I'm fine."

"It's Mavis. I think we're about the same age, thirties, right?"

"Yes."

We both took chairs. Candy had followed and stood in the doorway. "We're good, Candy." I gave her a look that I hoped communicated for her to leave us alone.

"I'll be in my office if you need me, Mavis," she said, flashing her eyes. "Nice to meet you, Mr. Dunn."

"Same, Candy." He smiled at her departing back. To me, he said, "I've seen her around the clerk's offices. Hard not to remember that multi-colored hair."

"She's worked for us for several years. Now that she's graduated from high school, she's full time. She's also graduated to serving most of the documents we're hired to serve. I don't think you're one of the lawyers who uses us, are you?"

"Not yet. Maybe I will now."

"That would be nice. Mr. Dunn, I take it you worked with Ms. Oliver on some adoptions?"

"I did. And over the years, there have been a few cases where I've had to go to a third party's home to see the child, the baby, or toddler, the subject of the suit."

I leaned forward, fisting my hands, anxious to hear what he'd say next. Melodramatically, I was thinking, *did I dare hope*? "You're going to tell me you have some idea where Ms. Oliver may have left the children we're searching for?"

"Okay, well, as I understand it, she somehow took possession of a set of twins. The ones the newspaper wrote about? Babies?"

I had no comment on the *took possession of* statement. "Right. Could you possibly know where they are?"

"I know where they might be. I haven't called the woman or anything. I didn't want to alert her. I mean, she's always seemed like a nice lady, but I don't know what she might do if she thought she could be in some trouble."

"My stomach is flip-flopping here, Mr. Dunn."

"Richard, please. I could go out there and see if she has them. I don't want to say anything to the police in case I'm wrong. I wouldn't want cops showing up to this woman's house and scaring the heck out of her."

"Yeah, we've heard of too many instances where that didn't end well." I stared at him for a minute, which was easy to do, the silence broken only by the murmurs of voices coming from the front of the office. Rain began to tap dance on our roof.

"Do you think I should go out there or what?"

He had crossed his legs, one ankle resting on the other knee. Now he switched legs and gripped his kneecap. I guessed the scenario probably made him nervous, too. Who in their right mind would want to be involved in a kidnapping and murder case?

I scratched behind my left ear. Then I scratched behind my other ear. "I'm thinking I should go out there. Could you give me the address?" I would drive out there no matter how late or how dark it was outside if I could get Connie and Dave's babies back for them.

"The woman lives outside of Liberty, in the country."

"Ugh. Not exactly the armpit of Texas, but a close second. I haven't been out there in, like, forever. Maybe I could take Candy with me for company. If the kids are there, I could call the police. You wouldn't have to be involved if that's what you're concerned about."

He was grim-faced. "I'm not really worried about that. I had nothing to do with how they got there, if that's where they are."

No one had said he did... "Would you want to be out there if that's where they are? I mean, do you want to go out there? Candy and I could follow you in my vehicle so once we recovered them, if we did, you could go home."

"I don't know... It'll be complicated. Social services will have to be called in addition to the police. It could take all night."

"Well, not all night, but several hours, especially with Liberty being an hour or so from here and rush hour traffic still going on. So, yeah, we would be a while."

"I want to help," he said. "Let me call my wife, and then you and I can come up with a definite plan. Do you mind?"

"I'll leave you in here for a minute. I'm going to call my, uh, boyfriend. Be back in a few minutes." I took my cell and walked into the kitchen. Candy sat in the chair nearest the hall. I was sure she had been trying to hear what was being said. I held up one finger and then used it to call Ben.

"What's up?" he said. "Are we still on for tonight?"

"No, listen. There's a lawyer here who thinks he may know where the twins are."

"No kidding, really? Where does he think they are? Is he listening to this call? Do you think he was involved in the kidnapping? Should I send a car to your office?"

"Hold on, Ben, will you?" I shook my head at Candy and rolled my eyes. She laughed. "Let's see. Liberty. No. No. And no. But here's what I'm thinking."

"Uh oh." I could imagine the expression on his face matching his 'uh oh.'"

"Come on, now. The house is out in the country somewhere. He knows where. He's been there. I'm thinking I'll go with him and take Candy." Candy's head bobbed up and down.

"You think it's safe to go with him? Do you want me to contact the authorities out there and have them meet you?"

"No. Wait. I'm still sorting this out in my mind. We could follow him, Candy and me, but I don't see why we can't just ride with him. If it's his car parked out front, then it's big enough. By the way, his name is Richard Dunn. And he's on our list of court authorized lawyers, so we know he's real."

"All right. How does he know they're there?"

"He doesn't, but he knows Ms. Oliver has had this woman take care of children before. That's why we're thinking we don't want to just send cops out there. Could be they're someplace else, and the poor woman could have a heart attack, if some cop didn't shoot her."

"Not funny," Ben said, his voice taking on his reprimanding tone.

"I know. I'm dead serious. Richard said, and I think he's right, we don't want to call her in advance in case she's somehow part of what's been going on. Like a criminal part. Who knows what would happen to the twins."

"What's your plan? I know you have a plan."

"Okay. Candy and I will ride with Richard if it's okay with him. When we get there, since the woman's met Richard before, he'll knock on the door. I'll be right behind him." Candy was motioning that she'd be right there, too, but I waved her away. "Then we'll go inside and if the kids are there, we'll explain to her what's going on. You know, she may not even know Ms. Oliver is dead."

"And if they're there, will you call me and let me know? I can contact the Liberty County welfare people."

"Not the police, if they have a police department? I know the town is small. And I guess your department hasn't called the FBI in yet?" Most police departments hesitated to get the FBI involved.

"No. If the house is out in the country, it might not be in the city limits of the town of Liberty, so the sheriff will have jurisdiction. And no, no FBI."

"Candy and I could do that, ride with Richard and call you if we find the kids. I'm guessing you might know some officials in that county?"

"You'd be guessing right. If they're there and the sheriff sends people out, they'll contact social services for that county or CPS, whatever exists there. And I hate to tell you, but they won't give the children to Mrs. Wite until they've been positively identified and checked over and so on."

"I'm not even telling Mrs. Wite there's a possibility we've found them. Just in case."

"Good thinking. I hope I hear from you."

"Well, if you never hear from me again, you know you can still find me, or at least my phone, with the tracker."

"Quit joking, Mavis. Do you feel like you're in danger from this guy? If so, don't go with him. We can call over there and have them do a welfare check."

"It's fine. I'll keep you posted on what's going on." I clicked off and slipped my cell phone into my jacket pocket. "You don't have a class tonight, Candy, right?"

"Nope! This is exciting! I'm going to move my Moped close to the back stairs and chain it up. I'll get my stuff and come out front."

"Good idea." I went back into my office and stood in the doorway.

Richard Dunn said, "Everything's a go on my end. My wife wasn't especially happy, but I've worked long hours before, so she's kind of used to it."

"Candy and I'll ride with you, okay? What kind of car do you have? Is that big vehicle parked outside yours?"

"A 4Runner. Plenty of room. Would that other lady—Margaret—want to come, too?"

"That's overkill, don't you think? She's going to be disappointed when I tell her what we're doing. Be right back."

I walked up to the front of the office and explained what was happening to Margaret. Surprisingly, she was okay. She and Barry had plans anyway. I sent Richard outside, grabbed my purse, bolted the back door when Candy returned, and we followed him out.

# CHAPTER

# THIRTY-TWO

Candy climbed into the smooth, beige-colored leather back seat, while Mavis took the front passenger seat, in Richard Dunn's 4Runner. They quickly buckled up, and he pulled out into Houston traffic, headed East. Rain drizzled on the windshield. He turned off the radio and turned on the heater.

"Hey, you warm enough back there, Candy?" Richard asked over his shoulder.

"Fine, thank you." She put her backpack between herself and the heavy-duty, black plastic base for an infant seat that was latched in behind the driver's side. She and Mavis made eye contact. Mavis' eyes cut over to the seat base. Richard hadn't mentioned that he had a little child, but then they didn't really know him.

A tiny tan-colored bear with embroidered eyes, nose, and mouth was in the base. Candy picked it up. It was soft and spongy and squealed when she squeezed the tummy. Mavis glanced at her again.

Richard and Mavis settled into polite conversation. Candy called her mother and told her where she was. Next, she texted Shaun.

*Hey, you won't believe this. We may find the babies tonight.*

Shaun texted back a thumbs up emoji. *I'm in class. TTYL*

Candy sat back and listened to Mavis talk to the lawyer. She asked him questions, like how many years he'd been practicing law, where had he gone to law school, did he do other kinds of cases besides family law?

Candy watched the lights whiz by out the window. Her chest had a fizzy kind of feeling in it, excitement filled her up. She was happy Mavis let her come with them.

Richard asked Mavis whether she'd always wanted to do investigative work. She explained how she used to be a social worker but got fed up with the bureaucracy and wanted to work for herself, so she opened her office a few years back. Then she talked about how Margaret and she had been friends when they were growing up.

Candy listened to their conversation, the rain on the windows, the hiss of the water under the tires, and drifted off to sleep. When she awoke, they were stopped parallel to the front porch of a wood-framed farmhouse-style home. A single bulb burned next to the door. The house looked like a face, with a window on each side of the door, like eyes, the door being the nose, and the porch being the mouth. Mavis had her hand on Candy's knee and was shaking it.

"Candy, are you awake? We're here."

Richard switched off the headlights and turned to Mavis. "How do you want to do this?"

The rain had stopped, but the wooden porch glistened and reflected the light. A brisk wind blew a wooden rocker backward and forward. To the left of the house sat a one car garage with an old Chevy two-tone crew cab truck like something out of an old TV show. A curtain moved in one of the front windows.

"I'll go up with you," Mavis said. "Candy, stay here. We don't know what we're going to find." Eyebrows raised, her eyes went to Richard. "I think we should be safe."

"Then why can't I come?" If Mavis wasn't going to let her come, she might as well have gone home.

Mavis gave her the side-eye. "Keep your cell phone out in case you need to call for help for us."

Richard gave a small smile and looked through the windshield. "Let's go. Her name is Janice Weaver. I'll introduce you, Mavis. It really should be fine."

They exited the 4Runner, closing their doors gently behind them. Candy opened her door and got out, standing behind it where she could see the action. Richard had parked close to the house, in the yard. It wasn't like the house was in the suburbs, and he had parked on the lawn. There were no houses on either side, just trees, grass, and a small flower bed below the porch.

I GLANCED over my shoulder at Candy as we approached the door, hoping she'd stay put. Richard knocked, and a short, gray-haired woman answered the door, a whoosh of warm air enveloping us.

"Hey, I remember you, Mr. Dunn. Ms. Oliver didn't tell me you were coming." She looked at me, clearly wondering who I was.

Richard said, "Ms. Weaver, this is a private detective, Mavis Davis."

I held out my hand, and she took it. Her hand was dry and wrinkled but soft. "Nice to meet you," I said. "Richard and I have some things to discuss with you."

Her smile faded as her face transformed into a frown. "That doesn't sound good."

"May we come in?" Richard asked.

The woman stood back and let us pass, closing the door behind us. An old person smell, together with a boiled cabbage aroma, threatened to overwhelm me. Just like what I'd smelled at my grandmother's when I was small. The front room, a small living area, reminded me of what my grandmother's house had been like, too.

"Why don't you sit down and tell me what's happening?"

Richard and I looked at each other. He knew her. I didn't. I'd let him break the news. We both perched on the edge of her well-worn easy chairs.

"Unfortunately, I have some bad news about Ms. Oliver."

Ms. Weaver's eyes flickered between us. "Don't tell me something's happened to her."

"Yes, ma'am," I said.

Richard said, "She passed away a few days ago. No one told you?"

Ms. Weaver's hands flew to her cheeks as she sucked in a deep breath, and her eyes flared wide. "Oh my God!" She shook her head. "No. No. I just saw her a few days ago." Her eyes welled up with tears.

We sat for a few moments before Richard continued. "She was—uh—found dead in her office last Friday."

I couldn't stand it. I piped up. "You saw her last week? When was that?"

Ms. Weaver reached for a tissue from a box on the scarred coffee table in front of the sofa. She dabbed her face. "Wednesday night late?"

Sounded like she was asking us, but that would have been the correct time, unless Ms. Oliver had kept the babies overnight someplace else. Like maybe in the nursery in her office? That raised other questions, but we could figure out all that later.

"Which leads us to the second reason why we're here, after informing you of Ms. Oliver's passing. Did she or someone bring you twin babies to care for?"

Ms. Weaver reared back. She whispered, "Yes. They're asleep in the back."

My body responded with an adrenaline rush. I jumped up. "May we see them?"

Ms. Weaver looked at Richard as if for permission.

Richard stood, also. "Will you take us to them?"

She rose and wobbled on her feet as she led us down a short hallway, turning on lights as she went. The small room she led us to held two sleeping babies, one in each baby bed. The tiny blond things lay peacefully, one with a thumb in its mouth. I tiptoed to the beds and peeked at them closer. Richard was right behind me. If I'd been a crying-type of person, I would have burst into tears.

CANDY HAD PLOPPED BACK DOWN in the backseat, closing the door behind her to keep out the cold. It didn't seem fair that she should ride all the way out there and be stuck in the truck, not knowing what was going on. She pulled out her cell phone and checked texts. Nothing from Shaun. She knew he had a six-to-nine class but thought maybe he'd text her during their break.

After about ten minutes, Mavis opened the front door and called to Candy, waving her in. Candy jumped out of the truck and ran through the wet, short weeds up onto the porch. "What's going on?"

"The twins are here," Mavis said.

"Holy sh—heck! My heart is beating so hard, Mavis. I can't believe it."

"Come inside." Mavis held the door for her.

"Hello," she said to a tiny old woman. Candy's nose cringed from the smell of the house, an ancient wood, ancient person smell. She glanced around the room for the babies, but of course they'd be in another room. She stood in a small room with a sofa, a couple of easy chairs, and a battered coffee table. That lawyer must not have paid the old lady very well.

"Hello, young lady. I'm Mrs. Weaver. I didn't want you to have to wait outside." She took Candy's arm and walked with her to the sofa, sitting down and patting the seat next to her. "I understand you're Miss Davis' assistant."

Candy glanced at Mavis. "Yes, ma'am. I've been working for her for a couple of years, since I was in high school. Is it true the little twin babies are here with you?"

"Yes, they are. Mr. Dunn and Miss Davis have explained what happened to Ms. Oliver, and why y'all are here. An awful thing. Just terrible. I didn't know. Of course, Ms. Oliver didn't tell me anything about the children, just that they would be with me for a few days to a week or so."

"Can I see them?" Candy asked. "Do you have a nursery?"

Mrs. Weaver stood and scooted around the coffee table. "Of sorts."

Mavis said, "I've already been in there. So's Richard. It's definitely them."

Candy followed the old lady down a short hall and into a room no larger than ten by ten. Two baby beds, an old play pen with a thin baby sheet covering the bottom of it and a rattle lying inside, a bassinet, a changing table, a four-drawer dresser, and a glider were crammed inside. A small lamp on the dresser illuminated the room. The old person smell had turned into a sweet, baby smell.

In each bed lay a small blond bundle, diapered and wearing a nightie, a light blanket draped across its body. Candy turned to Mavis, who stood behind her. "They look just like you said they would."

Mrs. Weaver said, "I was told their names were Fred and Frederika. No kind of names for babies these days. At least not any I hear on my television shows." She shrugged and sighed. "They are sweet little things."

Mavis said, "Let's go back out into the living room. The sheriff is sending out a slew of people, deputies and social workers."

The three of them stepped back into the living room where Richard sat in an easy chair. He stood when they entered. "I guess we just wait now."

"I can't stand it. I'm calling Connie Wite. Then Margaret. Then Gillian Wright. Then Angela Strickmeier." She turned to Richard, looking at him as though they were old friends. "You probably know Gillian. Angela is a supervisor at CPS."

Mrs. Weaver said, "Why don't I make a pot of coffee? I think it's going to be a while."

"Black, please," Richard said.

"Tea for me, if you have it," Mavis said. "I'm going out on the porch to make those calls."

"I don't understand. How does the sheriff of this county know to come out here?" Candy asked.

"Oh, I called Ben, and he knows people here. He called them and called me back. That's kind of what we were doing before you came inside."

"I'm just going to have a seat and call my wife. I want to tell her what's going on and give her an ETA for me tonight."

Mavis went out on the porch, a cold gust of air blowing in as she did so. Candy sat on a chair and looked around the room at some books and framed photographs on bookshelves, a stack of magazines, an open book facedown, a glass of water on an end table, and some inexpensive pictures on the walls. She felt like it was Christmas morning, and she had wonderful gifts under a beautiful tree. If this was how it felt to be an investigator or a social worker, she wanted to be one. She and Mavis had shared a few adventures since Candy began working there half a day, but none of them were happy like this one.

Mavis' voice rose and fell from outside. Richard spoke in a low tone to his wife. Candy checked the time on her phone. Could it be nine already? She texted Shaun an emoji with a party hat on its head:

*We did find the twins! Everyone's ok.*

Shaun texted back fireworks: *Very cool.*

Candy: *Just wanted to share the news.*

Shaun: *Celebrate this weekend?*

*Yes.* She took a risk and added a heart. *TTYL*

Richard scrolled through his phone, reading messages. Candy looked at Instagram. Mavis' voice continued its ups and downs.

Mrs. Weaver carried in an old, scarred tray that looked like a school lunch tray. On it were two cups of coffee and two cups with teabags hanging out of them. She set the tray on the coffee table. "You didn't say, young lady, so I brought you tea, also."

Candy nodded. "Thanks." She went out on the porch, holding the door open while she said, "Your tea's ready." Mavis nodded and held up a finger.

Richard gripped a coffee cup, as did Mrs. Weaver, who sat on the sofa again. Candy picked up one of the cups of tea and sat back down.

Mavis came inside. "The sheriff's deputies are arriving. I saw several sets of lights." She took a cup of tea and sat next to Mrs. Weaver. "Thank you for being so hospitable."

For a few moments, all four of them sipped and stared into space. Then Mavis said, "Angela Strickmeyer is going to pass the word along that Harris County CPS and Liberty need to get together tomorrow to get the baby issue settled and then they'll go back home to their mother."

Candy said, "Well, what did Connie Wite say?"

Mavis laughed. "Oh. I forgot. I called her first. She screamed and cried and laughed." A tear rolled down Mavis' cheek. Candy had never seen Mavis cry before. "I told her I thought she'd have them back by tomorrow night. I hope so. Then I called Gillian Wright."

"What'd Ms. Wright say?" Candy took a sip of her tea and set it on the tray. She wasn't a big tea drinker, but a few swallows tasted good.

"Three things," Mavis said, rising as the first set of headlights swept across the front of the house. "Finding the kids is wonderful news. She's going to kill me because the judge she talked to said he was going to appoint her to wind down Ms. Oliver's law practice, even though she told the judge it would be a conflict because of the criminal case. Third, she said for me to get out there tomorrow, go interview the people in Ms. Oliver's office building, and find out if anyone saw anyone who could have killed Ms. Oliver." She gulped her tea and fanned her mouth. Beckoning at Richard, the two of them went out on the porch to meet the authorities.

Candy stayed where she was, feeling awkward, but glad Mavis had come and gotten her so she could be in on at least a small part of the action. She and Mrs. Weaver stared at each other over their cups and didn't talk, just listened to the activity out in the yard.

# CHAPTER
# THIRTY-THREE

I woke up Wednesday morning, gasping for air. I had dreamed I was drowning, sinking to the bottom of the ocean floor, and trying to pull myself up to the surface.

I was alone. We had gotten back to town so late that Ben had gone home to his apartment, which was okay by me. More than a few nights in a row with company in my house was too much for me anyway. I often liked my solitude.

The night before, after we made statements, the social workers took the twins, and we had thanked Mrs. Weaver and left, Richard drove us back to the office. It was so late, I followed Candy to her house. I didn't like the idea of her driving her Moped through the Houston streets in the middle of the night alone. Then I went home, showered to get the stress sweat off my body, and fell into bed.

Now, I crawled out of bed and stretched, cleaned up enough to pull on running clothes, and drank a glass of water. I took off jogging. I needed fresh air, even cold and humid, to clear my head and energize my body. I had to plan how to find Ms. Oliver's killer. I'm not a runner, by any means. I'm a jogger. Sometimes a walker.

Sometimes a jogger and a walker, depending on how many days I've been a slacker.

By the time I returned home, an idea nagged at me, an inkling I wanted to follow up on without too much delay. My stomach, though, raged inside. We'd never stopped for a meal the night before. I hoped Candy wasn't upset with me about it. The thought had never crossed my mind. Putting the kettle and a pot of water on to boil, I ran to the shower to wash my hair and rinse off. I'd come up with some ideas of what I needed to do and who I needed to see to work toward getting Dave Wite off the hook.

Two soft boiled eggs with buttered toast and two cups of tea later, I was in my SUV. I'd promised Gillian I'd meet her at Ms. Oliver's office to, among other things, introduce her to Jean. In spite of Gillian being miffed about the judge making an order for her to dismantle or liquidate or whatever they were calling Oliver's law practice takedown, the assignment was fortuitous for Jean.

As for me, I had to interview all of the tenants of that office building. I drove around the block to see whether there was another entrance to the building and found one off to the side at the back of the building, almost behind the dumpster. That would be one explanation of how the killer had made an exit without passing Dave as he entered, or without people on the street seeing him depart. Not that I thought that was necessarily what happened.

For the third time, I parked along the side of the building. When I entered, I studied the directory of tenants and gave some thought to how I'd proceed. Walking around the corner, I could see through the glass panel that Gillian had already arrived. She was wearing black jeans and a sweater with a jacket over it. Obviously not planning to go to court.

"Good morning," I said when I swung through the door.

"Hi Mavis," Jean said almost shyly. She was behind her desk with her sleeves pushed up. The pen in her hand began tapping on the desk pad. She may have been afraid I'd told Gillian about that list of names of parents in pending adoptions.

I subtly shook my head and grinned at Gillian. "You want to bawl me out again?"

She gave me the stink eye. "No, but I'm going to figure out some way for you to pay for this situation you've gotten me into. The judge hasn't said how I'm going to get paid for the work I'm going to do."

I shook my head. "I really am sorry. I know I had suggested it to you jokingly, but I never thought a judge might really appoint you. You're defending Dave Wite for heaven's sake."

"That's what I told the judge. He asked me if I thought Dave was guilty, as if I could even really give him my opinion of that. Of course, I said no. Then the judge said, 'Well then, no conflict. All you have to do is get him off, find out who really killed her...'" Gillian flinched and glanced at Jean, to which Jean responded with a shrug. "Well, you see how it was. What could I do?"

"I'm not a lawyer, but even I can think of how you can get paid. Out of her estate. With all the big fees she was charging and all the people I suspect she was extorting money from, she must have money socked away someplace."

Jean said, "I'm not sure she had any relatives, Ms. Wright. No one ever came to see her. I don't think she was ever married or had kids. She never mentioned any family."

"We'll just have to see who comes forward. Huh. I'm wondering whether the probate judge will appoint me to handle her estate. That's how I can get paid, all right. Okay. I don't want to be accused of being an ambulance chaser, but I'm going to pay a visit on a probate judge today."

"So, I'm forgiven?" I engaged my best smirk.

"I'm reserving judgment on that. Now go away, go talk to the tenants in this building, or something, and let us get organized."

I looked at Jean. "Excuse us for a minute, Jean." I pulled on Gillian's sleeve and led her to Isobel's office, where I closed the door.

"What now?"

I twirled my keyring around my finger. "I have an idea. My first interview is going to be with Richard Alan Dunn."

"The attorney you were with last night when y'all got the twins back?"

I nodded. "Gillian, I thought I recognized his name. I came here directly, didn't go by my office and get the tote bag I've been filling up with documents and notes about this case. I left it at the office last night when we got back. I checked the building directory from the picture I had on my phone. Richard Alan Dunn's law office is upstairs on the second floor overlooking the atrium and this office."

She took a step back. "Do you have any reason to think he might have killed her?"

My eyes met hers as I gave some thought about what to say. I didn't want to tell her that Jean had given me the list of adoptive parents with pending cases. All the evening before, I kept thinking Richard's name was familiar but couldn't think why. When I was jogging, I thought I remembered his office was in the same building. Then, I remembered seeing the base of an infant seat in the backseat of his 4Runner. I didn't want to suspect him of any wrongdoing. I really liked him. He seemed like a good guy. But then I began to recall the names on the list Jean had given me. I still wasn't sure, but I thought Richard's name, as well as that of his wife, was on that list.

"It's odd that he has an office in this building, don't you think? He obviously knew Isobel Oliver, because he was an ad litem on more than one of her cases. But it's even odder that he would know where the twins were. I mean, it just feels off that he knew that."

She said, "What are you going to do?"

"I'm going upstairs to talk to him."

"That could be dangerous."

"Well, I have an idea. Before I go up there, I'm going to find that maintenance man who heard the arguing in her office last week. I'll ask him if he'd do me a favor by going to Richard's office. He can tell Richard the toilet needs fixing. When Richard responds that it doesn't need fixing, the maintenance man may recognize his voice and come back down and tell me. If he does, great, that'll help. If he doesn't, nothing ventured, nothing gained."

"Mavis, how do you know that Richard is even in his office?"

"Well, for one thing, I drove around the block before I parked and saw his 4Runner parked in the building parking lot. If he's not in his office, it's only because he's gone somewhere temporarily, walked, or ridden with someone else."

"I don't know. This whole thing's complicated."

"Yeah, but I have to know before I go any further. You want me to waste time and money with all the other people in this building if Richard's the guilty party? Besides, he knows I'm going to be here today. When I got off the phone with you last night, I spouted off and shouldn't have. I said I'd be seeing people in this building today. He knows that I know or will know that his office is here. He's a smart man. He'll know he's a suspect."

She rolled her eyes and shook her head. "I'll leave it up to you, but be careful."

"Tell you what. I'll ask Jean to see if she can find Mr. Perez and bring him in here, so if Richard looks out, he won't see me wandering around the building. I think I can persuade Mr. Perez. He won't be in any danger. He can just tell him, when Richard says the toilet doesn't need fixing, that he must have the wrong office."

So, that's what we did. Jean was happy to cooperate. I can't say Gillian and I relaxed in Oliver's office while we waited, but I, at least, sat down and tried to still my shaking knees. Gillian began going through the file cabinet.

Twenty minutes later, I asked Gillian to call the authorities—specifically Ben, who has come to my rescue before—if I wasn't back in fifteen minutes. Armed with the knowledge that Mr. Perez was pretty sure he recognized Richard's voice, I climbed the stairs to the second floor and entered Richard's office.

# THIRTY-FOUR

"ay I help you?" the young brunette at the reception desk asked. She couldn't have been twenty-one. The office was small. I guessed there couldn't be more than two lawyers in it. I tried to remember whether I'd asked Richard the night before how large his firm was.

"Yes. I'd like to see Mr. Dunn."

"Do you have an appointment?"

"That's okay, Dee Dee," Richard's low voice cut in. "This is the private investigator on Ms. Oliver's case, Mavis Davis. Why don't you take an early lunch?" Richard stood there in all his handsomeness, dressed in a dark brown wool suit with a tan turtleneck under the jacket. Stress wrinkles ran down his face like clown makeup.

"But, Mr. Dunn, I'm working up that petition you said you needed today."

"Take an early lunch, Dee Dee," Richard said, his voice firmer.

My heart gave a lot of thought to pounding in anticipation of our confrontation. Surely Richard wouldn't have introduced me to his assistant if he planned to do away with me.

Dee Dee looked from Richard to me and back to Richard. "Well, all right." She opened a lower desk drawer and retrieved her purse. "Nice to meet you, Miss Davis." She walked out the door, pausing to look through the glass for a fraction of a moment, and was gone.

"Why don't you come on back, Mavis?" He held out his hand, gesturing toward the back of the office.

I preceded him down the hall and when he prodded me, entered the office in the very rear. It looked like any other lawyer's office. The bookcases were filled with gold trimmed books that I assumed rarely got looked at anymore now that just about everything could be found on the Internet. Expensive frames held his undergraduate diploma, his law school diploma, his law license, and a document that said he was board certified in criminal law. Of course, there was the usual furniture. I took a seat opposite his desk. He sat across from me.

"To what do I owe the pleasure of this visit today? I thought you'd still be resting up from our trek last night."

"You knew I was coming to interview all the tenants in this building. You heard me say so last night just before the deputies pulled in. Why didn't you tell me your office was here?"

He shrugged. "Didn't think of it. Have you spoken to Mrs. Wite today? Has CPS taken her kids to her?"

Changing the subject wasn't going to work with me. "Yes, I called her on the way over here, and she said they were going to bring them early this afternoon. But as to why I'm here. I've been wondering something, Richard. How well did you know Isobel Oliver?"

The muscle at the side of his eye twitched. "Better than I ever wanted to."

"You didn't like her?"

"Nobody liked her. She was all about money all the time. She didn't care about anyone except herself."

"You think she was a sociopath?"

"A *narcissistic* sociopath. You've heard that term bandied about over the past half decade or so."

"Oh, yes. Way more than I ever wanted. Richard, we know Ms.

Oliver was buying babies from women in the jail and selling them to adoptive parents, even if the adoptive parents didn't know why their adoptions were costing so much."

"I had suspected that for a long time. I tried not to know it. I didn't want to know it."

"Why do you think she wanted all that money? Was she into drugs or gambling or something else?"

"She was just plain greedy. She had a condo in south Florida. Her house here is ostentatious. She had her eye on an enormous property in Costa Rica and was trying to raise enough money to pay cash for it."

I had never understood people like Isobel Oliver. What was the point? It made no sense to me. Greed did so much harm. I chewed on my thumbnail for a moment as I thought of how to approach my next few questions.

"How did you know about the Wite twins? When did you figure out she had kidnapped them—or had them kidnapped?" I watched his face for any sudden movement.

His fingers had been tapping on his desk. They stopped. Did that mean something? His jaw began working. He rubbed his chin. My knees shook.

"I was working late on Wednesday night when a woman I'd seen here several times came in with another person. They were Mexican women carrying two little blond babies who were screaming their heads off. Their screams caused me to come out of my office. It didn't feel right, but it wasn't any of my business, so I closed the door and finished what I was doing."

"When did you figure out who those babies were?"

"I had a hard time sleeping that night. The next morning, I went to Isobel and told her I'd been here, that I'd seen the women carrying the children who were obviously not their own. I told her I didn't know where she'd gotten them but that something wasn't right, and she needed to take them back where she got them. We had a huge argument. She finally agreed that she would."

"But she didn't."

He put his head in his hands. "Did you know that we have a baby, my wife and I? A little girl named Mia."

"I kind of figured that out when I saw the evidence in your back seat."

He chuffed, sounding like a dog. "Yeah. We're adopting. Our baby is almost nine months old. Isobel got her for us. We were paying her out, which is why the adoption wasn't finalized a long time ago. She agreed to let us pay that way since I did ad litem work for her, and we worked in the same building. She joked that she would always know where to find me."

I'd been afraid of that. "Richard, I'm so sorry. You're such a nice person."

"I'd been after her to finish our case. All the fees I was owed for the work I did she applied to her adoption bill. I was sure we were even-steven."

A chill ran across my neck and down my arms, so I crossed them, rubbing to keep myself warm. It didn't work. "Richard, when did you learn the babies hadn't been returned?"

A noise I can only describe as sounding like a drawer slowly opening came from in front of him. His hand slid from the top of his desk into the drawer. "Friday afternoon."

"Friday afternoon," I repeated what he said, realizing he'd confirmed my suspicions. My stomach churned when I thought about why his hand was inside that drawer.

His eyes roved down my face. He wore a ginormous frown. "I went down to her office and asked her about them. She said she had taken them out to Mrs. Weaver's, that the petitions for adoption would be filed this week."

My hand went to my mouth to stop myself from saying anything.

"We had a big argument. She said if I didn't keep my mouth shut, she'd make sure Mia was removed from our home. She said she was still managing conservator, and she could take Mia any time she wanted." His eyes became pink and watery. I could see the fear in his face at the thought that he and his wife were going to lose their baby.

"Richard, anyone could understand how provoking her words were. Anyone."

His eyes glazed over as if he didn't see me.

"Richard, do you have a gun there?"

He appeared to regain his sense of where he was. "Mavis..."

"Richard, you don't want to do anything to make things worse for yourself. You know you don't." I was so afraid of saying the wrong thing.

He took the gun out, a big automatic-looking black thing, and pointed it at me.

I almost wet my pants. I needed to remain calm. I knew that. There was no way I could escape. Being only a few feet from him, I was a perfect target if he wanted to shoot me. I folded my hands in an attitude of prayer and held them in front of my face, hoping some silence between us would give him time to consider what he was doing. His eyes met mine. They were large and wide as though he were hypnotized. His lips were pressed together so tightly they'd become almost white.

"Mavis..." His eyes stayed glued to mine. He had to see I was terrified. Drawing a deep breath, he pointed the gun up under his chin.

"Richard, please don't do that." His eyes still stayed on mine. "You're a criminal defense attorney, Richard. Think about what kind of defense you'd put on for a father who'd been in your position."

He drew another deep breath. His hand wavered.

"Think of Mia. And your wife." I rose out of my chair and stepped toward his desk. Putting out my hand, I said, "I'll testify for you. I'll find others who she treated badly, who she extorted. Any jury would understand your reaction to her threat."

I stood there with my hand out, standing my ground so to speak, for what felt like eternity.

Finally, Richard laid the handgun on the top of his desk. He put his face in his hands and wept.

I snatched the gun and put the safety on. When he didn't move from his position, I sat back down, the gun in my lap, and waited for him to grow calm. I thought the best thing would be if we went to the authorities together like Carmen and I had done. I was in no hurry. I wanted him to be ready to go, to get himself together.

We were still sitting in those positions when a door banged open, and Ben rushed in with two uniforms. All three of them had their weapons drawn.

Ben looked at Richard whose head was still bowed, looked at me and the gun in my lap, and shook his head.

# CHAPTER
# THIRTY-FIVE

After the two uniforms cuffed Richard and took him away, Ben took possession of the weapon. We stuck a note on the door telling the secretary to go home and locked up Richard's office. Ben walked me downstairs to Ms. Oliver's, giving me the same lecture as he had the previous week when I took Carmen to the authorities.

"Boy was I glad to see you, Ben," Gillian said when we entered. "Are you always so available?"

"No. I have special dispensation from my boss to look after Mavis." Ben wore a wry expression.

Jean watched us, her head turning back and forth like she was watching a ping-pong match.

"Really?" I was astounded. "Captain Milton? I didn't know that. I thought he didn't like me." I'd had a run-in or two with the captain in the past.

"No, not really. He tolerates it. And he doesn't like you."

Gillian laughed. "I wondered..."

"I have to get back to work," Ben said, squeezing my arm a little too tight. "We'll talk more later."

Before I left, I took a chair and breathed deeply a few times. My insides still quavered. Did I just talk a man out of killing himself? I had put on a strong front for Ben, but I could have wept harder than Richard once the situation was under control. When I settled down, I looked at Gillian and Jean. "Let me give you a rundown on what just happened." Both grew wide-eyed as I told them about the gun. After that, I was ready to get the heck out of there.

"Thanks for helping out with Mr. Perez, Jean," I said. "I appreciate it. You can catch him up on what happened."

"It was kind of exciting," she said, her eyes waltzing. "Hey, do you want me to tell Dee Dee what happened, too, when she gets back from lunch? We know each other. I can text her to let me know when she returns."

"Good idea," Gillian said. "Mavis, I would never have done what you did. That took a lot of guts."

"That's not what Ben called it." We laughed together. "I'll leave y'all alone now and go back to my office. What are you two going to do?"

"I'm keeping the office open and calling Ms. Oliver's clients and telling them that Ms. Wright is taking over. Is that all you want me to do, Ms. Wright?"

"For now. I'll be back tomorrow. You'll get me a set of keys by then for everything?"

"Yes, ma'am. See you, Mavis."

Gillian walked me out to my vehicle. She was parked not far away. "I'm headed to the district attorney's office to see about getting Dave Wite released. I think they'll do it as soon as the police say they have a confession from Richard Dunn."

"Well, you've got your work cut out for you with Ms. Oliver's office as well as your own. Hey, what are you going to do about that notary? Did Jean give you the name of the person who had been notarizing Oliver's documents?"

"We're going to make a list of everyone who we think was involved in this adoption ring and turn it over to the DA."

"What do you think will happen to Richard? I guess you can't represent him, but he'll have to have a good criminal defense lawyer."

"No, I can't represent him, but we're both members of the Harris County Criminal Lawyers Association. Once the word gets out about what he's charged with and what the facts are, someone good will represent him. Don't worry."

"He seemed so nice. It's hard to believe he killed her."

"Not for me. If someone was going to take my kid, I'd do it, too."

"You think people feel the same about adopted children as they do about their biological children?"

"Absolutely. I'm sure Richard and his wife are firmly attached to that baby, especially after having her for so many months."

I thought about that. I understood attachments. "Well, I'm going to my office. Margaret and Candy have no idea what's happened. I only called to let them know I was coming over here this morning."

"We'll talk." She waved at me and crossed the street to her car.

I climbed into my own and sat for a few minutes. I was still having a hard time believing I'd done what I did, too. A shiver ran across my neck and shoulders. I own a gun, a revolver, but the thought never occurred to me that I should stop off at my office and get it from the safe. Who knows what would have happened if I'd gone waving my gun at Richard. Not that I would do that. Anyway, the adrenaline rush had faded. I started up my SUV and drove to my office, stopping once for the largest pizza with everything on it that I could get.

When I arrived, I put my purse on my desk, my cell in my pocket, the pizza on the table in the kitchen, and walked to the front in response to their calling out to me. "Y'all want to follow me to the kitchen? I'm starving and brought pizza."

They did, and while we stuffed ourselves, I explained what had transpired that morning. They'd had no clue as to what I had planned. After I finished my story to their oohs and ahs and questions asked between bites of pizza, I sat back.

"Now, I could go for some chocolate chip cookies." Glancing from Margaret to Candy, I asked, "Where'd you put them?"

Margaret cleared her throat. "There aren't any," she said. "They're all gone."

"Awww. I really need some cookies in the worst way."

"We ate them."

Candy said, "Barry ate some too, and I took a few home to my sister and brother. I didn't think you'd mind."

"And to think I was going to offer to give you an engagement party, Margaret."

"That's so sweet." Margaret jumped up and ran at me, enveloping me with her arms. "Wait, you said it like it was past tense."

"No cookies. No party."

"You don't mean that."

I cocked my head at her. "Then you know what you need to do."

"Bake more cookies!" Margaret laughed. "You were just kidding. Will you really give me—Barry and me an engagement party?"

"Of course, she will," Candy said. "I'll be able to bring a plus one, right?"

Both Margaret and I turned to Candy and in unison said, "You have a plus one?"

"Yep. And that's all I'm going to say about that." With a few long strides, she left the kitchen, saying over her shoulder, "I'll be in my office."

Margaret and I looked at each other. "Who knew?"

I hoped that would be the last of the surprises for a while. Between Margaret's introduction of Barry into our lives and now Candy with a plus one, life was taking a complicated turn. But with a little rest and a handful of cookies, I'd be able to handle anything.

# Acknowledgments

Many thanks to my advance readers, a lot of special people who have taken the time to help me get this final draft polished.

Dianna Baker

Deborah Breen

Paul Ray Heinrich

Patricia Jakobi

Roseann Krannich

Sharon Marks

Lanette Pacheco

Liz (NLN)

Thomas Palmer

Saralyn Richard

Mary Kastle

And special thanks to my virtual assistant/editor: Mars Reyna

# ABOUT THE AUTHOR

Susan P. Baker, a retired Texas family court judge, presided over everything from murder to divorce for 12 years. Afterward, she traveled around Texas as a visiting judge for another 12. Prior to being elected to the bench, she practiced law for nine (9) years, and was a probation officer for two (2) years. Susan's works are derived from her experiences in the justice system or events in and around court in Texas, *fictionalized*, of course!

She is the author of 11 novels of mystery and suspense set in Texas, two nonfiction books, and an eclectic collection of short pieces. Her novels include five featuring Mavis Davis, a private detective; two Lady Lawyer mysteries starring criminal defense lawyers Sandra Salinsky and Erma Townley; and four standalones with court participant protagonists (including judges and lawyers).

Her two nonfiction books are Murdered Judges of the 20th Century and Heart of Divorce—Advice from a Judge. The title of the collection is Fly Catching.

Susan is a member of Alliance of Independent Authors, Sisters in Crime, Authors Guild, Writers League of Texas, Texas Authors, and Galveston Novel and Short Story Writers.

She has two children and eight grandchildren. She loves dark chocolate, raspberries, and traveling the world (and has lost count of the number of countries she's visited). An anglophile, Susan most enjoys visiting her cousins in England and Australia (where she was finally able to visit in September of '22). She hopes to finally drive

Route 66 in 2023. She is at home in Galveston with her rescue kitty, Tudi.

Read more about Susan, sign up for her mailing list, and find her books at www.susanpbaker.com. Like her at https://facebook.com/legalwriter. Follow her on Twitter @susanpbaker and on Instagram @suewritesandreads.

# ALSO BY SUSAN P. BAKER

**Novels:**

*My First Murder*

No. 1 in the Mavis Davis Mystery Series. A cafe owner hires Mavis as a last resort to discover who murdered his mysterious waitress.

*The Sweet Scent of Murder*

No. 2 in the Mavis Davis Mystery Series. Mavis' search for a missing teenager turns into a murder investigation in Houston's Ritzy River Oaks.

*Murder and Madness*

No. 3 in the Mavis Davis Mystery Series. Mavis takes on the cold case of a grisly ax murder of a cruise ship captain in Galveston.

*Not Murder*

No. 4 in the Mavis Davis Mystery Series. Mavis is hired to locate a lawyer's deadbeat client and finds a Pandora's box of problems, including a dead body.

***DEFENSIBLE MURDER***

*Death of a Prince*

No. 1 in the Lady Lawyer Mystery Series. Sandra Salinsky & Erma Townley defend the alleged murderer of a Galveston millionaire plaintiff's attorney who was Erma's best friend.

*Death of a Rancher's Daughter*

No. 2 in the Lady Lawyer Mystery Series. Sandra & Erma defend a family friend for murder while fighting gender and racial prejudice in a small Texas town.

*Ledbetter Street*

A Novel of Second Chances: Not just the story of a mother fighting for custody of her disabled son, but one of love, tragedy, and the relationships of the women of Ledbetter Street.

## *Suggestion of Death*

An investigative reporter who can't pay his child support searches for the killer of deadbeat dads, before he becomes the next victim.

## *UNAWARE*

Attorney Dena Armstrong wants to break out from the control of the two men dominating her life, unaware that a stranger has other plans for her.

## *Texas Style Justice*

Judge Victoria Van Fleet aspires to the highest court in the land, but is she willing to pay the price?

## **Nonfiction:**

## *Heart of Divorce*

Divorce advice especially for those who are considering representing themselves.

## *Murdered Judges of the 20th Century*

True stories of judges killed in America.

## *Fly Catching*

An eclectic collection of short pieces.

www.susanpbaker.com

Made in the USA
Columbia, SC
01 February 2024